YELLOW SKY REVOLT

BOOK ONE
of
THE THREE KINGDOMS
CHRONICLES

BAPTISTE PINSON WU

YELLOW SKY REVOLT:
The Three Kingdoms Chronicles (Book 1)
Copyright © 2022 by Baptiste Pinson Wu. All rights reserved.

No part of this book may be reproduced or used in any manner without written permission of the copyright owner except for the use of quotations in a book review.

ISBN: 978-4-9912768-1-1 (Paperback)
ISBN: 978-4-9912768-0-4 (eBook)

First Edition 2022

Interior formatting by Miblart.com

To my wife,

who will probably never finish this novel,

even though it's a story about her own culture.

CHINA, 2ND CENTURY

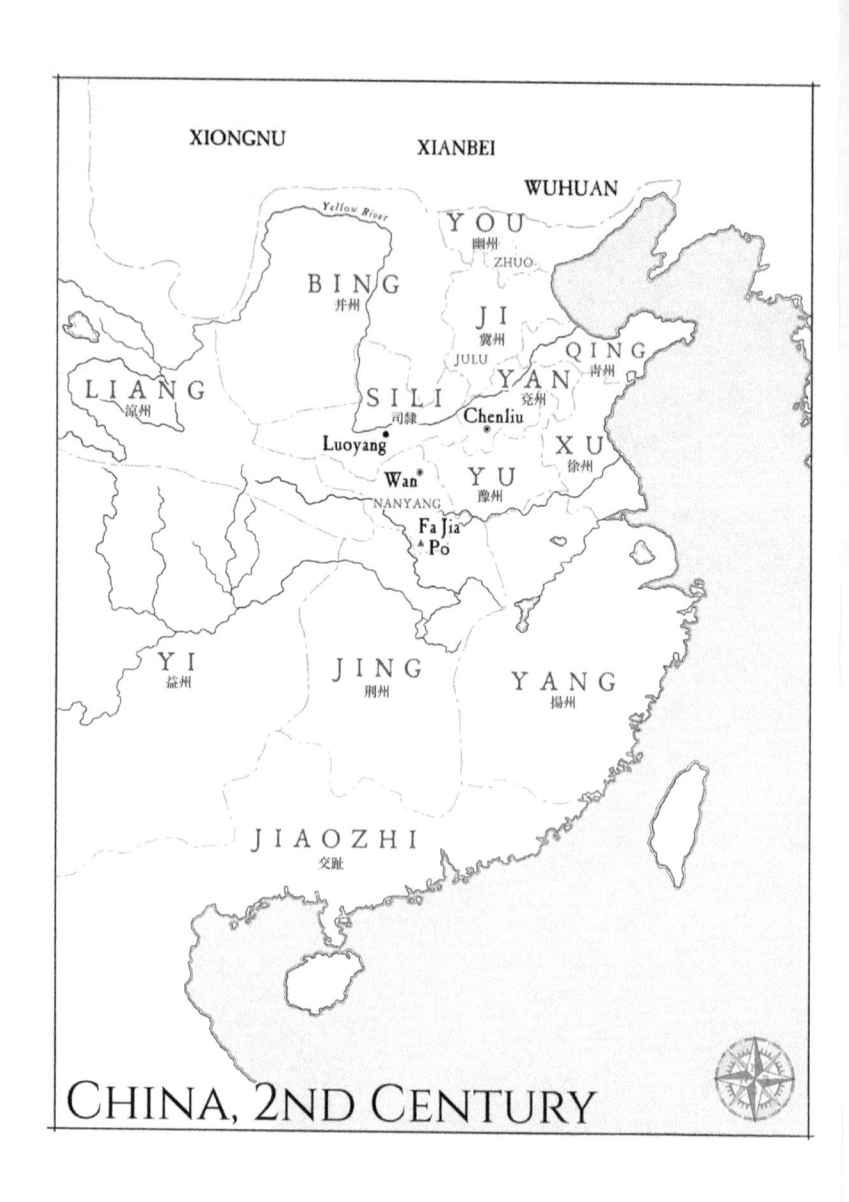

XIONGNU · XIANBEI · WUHUAN

Yellow River

YOU
幽州
ZHUO

BING
并州

JI
冀州
JULU

QING
青州

LIANG
涼州

SILI
司隸

YAN
兗州
Chenliu

Luoyang

XU
徐州

Wan
NANYANG

YU
豫州

Fa Jia
Po

YI
益州

JING
荊州

YANG
揚州

JIAOZHI
交趾

Though the tortoise blessed with magic powers lives long,
Its days have their allotted span;

Though winged serpents ride high on the mist,
They turn to dust and ashes at the last;

An old war-horse may be stabled,
Yet still it longs to gallop a thousand li;

And a noble-hearted man though advanced in years
Never abandons his proud aspirations.

Man's span of life, whether long or short,
Depends not on Heaven alone;

One who eats well and keeps cheerful
Can live to a great old age.

And so, with joy in my heart,
I hum this song.

Though the Tortoise Lives Long,
Cao Cao

PROLOGUE

Mianzhu, Yi province
11th month, 4th year of the Jingyuan era of the
Cao Wei empire (263)

I STILL CANNOT BELIEVE IT'S OVER. The three kingdoms are no more. To think we are the first of them to fall, I could die of shame. And yet, it is true. The worst, at least in my mind, is that I forewarned our defeat years ago, and very few paid attention to my warning. Yet, the signs were there for all to interpret. I guess it takes an old fool with more experience than energy to notice them, and this old fool has long been cursed with a generation of useless sycophants to guide.

Our emperor, or former emperor now, has spent his life heeding the wrong advice. Though in my case, more often than not, it was my fault for caring about the substance rather than the form. An old habit that never died, even when I thought I had gained in wisdom. And now, all we have fought for has vanished like a fart in the wind, as an old friend would have said.

Years, decades, generations of men have given their lives for the dream of our first emperor to become a reality. How many friends have I lost in that pursuit? How many great men have perished, slain too young or from an undeserved death? All for nothing.

No, not for nothing. Shu Han might never become the dynasty to unite the land of our ancestors, but the model of benevolence set by Lord Liu Bei will echo throughout the ages. This I swear.

"I'm sorry. What did you say?" the young man asks. I guess I was mumbling again. Another curse of age.

Young man … The boy in me laughs for thinking of him as such. Chen Shou is at least in his midthirties, though it is hard to guess. His candor, the smooth skin of his hands, his unmarked face, everything in him stinks of youth and privilege. His father was a real man. Not a smart one, but a good one. One of those with the undeserved death, while the son is one of those useless sycophants. He is clever, though, and highly educated, I'll give him that, and his calligraphy would meet old Zhong *laoshi*'s approval.

"I said, history is written by the victors," I manage to answer.

"This is very true," Chen Shou replies with the tone a teacher would use for his dumbest student. "And?"

"And what do they say about those they've defeated?" I ask in a harsher tone than he expected. I may not be able to use volume as I used to, but my voice still carries enough verve to scare a man with no life experience. "They say their vanquished enemy was weak, or evil, or dumb, and deserved their defeat. They say they brought light to a land of darkness. Tell me, *boy*, was our land dark? Were we any of those things they will make us be?"

Chen Shou takes a second to ponder, tilting his head meaningfully. Of course, he needs to think. He's part of the generation born in the Shu Han empire. He never knew the heroes who carved it with their blades. Names like Zhang Fei, Pang Tong, and Huang Zhong mean nothing more than the wind of the voices uttering them. They know of Lord Liu Bei, but mostly through his piss poor example of a son. Even Guan Yu, my beloved general, is but a name for them.

"We lost," he finally replies, "no matter what we were. And now we can have peace." I spit at that, missing his foot by a *cun*.

"*Peace!* There can be no peace. Not as long as these old bones carry my flesh. And not as long as a true son of Shu Han still breathes."

He's right about our defeat, though. It was absolute. Even Zhuge Liang, our great chancellor, must have been impressed from the afterlife.

"Which brings me back to my original question," Chen Shou says, a faint trace of anger in his voice. "Why did you agree to tell your story?"

Why did I agree? That's a great question. Another question I had been asking myself was why I had not used my own sword to open my throat when our "lord" surrendered to the enemy a week ago. The answer is the same to both questions.

I was chewing on the disgrace of being put in a wagon, pulled by oxen at that, to be brought to Luoyang and paraded in the capital as a new Cao Wei government member. I could have ridden all the way to Luoyang, damn it! There's never been a better horseman in this land, or very few, at least. Even past my eightieth birthday, I could have ridden through the empire.

That's when the enemy's general, Zhong Hui, a young upstart with much to prove, approached me. He asked if I would be willing to tell our story, being our original band of warriors' last surviving officer.

Him too, I had barely missed by an inch, though I had aimed at his face.

What were the chances *my* version of the story would make it to the imperial library?

But then, after a few *shi* of munching over it, I realized it was the best thing I could do for the memory of all those fallen comrades. As long as people whispered their names with awe, in a way, they would survive, and their fight would continue.

"I don't want the victors to write our history," I tell Chen Shou.

At least the enemy—for that is what they will remain in my mind until my last heartbeat—offered the assistance of a clerk from *my* kingdom. Oh, I could see from the moment he stepped inside my wagon that Chen Shou was already a member of the Cao Wei empire, down to the traces of golden color in his robes. But I hoped that a lifetime within the walls of Chengdu had given him enough pride that at least he would write the words I spoke faithfully.

"And I don't want Lord Liu Bei's dream to die yet. So grind your stone, you will need ink, and by the speed of this wagon, we have a couple of months, I'd say."

No, I can't let it happen, but not for the sake of this impossible journey my lord has sent us on. I can't let it die because I have given too much for our dream. I have bled and killed and led too many men down that path to let it happen. I have to tell the tale of the three kingdoms because I know that should I fail to, the fallen will greet me in the afterlife with disappointment. *Was it worth it?* some would say. *How could you let Shu Han fall?* others would ask. For that is the curse of being the last one alive, and I will take it. So, yes, I will tell it as I lived it, with all the stench, the gore, the gravity, and the moments of bliss my long existence has witnessed. No one might ever read my words, but I have to hope that someday, no matter how far in the future, someone will read the life story of Liao Hua, General of Chariots and Cavalry, and know that brave men fought for a just world.

This hope might be naïve, but that, too, is one of my traits. One that hasn't changed since my childhood years on a small farm of Nanyang commandery all those decades ago, when the Han empire seemed as certain as the setting sun.

PART ONE

DEATH TO THE BLUE SKY

CHAPTER ONE

Fa Jia Po, Nanyang commandery,
11th month of the 6th year of Guanghe era (183),
Han Dynasty

IT WAS A WINTER AS COLD AS ANY I could remember. Though being six, I only recalled a couple of them, and according to the village elders, it was actually a mild one. To me, it was as if the wind and rain would never stop chasing each other, leaving me confined to the walls of the shack we called home. We had two rooms in our house, one for dining and cooking, one for sleeping. Our great luck came from only three of us sharing that house: my father, my sister, and me.

Until a year ago, my *Yeye* was also with us, but a fever that people thought for a time to be a great plague took him, and I can't say it was a terrible thing. *Yeye* was a tough old man with little love for his son or grandchildren. Father said that he had always been sour as old milk, and only my mother could manage a smile on his wrinkled face. But she had died giving birth to my sister, Mihua, and being only two at the time, I have no memory of her. In my mind, she was a gentle woman with abundant love for her progeny, though I guess this is how all orphans picture their parents.

For all his bitterness, *Yeye* was the reason we had a roof over our head, sandals at our feet, and, on rare occasions, some chicken meat with our millet. Through a life of hard work and sacrifice, he had maintained the farm in the Liao's hands. It doesn't sound like much, but it was as close to a miracle as you could get back then, and now too, I suppose. Great landowners were buying farms like ours as if it meant nothing, turning previously independent peasants into tenants. One poor crop, an injury keeping a pair of hands from the field, or even an extra tax for constructing such or such a palace in the capital could leave a household in debt and force them to sell their bit of land. Sure, it meant better equipment and no more land tax, but it also meant giving away half your crop to your landowner. And if like where we lived, under the thumb of the Cai clan, the landowner happened to be a voracious, greedy bastard, it was only a matter of time before your land got absorbed. *Yeye* kept us from it, going as far as managing to buy two oxen with the savings of a life of hard labor and privation, one for us, one for renting to our neighbors. A miracle. A short-lived one.

When I was five, soldiers came to our hill, conscripting men to fight our unruly neighbors in the north, either the Qiang or the Xianbei, I don't remember. They called for my dad, who was still far from the fifty-six-year-old limit, and there were only two ways out of it, paying them off with the *gengfu*, the scutage tax, or exchanging his service with a gift, such as an ox. I remember my grandfather thinking about it, and if he had been younger, or if the conscription wasn't taking my father so far off, he would have agreed. But as it was, my father was still more important than an extra animal, especially with two children in his care. So we parted with the beast, which would most likely have been commandeered anyway. Officers always seemed to take from the independent farms somehow, though few were left in Fa Jia Po.

Still, seeing the result of his life's work taken by soldiers took a toll on *Yeye*, and his health subsequently declined.

Father tried, but he was not like his own father.

Liao Xiong, for that was his name, was a timid man who never freed himself from his father's shadow, had somehow married a good woman, and had lost everything when she gave him a daughter.

It would have made many a man bitter, but he did not have enough personality for that. Instead, he just seemed to vanish into his daily rhythm of hard work, cooking some millet, and getting everything ready for the next day of farming. There were few breaks, no pleasure, and though I could not see it then, he still found it in himself to love us.

Winters should have been the time for children to play together, as there was little to do on the farms. But, as I said, this year's winter kept us close to the stove, making the daily visit to the ox my only distraction.

Yet I was happy as a flea on a dog's back, for Uncle Cheng would be back any day now.

To a six-year-old boy from the countryside, Cheng Yuanzhi was the pinnacle of manliness. And not just children; everyone loved him.

First, he was a former soldier. Not a conscript being called whenever the need arose, a proper soldier. He had served on the northwestern frontier and even ventured into Qiang territory, where he must have killed his fair share of barbarians. Judging by his scars, which he got aplenty on his thick arms, he also had brushed with death on several occasions. Uncle Cheng had served for ten years before resuming his civilian life. But ten years had been enough to fill his mind with stories to please the crowds of peasants joining him wherever he went. He never spoke of the battle, only of the camp, and that was enough to ignite a bright fire in this young boy's soul. From the day I met Uncle Cheng, I knew the farm wouldn't be my life. The army would.

The second reason for Cheng's popularity mattered less to children but had everything to do with adults, for he was an Adept of *the Way of the Taiping*, the Great Peace.

Even a boy such as I knew of the Way. Folks seldom spoke of anything else back then. It was said that its founder, Zhang Jue, could cure any disease. Millions of people followed him throughout the empire, and he even had ears listening to his teaching in the court of Emperor Ling. He and his two brothers had created a movement the size of which had never been seen before, and since they mostly cared for the poor and the sick, the government did not care that much about them. As they grew, from their base all the way up north and east in Julu commandery, the three brothers organized their followership to expand, thus giving some teaching and authority to Adepts, who were sent throughout the empire to spread the word. Cheng Yuanzhi was one of those.

You could hardly believe him the religious type, with his unruly mass of hair, thick beard, and bear-like chest. Uncle Cheng, though he had left the army almost ten years ago, was obviously a warrior. So when he arrived in Fa Jia Po, people had welcomed him with a certain sense of doubt.

Apparently used to it, Cheng Yuanzhi had pointed at an old woman who had joined the circle of onlookers a little late for her bad hip and had invited her back to her own house, where he accompanied her. Less than half a *shi* later, she left her house again, almost jumping like a goat kid, tears streaming down her smiling face. The folks had fallen on their knees and begged Uncle Cheng to stay.

I do not know why, but he chose our house to stay in for the night. My grandfather had passed away a few months before, so he had no one to treat in our household, and maybe that's why. Whatever the reason, I could barely fall asleep that night, drowning our guest with a flow of questions about the land, the army, and battle, of course. My father, contrary to his habit, spoke too, though he always came back to Zhang Jue and the Way. My sister cared about none of that and fell asleep even faster than usual.

About Zhang Jue, Uncle Cheng said something like, "He is the greatest man that ever walked the land, and we would be the luckiest people of our history if such a man led the empire." Those were dangerous words, but he must have measured my father by then and knew he would make no wave.

I believe he liked the attention of this spirited young boy and decided to stay a few more days. By the time he left, I was beaming with a new sense of purpose. All the other kids, and some grown-ups too, came to me so that I could recount our guest's words.

For the next two months, I must have checked the path stretching from the main road to our hill at least once a *shi*. Then one day, he came back and bear-hugged me in his muscular arms. I had never been so happy in my life.

Being an Adept meant that Uncle Cheng handled an area the size of a county. Ours was home to roughly ten thousand households, and he could, of course, not spend his time exclusively on the Fa Jia hill, where a little less than two hundred people lived. And yet, whenever time allowed, this was where he would be. Though I hoped he came back because this was where I lived, I now know the hill was just perfect for his tasks, the official one and the other as well. It was remote enough to avoid suspicion and yet close enough to the city of Xiangyang for his dealings.

Uncle Cheng was not simply using our house and our food; he worked for it. Of course, he would help all he had the power to, mostly the old and those with light sickness. For the others, with an unfeigned tone of sorrow, he would recognize his lack of power. He advised them to make their way to Julu, where Zhang Jue was certain to heal them, but few could afford it. And when he did not act as an Adept of the Way, Cheng Yuanzhi worked the field. Farming had never been as interesting.

"How do you work your miracles?" one boy asked as we took our lunch break. It was early in the year, and we were weeding the fields, as back-breaking a task as you can find. Weeding and reaping are the two times of the year when neighbors help each other, and also when we have something to eat halfway through the day. I think on that day, we were working in the Fa family's field, after which the hill was named.

"You know it's a secret," Uncle Cheng replied, stuffing his mouth with some wheat porridge. It was indeed a secret. He had made all those he had helped swear never to reveal his methods. Those who sat around the pot at the moment looked at each other, faces riddled with embarrassment. The boy looked disappointed, and so was I. Again, I cared little about the miracles of the Way, but I too was curious. Only magic could heal people so fast, and I know no child who wouldn't beam with curiosity at the idea of magic.

"But," Cheng Yuanzhi said, raising his chopsticks, "I can teach you one of our secret techniques." Now I was positively radiating with jealousy, but I knew

Uncle Cheng enough to know he had something in mind, so I kept quiet.

The boy—he was from one of the Zhang houses, I believe—stood up at once, eyes wide with excitement, and joined Cheng Yuanzhi. He knelt by the Adept's feet, who sat on a log turned bench. Uncle Cheng licked his thumb to remove some of the porridge, dropped the bowl, and rocked his shoulders.

"Now, you raise your hands like that," he said, placing both hands palm to palm in front of his face. The boy did as such. "You curl your last two fingers inside. You close your eyes." They both did. "And you repeat those words. *By the power of the western wind—*"

"By the power of the western wind," the boy said.

"I expel you!" Cheng Yuanzhi shouted. What followed was the loudest, most disgusting fart I had ever heard.

The gang of boys and men sitting together erupted in a loud burst of laughter. It took a few seconds for the Zhang boy to realize he had been duped, and though he looked petrified with shame at first, he soon followed us in our hysteria. And while we were calming down after a long minute of laughing, we went at it again, louder even, when Uncle Cheng stood urgently and claimed he needed a bush or something. The joke had turned against him, to our great pleasure. If life on a farm was always like this, I could have been content with my lot.

Cheng came back every two or three months, looking more tired and worried every time, though he pretended otherwise when he saw me. Until it was the winter where my story really began. Finally, Uncle Cheng marched down the small path leading to the hill, though it had been pouring rain, and he had been running more than walking. He looked utterly pissed, and as I was to learn a couple of days later, it had nothing to do with the rain. He also came with a strange request for my father, one I begged him to accept.

"Dun, wake up," Cheng Yuanzhi said. I was still many years from being Liao Hua. Back then, my name was Liao Dun. "We have a long road ahead."

And that we did, for we were going to Xiangyang.

Waking up proved harder than ever, for I had fallen asleep late at night. I was now seven and had never gone further than the nameless village Fa Jia Po belonged to. So to think about a journey with Uncle Cheng to the greatest city not only in the commandery but in the whole province of Jing had been enough to deprive me of some much-needed sleep.

This was the only time I saw something resembling anger on my dad's face. He had not liked the idea of his son traveling the road to Xiangyang, even in the company of a fierce-looking veteran. But at this point, Father was already a devoted member of the Way and could not refuse an Adept, the voice of Zhang Jue. He let me go with a pat on the head just before Uncle Cheng gently slapped the donkey's rump, forcing it to pull the small cart. We were going to sell our hill's crop of onions, cabbages, and garlic at the big market in Xiangyang. Even I knew it was odd. There were several markets from here to the city.

"Why do we go to Xiangyang to sell those?" I finally asked, just as the sun rose on our left. For each of his steps, I needed two, which left me struggling for air as I spoke.

"They'll sell for a better price," Uncle Cheng replied.

"But is it worth the extra time?" I asked. Xiangyang was a day and some from Fa Jia Po.

"Don't you want to visit an actual city?" he asked, his lips turning into a smirk.

"Of course I do," I said. I did want to see Xiangyang, but more than that, I wanted to spend time just with Uncle Cheng, away from my father and the folks. Secretly, I hoped to finally hear of the battles he had been part of, of the enemies he had killed, and all those things he had never mentioned before. I did not ask about our real purpose again; just glad to be part of the journey. I was far from knowing it, but the next two days would change my life and that of many others.

We quickly passed the village, where Cheng Yuanzhi waved at many other folks. It was like he knew everyone. Then we turned on the main road heading south. It was the furthest I had ever gone in my life. The road linked Xiangyang in the south to Wan, Nanyang commandery's capital. We followed the Bai river for the whole day, munching on grains and drinking the river's water until we reached the point where the Bai met the Tang to become the Tangbai, where Uncle Cheng called a stop. He chose one of the three inns cluttered where the bigger river began, and for the first time in my life, I stepped inside such an establishment.

Being winter, it was fairly quiet, but to my unknowing ears, it felt like chaos. Five of the eight tables were busy with customers, a server carried pots and bowls, and a big burly man sweated over a stove in the open kitchen. I shivered with hunger as I discovered the smell of pork cooked in oil.

"Can I really eat this?" I asked, the pit in my stomach growing double as I glanced down at my bowl of millet, cabbage, and pork.

"You'd better," Uncle replied, "or I will."

I did eat it and some more. Even all those years later, I can still recall the little part of me that died that day. I told myself I would not live if I could not eat like that for every meal. I apologized when I asked Cheng if he could order more, and the way he laughed told me it was all fine. This would cost him a fortune, but as he explained, it didn't really matter.

"The owner is a friend," he said, meaning a member of the Way. "I'll pay for the pork because it would be unfair otherwise, but he'll let us stay for the night for free if he has some room to spare. And he'll feed the donkey. I'll give him a few onions and cabbage if you don't mind, and if you don't tell your folks."

I told him I didn't mind and would tell no one. It seemed fair enough, and as I received my second serving, I tried to picture the face my sister would make when I told her I had eaten pork twice.

"The Way has people everywhere," I said through my chewing.

"It does," Uncle replied, though not before checking over his shoulders. "At least in this part of the land."

"So, when do we fight?" I asked.

It was like I had dropped a bucket of cold water over his head. He slightly bent over the table to lower his voice and invited me to come closer.

"Why do you say that?" he asked.

"Well, everyone knows there will be a fight," I answered. "Old Zhang says that's why a big brute like you was made an Adept."

"Old Zhang said that now?" Uncle Cheng asked, smirking. "What else do people say?"

Now I was truly sorry I had started the topic. He was putting me in a corner. Honesty was my only viable path.

"They say the government cannot tolerate the Way of Taiping much longer; it is growing too powerful. One day, they will make it unlawful and punish some of its members as an example." While I spoke, Cheng Yuanzhi made a low hum. I was right, but he did not like hearing it from a child.

"They also say that it would mean war. The people won't tolerate being deprived of the one thing making their lives a little better." I was proud of myself for having correctly used the word "tolerate" twice and for making it sound like I cared deeply about it all. There was much more to it, of course. The people had always worked and lived at the whim of the powerful, but even the elders agreed things had never been worse. New taxes sprung up arbitrarily for purposes the people couldn't care less about. Too often, the men were called away from the fields to fight in the north, repair some bridges, or take part in the occasional punishment expedition against local bandits. All the while, the rich landowners, through a clever game of marriage and corruption, kept their people away from all this. In short, the rich were getting richer and the poor poorer. Even a child could pick up on those things, and I guess I missed a lot more.

"Dun, I'm not saying there will or won't be a fight," Uncle said gravely, "but this kind of conversation needs to remain quiet for the time being, you understand?" I did, or at least I assured him I did. "Did you hear anything else?"

I took some time to think about it. The truth was, I only cared about the conversation regarding the fighting. The rest flew over my head. I was not a particularly big or strong kid and had rarely fought with other boys of the hill, usually following some comments regarding my eyes. Some people claimed they were so bright it looked like they were burning. I did not mind those comments, but when boys my age used it as an insult, I would defend my honor. The truth is, I was always itching for a fight. In my young mind, it was how I would prove myself a man. The battle would be the test where I would shine, and Uncle Cheng would recognize me as a great warrior someday. I knew it would not happen for several years, but I also knew the Way would get me there, and in this, I was not wrong, at least.

"Old Zhang said we would be fools to believe the government could be beaten," I said. "But everyone knows old Zhang is a lackey of the Cai clan."

"He might be right, though," Uncle Cheng said. I did not reply. He had spoken mostly to himself.

The server came and served us a small bottle of *huangjiu*. I was years from developing a taste for wine, so I was left to drink some hot water.

"When—if it starts," I resumed after a few more minutes, during which I finished my second serving, "you won't leave me behind, will you?"

"Battles are no place for a child," Uncle Cheng said. His cheeks had turned slightly red already.

"You could teach me to fight," I blurted. There it was, my secret wish.

"I could," he replied, bringing a wide smile across my face. "But that's not the problem. Can you imagine what your father would say if I brought you to battle?"

I blew air through my pursed lips in a very childish yet arrogant way.

"My father is weak," I said. "He could never—"

I got no further.

Faster than a lightning bolt, Uncle Cheng's hand shot above the table and slapped me across the left side of the face. I had never been hit so hard before, not even by *Yeye*. It took me a second to realize what had just happened, so I remained petrified when my eyes returned to Cheng's.

"Never," he said through his teeth, his finger straight as a nail pointing at me, "never speak of your father like that." He was angry and sounded as if *he* had been hurt. "Your father is a brave man, more courageous than I will ever be."

"You don't know him," I shouted, "he's—" The second slap came even faster, though not as hard.

"Do you think waving a sword is bravery?" he asked, shaking. "Your father, like millions of other men and women, is grander than any warrior I've ever met. They work worse than slaves every day without fail, toiling the earth, pushing their plow, eating the same shitty food, day after day after day. They slowly break their bodies so their children may have a piece of something by the time they're too old to continue. At best, they get an average crop and will go a few months without knowing hunger. At worst, they fail, through no fault of their own, and the results are terrible. Some might even have to sell themselves or their child not to die in winter. Do you know, *xiao* Dun, what *I* would have done if I was your father when your mom died?"

I shook my head, for I could not speak. The tears were prickling the back of my eyes, and a ball had formed in my throat.

"I would have left, abandoning you and your sister. Or worse, I would have sold you first. That's my bravery for you."

"But you can fight," I said, though my quivering lip made the sound difficult.

"Aye, I can fight. I can impose my will on a foe. But fighting requires a few seconds of courage just before the battle begins, and most of us are drunk enough that courage is no longer an issue. Being a warrior is like throwing a die. Either you follow the right leader, and you might survive the fight, or you come short and die, that's it. It doesn't take a man to throw a die—believe me—only a fool. But your dad, despite all the shit the world has dropped on him, still loves his children and worries about them. If I had your father, Dun, I would have become a good man."

I meant to say he was a good man, but all that came as I passed my sleeve over my first tears was, "I wish you were my father."

"No, you don't," he said in a softer tone now. "But, Dun, if I had a son, I'd be glad if he was like you."

Now there was no stopping the tears.

Uncle Cheng pushed his stool next to mine and passed his arm around my shoulder while I cried out the tension he had built. And while I took some time to recover, he told me more about himself, maybe so I would understand his point better.

Cheng Yuanzhi was from Ji province, the son of a farmer as well, and just like me, he had always known farming wasn't his life. But while I could see my path as a soldier, Cheng's found his in banditry. They had caught him early on, which earned him a five-year sentence in Liang province, near the border with the Qiang tribes. To his great surprise, he took a liking to the army life and signed on for another five years when he became a free man again. The first five years had been relatively peaceful, the next five, not so much. Bitter and broken, he left the army and meant to resume his life in Ji province, though not as a farmer. Less than a year later, he fell back into his life of banditry. When his gang got caught again, Cheng Yuanzhi managed to escape—he would not be given the same second chance this time. With little hope, he followed the rumor of a miracle maker and was accepted within the close circle of Zhang Jue's disciples.

"I was extremely lucky," Uncle Cheng said.

I know he meant to discourage me from following in his footsteps, but the boy in me only retained that he had fought great battles, survived them, and found his way through hardship. Now more than ever, I wanted to be like him.

He slapped me again while I daydreamed of a similar life.

"What was that for?" I asked, rubbing my tender cheek.

"That was for letting me slap you twice," he said. "You want me to teach you how to fight? We'll start by making sure you learn how to defend yourself." Thus began an unending game between us. Out of nowhere, Uncle Cheng would try to slap me, usually succeeding, and I was to hit him any way I wanted, which never seemed to work. Though that would start on the next day. We had a good night of sleep ahead, and I was more tired than ever.

My head was spinning from the moment we passed Xiangyang's northern gate halfway through the next morning. Never in my wildest dream had I imagined so many buildings and people crammed together. The city was swarming with life, and according to Uncle, it was as quiet as it got, it being the middle of winter and not a great market day.

The guards at the gates had given half a glance at our cargo and even less at our faces, clearly not bothered with the idea of a boy's presence on the road. Maybe it was why Uncle Cheng had requested my presence, I thought, to look less suspicious.

Then it was a perfect grid of streets going north to south and east to west. Some buildings even had a third floor! Smells I had never encountered came out of the establishments serving food. There was more meat than I knew existed and so many guards on patrol. Why, I asked myself, would anyone choose to live in the country when he could live here?

I knew nothing of it back then, but Nanyang commandery, and by extension Xianyang, was considered a place of knowledge and refined men. For the peasants, whether they lived in Nanyang or in faraway You province, life was the same, but when you stepped into cities, the difference was obvious. Xiangyang was bursting with life and trade, even in those days when it wasn't as important as it would become. Over the years, due to the events linking me to it, I would come to hate this place more than any other, but back then, it was as if heaven had opened up in front of my eyes.

We parked the cart and donkey in the walled backyard of what I assumed to be an inn, but since we didn't get inside, I didn't know for sure. The owner came with us and inspected the cart after saluting Uncle Cheng with a respectful *zuo yi*, a fist inside an open hand, which Uncle returned. I forgot what they said exactly, but I remember the man inspecting our vegetables while Uncle Cheng's patience turned thinner by the second. We had something to attend to, and it would not wait for us. They agreed on a price, saluted each other again, and we left the cart and donkey in the small courtyard. We ran more than we walked, and though I did my best to keep up with Cheng Yuanzhi, he had to slow down and grab my hand to ensure I did not get lost among the growing number of people.

"What you'll witness," Uncle Cheng said, "you have to remember all your life, understood?"

"What is it?" I asked. How could I make such a promise if I didn't know what we would see?

"Injustice," he simply said as we reached the back of a gathering crowd.

I barely heard his voice, so strong was the hubbub of the onlookers, all staring in the same direction. Further down the impenetrable wall of people, standing higher on a kind of stage, I could spot the tip of the *liang guan* hat marking a man representing the government. But soon enough, I was shoved against Uncle Cheng by an elbow and could see nothing besides the back of the man in front. Before I realized what was happening, Uncle plucked me effortlessly and dropped me on his shoulders. I could see other boys carried the same way here and there. I dare say we had the best point of view of the assembly.

Next to the official, a gray-bearded man wearing black and red robes standing with his hands behind his back, stood two groups of ten soldiers, two of whom surrounded another man on his knees. While the official and the soldiers looked their best, with their uniforms, armors, and *hanfu* clean and polished, the man on his knees looked anything but. His hair fell pitifully over his shoulders, and though in other cultures it doesn't matter as much, nothing is more humiliating for a proud Han than having his hair unbound in public. His clothes were poor rags of hemp, probably the color of sand in the past, now piss-yellow, and though he did his best to hide his shame behind the curtain of his hair, he had obviously been crying. I also remember thinking he was incredibly slim and had lost small patches of hair.

The official, who I would later learn was the administrator of Nanyang commandery, nodded once over his shoulder and soon followed a bang of the big drum standing at the back of the stage. Years later, I would love this sound, but on that day, it filled me with dread. The administrator's name was Chu Gong. This I knew, for his name was whispered with hatred in the hill, and according to my folks, he must have been the greediest, most corrupt bastard that ever administered a commandery. He didn't look like much, besides the quality of his clothing and jewelry, but he was one of the most powerful men in Jing province, probably just under the inspector, who, though being his junior in the government hierarchy, had power over him in front of the emperor. No matter what I thought of him at this moment, he had come all the way from the commandery capital in the north, Wan, and this meant serious business. County magistrates were enough to rule most cases brought to justice, and sometimes even they did not bother.

There was another series of drumbeats, each throwing a wave of anxiety through my chest. Then Chu Gong raised his hand, and the people became quiet.

"People of Xiangyang," he called, making it sound like they were foreigners to him. "This man here, who goes by the name of He Luo, has been found guilty of black magic."

The crowd erupted with a low ruckus, and even Uncle Cheng joined in, shaking his fist toward the stage. The administrator must have confused the meaning of their reaction, for he shook his hands down as if to say he agreed and understood. In reality, those people were angry at him. Everyone knew an accusation of black magic meant that nothing wrong had been found. It was one of those unspoken rules of our legal system that folks hated, because it could be used against anyone the government deemed troublesome but for no legal cause.

"This filth," he continued, playing along with what he thought was the mood of his crowd, "was plotting to use his magic to sow discord in our good commandery."

My heart beat even faster, for I now knew where this was going. There was only one sentence for an accusation of black magic.

"Per our judgment, this man is hereby sentenced to death by beheading."

He Luo shook with a violent sob but even then did not show his face. He had known of his fate, of course. Executions were extremely rare back then. People were worth more as convicts, which is basically another word for slave, than dead. Officials would usually give a sentence of five years of forced labor, rather than this kind of punishment. He Luo must have seriously angered the local government to earn this fate. And even for those sentenced to corporal punishment, the usual was a flogging, which frequently killed the guilty, though officially, it wasn't the point. To deserve a beheading meant the man was too dangerous to be left alive.

When the executioner, one of the ten soldiers, stepped forward, a broadsword in hand, I turned around.

"Dun," Uncle Cheng said as he yanked on my leg, "keep looking."

I forced my attention back to the stage, where He Luo was made to bend over until his head nearly touched the ground. The drum resumed its beating, slow at first, then quickly increasing in speed. I found my heart matching the drum, and my mouth turned as dry as the summer wind. The administrator raised his hand. The drum reached a rhythm worthy of a festival day. Chu Gong opened his hand and waved his arm as if signaling a pennant on the battlefield. The drum stopped with a last bang.

"Death to the blue sky!" He Luo shouted. The last word died with him.

The broad sword came down in a big whoosh, severing the man's neck. For a couple of seconds, nothing happened. Then a gush of blood flowed from the severed neck and splattered the stage. The crowd gasped at once, even before the blood came, but otherwise remained silent.

I felt a strange sensation down my legs, running up my belly, a certain kind of heat. Then I saw the soldier had botched the job, for the head remained attached to the body by a piece of the throat. Another soldier stepped up and held the head of the dead man straight so that his comrade could finish his gruesome task. When the sword came down again and the second soldier nearly fell on his ass, the heat in my belly quickly rushed to my head. All I heard as the world turned black was the deformed voice of Uncle Cheng calling my name and the echo of He Luo's last words.

Death to the blue sky.

I blacked out for a few minutes, though I still remember Uncle Cheng turning me down so I could puke, then carrying me away. I had soiled myself and, by extension, Uncle as well, and I believe this is what I kept apologizing about as he held me in his arms.

My next clear memory came maybe half a *shi* later, as I lay inside the now empty cart in the inn's courtyard. I sat up as best I could, checking the mess I had made of my clothes. To my surprise, it had been cleaned, more or less. Uncle Cheng was nowhere in sight.

"Woke up for real this time?" asked the man who had bought our vegetables, though I had not spotted him. He came closer from the back door of his establishment, gratifying me with a sorry smile.

"Where is Uncle Cheng?" I asked, sitting straighter.

"A few people to meet," he answered. The man wore an apron, and this apron was red with layers of old blood. The image sent me a flash of the execution and I thought I might pass out again, but I managed to keep the taste of bile in my mouth with a violent head shake. He must have understood, for he removed the apron and threw it in a ball back inside the building.

"Adept Cheng told me to feed you if you asked, though he said you might not be hungry." He had a nice, soft voice. The kind I imagine my mother had. He had called Uncle *Adept*, meaning he was of the Way too.

"I don't think I can eat," I said, though in truth, I was shaking with hunger. It was a new feeling; one I would experience many times again in my life. A mix of disgust and anger.

"That was bad," he said, though it sounded like a question as well.

"It was horrible," I replied. "Why did Uncle Cheng want me to see that?" I asked, for that was the loudest question in my head. The man shrugged.

"You'll have to ask him," he replied. "All I know is that it wasn't supposed to happen like that. Until this morning, the man was supposed to be beaten to death. It ain't pretty either, but it's less… gruesome. You sure you don't want something? A soup maybe?"

"What's the *blue sky*?" I asked. The second question in my head.

The man took a nervous glance over his shoulder, closed the door behind him, and came a little closer, going as far as crouching to my level.

"The *blue sky* is what we call the Han government," he said, meaning how the people of the Way of the Great Peace referred to our rulers.

So He Luo had indeed been a member as well, and this was probably why Cheng Yuanzhi wanted me to witness his end, I thought.

The man stood up, making his knees crack with the effort.

"You look a bit better," he said after peering into my eyes. "The Adept should be back in less than a *shi*. You can wait here or inside, but it's quite busy right now. And if you want—"

"A porridge please," I asked, surprising both of us. He seemed to understand.

"Millet or wheat?"

"Millet," I answered. For the first time in my life, I just wanted to be home.

Uncle Cheng came back nearly two *shi* later. It was late afternoon by then, though I felt like I had spent days in Xiangyang. A piece of me had been curious to discover the city, but I was also too afraid to get lost, or worse, unknowingly find my way back to the marketplace where the execution had been held. So I waited in the cart, only stepping out of it to pat the donkey.

When he arrived, from the establishment's back door as well, I could see that Uncle Cheng was not his usual self. I could not understand if he was angry or disappointed, either by my reaction or because I had peed on him, but it was clear that I was to remain quiet. We left without a word to each other. He carried a bag of linen that we did not have on our way here and dropped it in the cart just as I left it. I took my place on the other side of the donkey, and we went.

To say that the mood was tense would be a euphemism.

For the best part of a *shi*, as we followed the *Tongbai* upstream, none of us uttered a word. The rhythmical clip-clop of the donkey marked the tempo, and it was a slow one. I don't know what made him speak first, but he was the one who broke the silence.

"I'm sorry, Dun," he said. "I didn't think it would be so bad."

"Your friend said it wasn't supposed to be a beheading," I replied, after recovering from the surprise of his apology.

"Yes, and I don't think it was supposed to be such a spectacle. You were out by then, but the silence was deafening when the head was presented to the crowd. Usually, executions bring a kind of exultation. People like to get rid of criminals, and it helps with the reputation of the *yamen* and whoever is in charge, but this time… I thought they might tear him to pieces."

"Why did they kill him?" I asked. I remember making a conscious effort to avoid the word "execution." In my mind, it was a murder—a brutal one at that.

"Didn't you hear?" Uncle Cheng asked ironically. "For black magic."

"I know what *black magic* means," I said. "It means he was a threat to them. Is it because he was from the Way?"

"You picked up on that as well, huh?" Cheng asked, sounding impressed. I simply nodded, for I wasn't sure if the innkeeper was supposed to tell me as much as he did, and I didn't want to bring him any trouble. Especially since he had been kind enough to add some chicken to the porridge. "Yes," Cheng went on, "they killed him because he was one of us. They had nothing but his function within the Way, so they made something up. What they did not expect was how many of us would be present to witness his death. When he left, that bastard Chu Gong probably realized he had made a mistake. He thought that would send a message, and it did, just not the one he wanted. I'm guessing he is halfway to Wan by now." He laughed discreetly, probably imagining the administrator killing his horse to leave the neighborhood as fast as possible.

"What was his function?" I asked, killing the laughter.

"He was an Adept, Dun," Uncle replied, looking my way for the first time. "Of Deng county." I gasped with a new sense of terror. Deng county was the one right west of Xinye, Fa Jia Po's county. Which meant He Luo was the closest comrade of Uncle Cheng. If they could execute such a man, Uncle was in danger too.

"Do you need to leave?" I asked in a panic, for that's the logical conclusion I came to.

"Leave? By *Huang Lao,* no. It means I'm needed here more than ever," he answered, and I don't know if I was relieved or terrified. "It just means that things are moving faster than we thought."

"So, there is going to be a battle?" I asked. The same question I had asked the day before. The answer was different.

"Yes," he simply said. "But it won't be just a battle. Until today, I didn't know how the people would respond to the Way, so far from Julu and our Grand Master. But it is clear now; the hay is dry. It will only take a spark for the fire to take."

"What do you mean?" I asked.

"I mean war, boy, I mean war."

Somehow, the word "war" gave me an entirely different feeling than "battle." I found it dangerous, far from the ideal of heroism and courage I could picture finding in battles. It's funny how two very similar words in their meaning can create contrasting impressions.

"I guess I have to tell everyone what I saw," I said, for I finally understood my purpose in this journey. I was a witness. I was to ignite that flame in the heart of the people in Fa Jia Po, who in turn would spread the heat to the neighboring villages and maybe to the whole county. By the mouth of a young boy, He Luo would become a martyr.

Uncle looked at me with sorry eyes over the peacefully ambling donkey. "You're growing fast," he said. I did not get it then, but now I do. He was sorry I understood this kind of complicated matter. Children should not have to bother with the world of men. But so many get thrown into the wheel of hardship before they are ready, and I was one of them. "But please wait until I leave your hill before you tell them about the beheading part. Your dad will chase me out otherwise."

I did not tell him, thinking about our previous conversation on the matter, but I doubted it. I was wrong. When I finally told my father, right after Cheng's departure, his temper reached nearly as high as *Yeye*'s used to.

As I walked, my hand rested on the donkey's shoulder, and I guess I sensed something through it, for I ducked right as Uncle Cheng tried to cuff me behind the head. He whistled, impressed. It was the first time I managed to avoid one of his strikes.

"Not bad," he said, smiling. "Now, why don't you step into the cart and change your clothes?" I frowned in confusion, so he just waved for me to climb inside the cart.

I did and found in the new bag a ball of fabric. Clothes to replace the ones I had soiled. It was a cold winter, as I said, so I kept the same cloak of dirty wool, but under I was now wearing a shirt made of hemp and a pair of pants of the same material. My old, now ruined clothes had reached a color between brown and yellow because of overuse; truth be told, the pants did not go lower than mid-calf anymore. The new ones, however, were purposefully yellow. They were not of great quality, and I wondered how much of the hill's money had been spent on them, but I instantly liked them. This was the first time something had been bought for me. Not something some neighbors made or remade, but actually new clothes. There was also a long piece of fabric of the same color, which I used as a belt. And of the few memories of my childhood, this is the last I still own, almost eighty years later.

"One more thing," Uncle Cheng said as I tightened the "belt" around my waist. "Never forget what happened today. Promise me, no matter what happens to you in the future, never forget what you saw. Never forget how the people with power act with those who threaten it. And never become that kind of man."

I promised.

I would lie if I said I made good on my promise, and I have broken it on several occasions. But I hope Uncle Cheng knows in the afterlife that I kept his lesson in my heart and lived my life remembering his words.

CHAPTER TWO

THE NEXT THREE MONTHS PASSED IN A FLASH.

Folks from the village and beyond came to hear my account of He Luo's murder, and as Cheng Yuanzhi had hoped, the story spread like wildfire. It soon did as it always does when a story is being passed from neighbor to neighbor; it became a new version of itself, with gross exaggerations and distortions. He Luo had not only lost his head but had been dismembered, his body dragged in four directions by as many horses. In other versions I heard, the evil administrator had cut his nose and feet, as they used to do in the past. I let it be said. As long as the people's anger rose, it was all fine with us.

I say *us* because I considered myself a full member of the Way of the Great Peace. After He Luo's death and other atrocities of the kind, the rumor of violence traveled fast within the country, and farmers who should have been entirely focusing on weeding, plowing, and getting the seeds ready were now busy sharpening tools and practicing whatever they had learned during their meager military training. Few of the folks had actually taken part in any military campaign, and it usually had been of a local scale, but they soon became the most important members of our communities. Every morning in Fa Jia Po, Ling Jun, whom we called Fat Ling as a joke, for he was as thick as a twig, and Old Mi, who was indeed fairly old, were training us to the best of their memory. I took part in the training, though I laugh now at what we considered a military drill back then. Basically, we learned which end of a weapon goes into your enemy and how to stand in groups without walking on each other. Even though it was clear our two instructors had little more experience than any of the others, Cheng Yuanzhi had left them in charge of the ordeal, and so we listened.

Another task kept us busy, though it mainly concerned the women. Gathering laurel leaves and some tree barks, they dyed as much fabric as possible in yellow. Slowly, we were earning the name that would make us famous throughout the land, and probably for many generations, the Yellow Turbans. We didn't know about the turban part, only that each member of the Way who wanted to fight for his or her freedom was to receive a piece of yellow fabric the size of my belt. For a time, the countryside around the hill was filled with peasants wearing bright yellow belts, and it is one of the fondest memories of my childhood.

Cheng Yuanzhi had come back once, during the last month of winter, shortly before the new year. This was when he told us of the yellow fabric. There was fire in his voice when he addressed the crowd, and I guess by then his speech was honed to the bone.

In the early summer, he told us, the signal would be sent for the people of the Way to rise against the oppressive Han rulers. This upcoming year was a *jiazi*, the first of a sixty-year cycle. According to our Grand Master Zhang Jue, this would be the cycle during which the sky would metaphorically turn yellow instead of blue, meaning the end of the Han dynasty and the beginning of our era. In response to this celestial favor, the characters of the *jiazi* appeared on the gates of cities and the buildings of the government, the *yamen,* all over the empire. A warning of their coming end.

Uncle Cheng urged us to maintain the farm work as long as possible, for the war would keep us busy from after sowing to harvesting, a few months during which even a limited number of people can care for the growing cereals. We needed no urging, and never before had the fields of Fa Jia Po been ready so fast, or so clumsily, for that matter.

Even my father gained in aggressivity as the winter made way for spring. He would never be a warrior, and even I could see his weaknesses when he practiced with his flimsy, self-made spear, but at least he walked straighter and looked the part. During our short family times, we spoke with more ease as well. My sister, who was barely five, did not seem to understand what was happening to our quiet hill, but since she got to spend more time with other kids, she was fairly happy. I regret it now, but I didn't care much about her during those months.

Then, a little more than a month after his last visit, Uncle Cheng came back to the hill, and from the moment he stormed the narrow path, I knew something was wrong.

First, he was riding a horse, something I did not know he could, despite his apparent ease. And second, he held a sword in his hand. Not just any sword, but a proper *jian* double-edged sword. The kind used by officers and nobles, with the particularity that his was covered in red.

Uncle Cheng's hair clung to the side of his face because of the sweat, and a few bruises showed from under his upturned sleeves. The steed, a strong-looking, sand-colored mare, breathed heavy clouds of hot air through her dilated nostrils, and though I knew nothing of horses, it was clear this one had been hard ridden.

The folks gathered around Cheng Yuanzhi in no time, and his voice carried far.

"Remove your belts! Hide them!" he screamed. He had to say it one more time before we all obeyed. I gave mine to a woman of the Wu family, who then ran back home with a ball of flying ribbons clutched against her chest.

"Listen to me!" Yuanzhi said, calling for people to stop asking their thunder of questions. "We don't have much time. The county guards came to me on my way here. It was a trap. I managed to slay their captain and steal his horse, but they'll come here soon." I suddenly held my belly with apprehension. Everything was turning real again, just like in Xiangyang.

"Get your weapons!" Fat Ling called with authority.

"No!" Uncle Cheng barked even louder. "This is a platoon of thirty men. You're not ready."

"We are a hundred fighters," Fat Ling said, looking left and right for support.

"They have trained for years," Cheng Yuanzhi said. "They have actual weapons, solid lamellar armors and helmets, and even a couple of crossbows. You're not ready."

I think the mention of the crossbows was what undid us. With numbers on their side, most people believe they will make it out of a fight, but when artillery is part of the fight, even a ragged band like us knew we would suffer casualties.

"So why did you come here?" a man asked. His question raised a few voices in agreement.

"I have a plan," Cheng said. I was standing right in front of him then, and I saw his left fist tightening. "You'll tie me and hand me to the guards. You'll say I appeared and threatened you, but you resisted and unhorsed me."

"Uncle!" I called after letting out a gasp.

"Dun, not now," he replied, and his eyes, more than his voice, told me to be quiet. "When they leave, you wait for a few minutes. Then, by groups of two, you scatter in every direction, go to every hamlet, village, hill, valley, wherever folks live, and tell our brothers and sisters to head for Wan."

"Wan?" I asked. "Not Xiangyang?" I wanted to burn that city to the ground, but such was not the plan of our leaders.

"Why Wan?" someone asked behind me.

"It's a long story, but that's where the war starts for us," Uncle Cheng said, and I saw all the regret of the world on his face when he used the word *us*. "You gather men wherever you go, and you head straight to Wan. Find one of the Adepts, if possible Deng Mao or Han Zhong, and tell them you come from me. And Liao Dun needs to go with you."

I was so surprised by what he just said that I barely heard my father asking why in a high-pitched voice.

"I told those two Adepts about him. If they see him, they'll know you are not spies and are my brothers from Xinye county." My chest filled with pride at the idea that not just one, but two more Adepts of the order knew of my existence.

Just then, we heard the ruckus of men running and a voice yelling orders.

"Dun, you'll remember?" Uncle asked urgently, grabbing me by the shoulders.

I nodded. "We go to Wan. We find Deng Mao or Han Zhong."

Uncle stood straighter and checked around him for a second, stopping his gaze into the eyes of my father. "Make it believable," he said, and before I could understand what he had meant, my father punched him straight in the nose. I say punch, but it was one of those blows that hurt the puncher more than the victim. My father shook his hand while wincing, and Uncle Cheng dropped on his ass, blood running freely from his broken nose.

Old Mi then rushed to Cheng Yuanzhi, and though I thought he meant to help him, he was actually working a thick rope around his wrists. Just as the noose was tightened, the first soldiers appeared on the small path, running two by two. The first two were carrying *ji*, dagger-axes, a weapon unique to our people, a spear with a second blade of the same length perpendicular to the first one, making the whole thing into a half cross. A *ji* is a wicked weapon if I ever saw one, though I would learn about its full potential later in my life. The others were mostly walking with regular spears in hand. Half of them carried shields, the ones we call *gourd shields*.

The platoon slowed down when they saw the mass of people gathered further down the path, and with the angle of the hill, I could see all those soldiers. Now I knew why Uncle Cheng had not wanted us to fight. Their armor looked solid, most of it made of iron, with hundreds of lamellar pieces sewn together on each man. Some even had this iron pattern sewn onto their helmets, though most wore leather caps or a simple pin to tie their hair in a bun. A man walked by himself on the third rank, and I guessed he was their new leader. His armor wasn't any different from the others', but his helmet looked more refined. He also carried a *jian* sword, the same that Uncle Cheng had dropped when my father punched him.

The two closing the march were indeed carrying crossbows, and even from where I stood, it sent a shiver down my spine. The way they all marched in unison made the procession all the more impressive to our untrained eyes.

They stopped at once when their leader called the halt, and he alone continued to walk our way.

"What happened here?" he asked, pointing his sword toward Cheng Yuanzhi, who feigned his struggle with talent. This man was easily in his late thirties and had bovine eyes that did not shine with cleverness. It was easy to see why he had not been an officer until now.

"We stopped him," Old Mi said, his knee on the back of Uncle Cheng.

"The bastard came galloping here like a mad Xianbei," Fat Ling added to sell the story. "Almost cut my wife in half before we jumped him down. Isn't that right, folks?" Some of us agreed with him, which was funny because Fat Ling had no wife.

The officer chewed his bottom lip as he tried to make sense of the scene in front of his eyes.

"Let me go, you ugly bastard!" Cheng spat, thrashing his feet in anger. "Huang-Lao will curse you for that!" I saw Old Mi's eyes turning round, probably wondering if this part would be true despite the situation.

"This man killed an officer of the county's guard," the soldier said. "We will take him."

"Is there a reward?" Fat Ling asked, his hands on the rope tied around Uncle's wrists. I thought he might have ruined everything, but the face of the officer took on a slightly disgusted smile, and my respect for Fat Ling increased a notch. Of course, in this situation, folks would try to haggle something out of it.

"Come to Xinye in a couple of days," the officer said. "I'm sure we can arrange something." He then held his hand out, and with a feigned air of regret, Fat Ling passed the rope to the soldier, who then waved his hands toward his platoon. Two guards passed their spears to their comrade behind and moved up, taking Uncle by the elbows and forcing him up. I thought he might headbutt one, but he just slumped his shoulders and dropped his head in defeat. I watched him being walked between the two lines of soldiers, and I told myself that it could not be. Surely this was not the end of Cheng Yuanzhi's path. An image of my uncle kneeling in front of a crowd, and a broadsword slicing through his neck, flowed through my mind, and I tried very hard not to yell at them to stop.

I looked down. It was unfair. We were but a month or two from the war, and everything Uncle had fought for would be taken from him. I fought the tears, and that's when I saw it again—Uncle Cheng's sword. He had dropped it, and somehow the blade had landed between the feet of a few folks. We would need that blade, I thought. But just then, I saw the officer's head slowly turning in its direction.

"Officer!" I called. I heard my father's breath being sucked in, and I thought he might cuff me, but he did not.

The officer turned his attention to me, and his frown told me it had been a bad idea.

"Don't forget the horse," I said, going toward the beast and dragging the man's eyes away from the blade. I took the bridle from one of my neighbors' hands and held it toward the officer.

His frown vanished, and a genuine smile cut through his unkempt beard.

"Thanks, lad," he said before patting my hair and taking the horse from me. If any of us knew how to ride, the horse might have been a better deal than the blade, but none of the folks could, so I still believe I had a good idea. The officer wasn't a skilled rider either, as he showed when he took three tries before he got on the saddle.

"Your name?" he asked from atop the horse.

"Liao Dun," I answered.

"You?" he then asked Fat Ling.

"Ling Jun. Though people call me Fat Ling."

The officer smiled, and it wasn't an unpleasant smile. Surely the man came from a community just like ours before turning to a life in the army. It is interesting how even then, as my hate for the Han government had reached its peak, I felt no anger against the army. I knew they just tried to make a living and had found a better deal than toiling the earth all their life. It might sound strange to think a kid had this kind of maturity, but I truly understood that point. And I still hoped to become a soldier when we were in power.

The officer turned the horse as best he could and trotted his way up the hill again. The soldiers followed two by two, in the same order they had come, making it look like they were peeling from the path.

Uncle Cheng looked backward as they pushed him and nodded discreetly in my direction.

The second they vanished, I picked up the sword. It was not as heavy as I originally thought, but I could imagine how tiring wielding this thing could be. Fat Ling took it from my grasp, but not before telling me it had been some nice thinking on my part.

"What do we do?" a panicking voice asked within the small crowd.

"What do you mean?" Old Mi asked. "We do as he said. We go by two and tell our brothers to meet near Wan."

"Why now?" someone else asked. "The war isn't for another month or two, at least."

"Who cares?" another replied. "Cheng Yuanzhi gave us an order. We follow it."

Several people agreed with that, but I wasn't part of them.

"Are you all mad?" Old Zhang said. We all turned in his direction. Old Zhang wasn't a bad man per se, he was just a lackey of his landowner, the head of the Cai clan, and since he had his master's trust, he wasn't as invested in the cause as the rest of us. "Don't you see? This war is over. The government found out about Zhang Jue's plan and acted first. We can't fight them if they're ready."

I'm not saying I disagree with his assessment, and he proved to be right in many ways, but at that moment I couldn't have cared less about his doubts and felt a ball of anger forming in my stomach. But what he said next truly made me furious.

"Just take the reward this officer mentioned and wait for things to settle. This is what I say."

I grabbed the sword back from Fat Ling's hands and ran like a mad bull, lifting the weapon above my head and screaming with all my high-pitched voice. Old Zhang gasped in terror when he saw me charging, and I still laugh that a seven-year-old boy could turn a grown-up's face white with fear so fast. Before I could land a blow, my father caught me from behind, nearly getting the tip of the blade in the eye. I struggled, never leaving Old Zhang's eyes from mine.

"I'll kill you, coward!" I barked.

"Dun!" my father said, shaking my body in one swift motion. "Stop it!"

After a few seconds of trying, I released all the tension in my body, and my father let me go. The tears came next.

"It's unfair," I said, wiping the tears with the back of my hand. "Uncle Cheng will never see the yellow sky."

"Dun-*er*," my father called softly, "I know it's not fair. But we should do as he asked." It was unfair, but my anger switched to him. Thankfully, before I could say something, Fat Ling spoke.

"We don't have to," he said as he picked up the blade again.

"What do you mean?" asked Old Mi.

"You saw them," Fat Ling replied. "They were boys. Barely better trained than we are."

"They have crossbows," someone said.

"And good blades," another added.

"We will have to face them anyway," Fat Ling said. "What did you think would happen? We would just show up and Emperor Ling would give us the keys to the palace? Many of us will die before this war is over. Don't think otherwise." He was getting angrier as he spoke, or sounded like it at least. Fat Ling had always been tall, but somehow he looked as if he had just gained a *chi* of height. "At least today we have the advantage of surprise."

"And we know the land," Old Mi added.

"And if we act now, we not only save our leader, but we also gain good armor and blades for the next fights. This might save some of us in future battles. And we would be weakening our enemy in the process. Those boys will face us, either today or tomorrow."

Fat Ling had spoken well, and it was hard to argue. Not that many people wanted to. I think what helped us make our decision was the fact that it would be our first fight. None of us could imagine falling in battle.

"So those who want to fight, follow me. The others can do as Cheng Yuanzhi said and spread the word to the folks around. Who fights?"

Voices and hands were raised in loud cheers, so many that I was wondering if anyone would be actually going to our neighbors.

"Get your weapons, get your belts, and tie this man until we come back," Fat Ling said, pointing a dirty finger at Old Zhang.

Children believe they run better than adults. Of course, they know grown-ups can run faster, but they believe they have more energy and endurance. That's because adults never run if they don't have to. When they *do* run, they can leave kids in the dust, which is exactly what happened on that day.

I had never seen my father run before, and a new sense of pride flew in me when I saw his slender silhouette outdistancing all the others. Then he was followed by all the others, leaving me to curse internally for being abandoned. If discretion hadn't been a priority, I would have cursed a lot louder. But we were in a hurry, and I also understood what mattered, which wasn't to keep a child in the loop.

In the time it takes for a man to finish a bowl of millet, our ragged band had gathered their weapons, recovered their yellow belts, and left in pursuit of the platoon of soldiers. Fat Ling gave a plan and left no option for a discussion. There was a part of the road leading to Xinye, the capital city of the homonymous county, which belonged to no village in particular, and thus was never taken care of. As such, the vegetation grew wild on both sides of the road, with thick bushes and lush trees. Even in this season, there would be enough cover for an ambush, Old Fa explained, and since he knew the county like the back of his hand, we believed him. Of course, that was if we could make it on time, and that was a big if. And we could not use the road but had to keep to the beaten path and fields across the land. It was more direct but not nearly as practical, which meant men not only ran, but jumped over the irregularities of the land, and more than once, a curse would be uttered when one of us fell.

Halfway through, maybe, I could no longer see anyone. I was truly alone. My father had barely argued my presence, keeping it to making me swear I would stay hidden. But seeing how things went, I would just not be there at all.

Even though this was the second month of spring, the morning air was still fresh, and the mud splashing around as I followed the path of tumbled grass kept my skin even colder. The left side of my ribs hurt, I tasted blood in the back of my mouth, and my vision was tunneling, so I slowed down a little. I wanted to cry but kept the tears at bay, if only to avoid making noise. I more or less knew where the ambush would be held, though I had never gone as far in that direction. I only had to follow the track left by the folks anyway, but a sense of despair took me in.

Out of the hundred or so warriors in Fa Jia Po, maybe sixty left to the rescue of our leader. The others were either absent from the hill on that day or chose to remain behind. I hoped the latter would at least be on their way to honor Cheng's request.

For the fighters, Fat Ling had given clear and simple recommendations. Fight by two, first kill the crossbowmen, then the officer. He kept the sword and selected three men to help him in a focused effort aimed at liberating Uncle Cheng. Fat Ling might have been a terrible instructor, but he was slipping into the role of gang leader like a fish in the water.

I also entertained the worrying idea that maybe those soldiers were not going to Xinye at all. The officer had invited Ling Jun to Xinye, which didn't mean this was their current destination. They might have taken him to Xiangyang, or even possibly to Wan, though that was doubtful. There was nothing to be done about it, so I just prayed internally that we had taken the right way.

My prayer was answered a couple of minutes later, when the sounds of battle resonated in the valley. I dashed through a lush stretch of land, then into a thicket of leafed trees. The sounds were slightly distorted by the vegetation, so it took me a few seconds to find the right direction. When I did, the sounds were fading already. I heard screams, mostly of pain, though also of rage. I thought battles would be filled with the sounds of metal on metal, but I heard very few of those. Men were far noisier than their weapons on that day. It made sense; this was an ambush after all, not a pitched battle.

By the time I came into view of the battlefield, the fight was done, as far as I could tell. I stepped back on the road, not far from where my folks had launched the attack, and it almost killed me. Just as I stepped away from a thick ground of bracken, I heard a horse galloping toward me. The wind produced by its speed brought the scent of its sweat as it grazed me. I fell on my ass and barely caught a glimpse of the horse bolting away, pushed hard by the panicking officer from before.

"*Tian-na!*" cursed one of my neighbors who had meant to pursue the horse rider. He was panting hard and sweating profusely, though the fighting could not have lasted more than a minute. He wiped his forehead with the back of his hand and left a long brush of red. I suddenly felt very cold and heard a buzz in my head. Was my father all right? A battle had just taken place, people had died, and it just registered in my mind that he could be one of them. I dashed past this neighbor and quickly came in sight of the slaughter.

As I grew older, I became accustomed to such a spectacle, but back then, as I first laid eyes on a battleground, I thought I might die myself. It was all so eerily still. Corpses were lying where they had fallen, most of them in positions suggesting their pain at the moment of their death, some carrying the shock of the event on their faces. Men barely out of their boyhood were clutching the pole of whatever had killed them, but nothing would make it all right for them. And among the bodies, two belonged to Fa Jia Po.

The first I noticed was that of Fa Deng, the son of Old Fa, a bolt from a crossbow lodged into his neck. The blood was still oozing out in lazy pulses. Old Fa only had one son, and this son was now dead. Soon, no Fa would live on the hill bearing their name. The father was kneeling, rocking his son's head against his chest as the tears poured freely.

The second of our dead, to my relief, was not my father. I could not recognize who it was, for he had taken a spear through the face, but I knew from his gray hair that it wasn't my dad.

I stepped over a soldier's body on my way to a large group of our men gathered at the front of what had been the platoon, when this body gave a spasm and startled me so badly I let out a shriek. He raised his head, and I saw the pool of blood gathering in his mouth, then the light in his eyes vanished.

"Dun-*er*," my father called from the main group, waving me to them. He seemed unhurt. He still carried his spear, which was unbloodied, but at this point I was just glad to see him well. Finding the comfort of his arms, I was amazed at the speed of his heartbeat against my cheek.

"What are you doing here?" asked the angry voice of Uncle Cheng, whom the folks had been gathering around. Old Mi cut through the ropes tying his wrist. Right after, Uncle stood back up, and the assistance stood straighter with him. His eyes filled with rage, and I thought he would yell at us for saving his life. "I told you to gather the men and leave for Wan!" For a few seconds, all we could hear were the sounds of our folks busy looting the dead or making sure they were truly gone, plus the breathing of Uncle Cheng, who could no longer inhale through the nose since my dad had broken it.

"That's the direction to Wan," Fat Ling said, in what must have been an attempt at humor. Cheng Yuanzhi looked straight at him, and Fat Ling took a step back. Then, to our great surprise, Uncle let out a laugh like the bark of a big hound. Then another, and finally he broke into a guffaw quickly picked up by everyone.

Cheng Yuanzhi went from rage to gratitude in the blink of an eye, embracing the closest men without shame, pulling even Fat Ling into a bear hug. His relief had completely overcome his ire.

"That was brilliant," Uncle said when he ran out of men to cling to.

"Aye, well, the kid wouldn't shut up about you," Old Mi said, which got a good laugh from everyone but me.

"I should have known you were too stubborn to let me go," Uncle Cheng said as he patted my hair, which made me feel absurdly happy. "It was brilliant," he then said again. The credit was given to Fat Ling, who deserved it.

In reality, as I learned later, it hadn't gone perfectly. One of the folks had lost his nerve and left the cover of the thicket too fast, forcing the others to charge before the entire line of soldiers was in a perfect position. This mistake had cost Fa Deng's life. Still, two lives against the nearly thirty of them was a great start for our rebellion.

"One of them got away," said the man who had run after the horse.

"Doesn't matter," Uncle Cheng replied. "We need to go anyway, and not just from here. He will know where you came from. Fa Jia Po is no longer safe. We all go to Wan now."

"What's happening to us?" Old Mi asked, and by us, he meant the members of the Way.

"I'll explain on the way back to the hill," Uncle Cheng said as he prodded his painful nose. "But first, gather their weapons, their armor, and for the love of Huang-Lao, remove those from your waists and put them around your heads. They are turbans, not belts."

I blushed when he said so, for I was the reason we wore them this way. Fortunately, no one mentioned it, and most chose to laugh at our mistake. This was the first thing we did. We had no uniform, almost no training, but as soon as we tied our yellow turbans, we did look like an army. At least in our collective mind.

Someone offered that we roll the bodies away from the road, which we did, if only because we would need to come this way again soon, on our way to Wan. Once done, we walked back to Fa Jia Po, and Uncle Cheng told us what was happening over the empire.

The revolt had not been planned to start for another month and some days, but things were moving differently. The Adept in charge of the capital, a man named Ma Yuanyi, got betrayed by one of his closest advisors, just as he was visiting one of our patrons in Luoyang. Ma Yuanyi had accomplished an amazing job in the name of the Way, getting even some of the emperor's beloved eunuchs to support our cause. This brought him no luck in the end, for he was dismembered, and most of his supporters shared a slightly less gruesome but just as fatal fate. Remembering how He Luo's story had morphed over a few days, I expressed some doubts about Ma Yuanyi's actual end, but Uncle promised it was the truth.

This had been less than a week ago. As they tortured Ma Yuanyi and interrogated the traitors, the government learned the plan for the rebellion and decided to act before we could. Uncle Cheng had heard all of this on this very morning, from a messenger sent by the leader of the Yellow Turbans in Jing province, the Grand Adept Zhang Mancheng. He was on his way to the hill to organize our next step when he stumbled on the platoon sent to arrest him, and the rest was known to us.

"So why Wan?" I asked, repeating the question from earlier.

"That's where the administrator of Nanyang is," Uncle answered. The one man I wanted to see dead was in Wan, meaning that my anger for Xiangyang was misplaced.

"Will there be many of us?" Old Mi asked not long before we reached the hill. Already we could spot the families gathered at the tip of the path.

"We will be an army like this land has never witnessed," Uncle said, his fist clenched in the air. "Though how many are fighters and how many are simply following, I don't know."

The folks from the hill ran our way when they recognized who was coming, and I saw more than one face filled with tears.

"Adept Cheng," called a woman. Fat Ling's sister, I believe. "We kept Old Zhang in his house, as requested, but we can't find his wife." At the back of the line, I heard a scream, which I knew was from Fa Deng's mother.

"Damn it," Cheng said, and for the first time he looked worried.

The county's guard was one thing, with less than two hundred soldiers and a whole territory to cover. But the private militia of a great landowner like the Cai clan could number close to a thousand, and they could be gathered with ease from villages and farms. Even in Fa Jia Po, many folks owed the Cai clan, though this arrangement would probably be revised at the end of the war.

"We need to hurry," Uncle said, waving the entire group toward the hill. It was time to leave our homes, many of us for the last time, and head to war. We had won the first battle, but many more were waiting for us, starting with the great battle of our province, in Wan.

CHAPTER THREE

AFTER A DAY ON THE MARCH, Uncle Cheng, and by extension all of us, stopped checking over our shoulders for any militia. He still believed they might come, but we were enough to repel any idea of attack from them. People flocked from all over Xinye county at our approach, pushed on by the small groups of men Cheng Yuanzhi had sent ahead and away. We stopped near the last village of Xinye county on the northern side. A few steps further, and we would be within the next county. Another two counties to cross, and we would be at Wan's gates.

The atmosphere was strangely euphoric on that evening. I can't say how many people had gathered, but I guess at least two thousand. It might sound like a lot, but Xinye was a well-populated county, as the rest of northern Jing was, with over ten thousand households and probably fifty thousand inhabitants, most of us being farmers. Cheng Yuanzhi seemed content with the way things had moved during the day and knew more would join soon. He was right; even during the night, large groups of men melted in the mass of Yellow Turbans. The first of them gave us a fright, making some of us run for their lives, so Uncle Cheng sent a good hundred men to watch the surrounding area in groups of three. One of them would report to him every time people were approaching, which meant he barely slept that night. Our numbers increased by at least six hundred before we resumed the march.

I had turned into something of a hero by that time, at least to the other children, of whom they were many. They came by the dozens to hear of the great battle *we* had fought, and of my role in this event. I must admit I liked the attention, and by the end of the day, I was willingly telling those who would listen that I had been part of the ambush and even had killed an enemy.

I marched in front, next to Uncle Cheng and Fat Ling, the de facto right arm of our leader, both of us walking as if we owned that land.

But in the evening, as children went to sleep among their people under the stars and clouds, which thankfully were few, I felt very lonely. Uncle Cheng had no time for me, though he always shared a smile and a nod when we exchanged a glance. So I went back to my little family.

Mihua slept against my father's chest, and they lay in the cart we used to carry all our meager possessions. Our ox, which had pulled the cart all day, slept ahead of it, his loud breathing marking a soporific tempo.

Father opened an eye when I climbed in the cart and invited me to join my sister. I refused and lay with my face to them, with as much space as I could put between us. He shook his head, but I did not react. I wasn't mad or anything. He had been part of the action during the ambush after all. It's just that as soon as the fight was over, he became his quiet self again and went back to caring about a little girl rather than trying to join Cheng Yuanzhi's circle. Then he said one of the worst things he could have said.

"Once this is all over, maybe we will have earned enough to buy a second ox again."

How could he talk of such things? I wondered, baffled beyond words. We were going to war, on the march to topple an empire and bring justice to the land, but all he could get himself to consider was the growth of his farm. I'm sure he said it thinking I would appreciate his ambition, while I truly hated the idea of a second ox, or anything related to farming. Once the war was over, I thought I would stay with Uncle Cheng and make my way to the top with him.

I rolled over and remained silent rather than speak my mind, but I could feel the ball of anger in my belly again.

I fell asleep to the sound of my sister's breathing and to that of a man playing a soft air with his *dizi*.

The next two days more or less followed the same pattern. We had a bit of rain on the second morning, and we also moved slower, not that we had been moving fast to begin with. Oxen cannot be pressed on, that's a fact, but from day two, a few donkeys and mules went lame, and some carts' wheels broke. All those things happened while more and more people merged with our army of peasants. We crossed into the next county late on the third day. Though Uncle Cheng grew more anxious by the *shi*, he started feeling better after finding one passable rider among the newcomers and sending him toward Wan to warn his collaborators of our approach.

I got a few minutes by his side when he relinquished his command to Fat Ling to eat his soup of cabbage and onion.

"Everything all right?" he asked, letting some of the soup drip on his beard as he spoke.

"Of course," I replied, determined to sound the perfect soldier. Back then, I had this twisted impression that soldiers never complained and obeyed every order without as much as a grumble. Nothing could be further from the truth, and knowing this, Uncle smiled. It was the first time I saw him smile that day.

"I saw a lot of children around you," he went on. "How is fame treating you?"

"I don't want to be with the children," I said as if I wasn't one of them.

"You want to stay with me?" he asked, somehow looking surprised.

"Of course!" I shouted. "But not just on the road to Wan, even after."

"Dun—"

"No, I know," I said, interrupting him before it could turn into a lesson again. "I'm not complaining about my dad. It's just that I'm not like him. I hate farming, and I hate this life of a peasant. I want to be a warrior."

"There is no shame in being a farmer," Uncle said weakly.

I wanted to say that there wasn't much pride in it either, but I swallowed the argument on time. Old as I am now, I know the pride of a farmer is far greater and more deserved than that of a warrior, but children can't understand that, least of all me.

"So why didn't you become one?" I asked instead.

"I did not have a loving father to support me," he said, meaning that I did have one.

"But I bet even if you did, you would never have felt fulfilled with your lot in life. Am I wrong?" I wasn't, and we both knew it. "So look, either I go with you, or I flee and become a bandit." I meant nothing of it but turned my eyes to steel. He searched through my soul, and I thought I might break our gaze, so I nailed the point harder instead. "And since the Yellow Turbans will be in power, it means you might have to chase me down someday."

After a few seconds during which the muscles of his jaws twitched, Uncle Cheng finally breathed out, looking suddenly exhausted.

"That was a clever argument," he said, which I took for an agreement on his part. "As long as your father is with us, you'll stay by my side." I did not like the sound of that, but could not argue against it. Besides, I did not see where else my father, or anyone from Fa Jia Po, could go in the near future. We had made ourselves enemies of the Han government, and there would be peace only once the power in place had been removed.

"You will make a great father someday," I said, just as an idea popped into my mind. Cheng nearly choked on his spoon when I spoke, which was exactly the reaction I was looking for. My punch came with all the strength of my young arm and landed clumsily on Cheng Yuanzhi's cheek. I don't think there was much force in the punch, but his sitting position wasn't stable on the bucket he used as a stool, and he collapsed backward, his arms waving in circles as he tried to gather some sort of balance. He fell on his ass, dropping the content of his soup all over his chest. My pleasure vanished fast when he leaned on his elbows and shot me the same look a dog would have if I was about to steal from its meal.

I ran before he could stand and scared more than one of the folks as I dashed my way through our camp. I nearly tripped on a bunch of stretched legs and received a fair share of curses while I tried to maintain my distance on Uncle Cheng, both of us laughing like drunks. I didn't make it far.

"That's the second time you soiled my shirt," he said as he picked me up and shoved my face against his soup-soaked garment.

"I got you though," I meant to say.

That night, I remained within the close circle of warriors around Cheng Yuanzhi, and I was exactly where I belonged.

The next day, as soon as Uncle Cheng called the march, it was clear things would not go as quietly as before. He increased the speed at the front of the line, hoping it would pull the mass of followers, but by then we were close to four thousand people, and all he did was create a gap between the warriors in front and the rest. To remedy this issue, he sent men to surround the folks and with little persuasion, brought a certain sense of urgency to our advance.

I thought he must have received some news of pursuers and meant to reach the safety of our larger army in Wan. But when we stopped next, someone asked him why he had forced his old neighbors to abandon their lame mule. Cheng simply pointed ahead, and that's when we noticed a few glints over the horizon. It was faint, but it had to be another large group of men, and since we were now using the main road and had followed the Bai river, we knew those men stood between us and Wan, meaning they had to be Yellow Turbans as well.

"Our brothers await," he said.

And though they had to wait for another *shi*, we finally reached the back of a massive crowd of folks, twice larger than ours and even less organized. Closing their march and facing us was a single man, arms crossed over his chest until he recognized Uncle Cheng. At that point, he stretched himself backward and opened his arms while laughing in a roaring voice worthy of a thunder spirit. This is how I met Deng Mao, and if I had thought Uncle Cheng to be a peculiar man, he was subtle next to his companion.

"Thought you'd never arrive," Deng Mao said as he finally let go of Cheng Yuanzhi. Deng Mao was about the same age as Uncle but looked much older for his hairless dome and sun-tanned, wrinkled skin. He was the kind of man who laughed a lot, or so said his wrinkles, but he had an air of violence about him. He was also short, a good head and a half shorter than Cheng, but what he lacked in height, he made up for in width. His shoulders looked as if set on a pole, and his heavy muscular arms dangled helplessly by his sides. His shortness, coupled with his thick chest, gave him a cubic shape that could have been funny but made him all the more impressive from up close.

"We had a long way," Uncle replied almost apologetically.

"So did we," Deng said, hands on his waist.

"And we had a fight."

"We heard," Deng Mao said. "Some poor bastards thought they could arrest Mad-Cheng. I pity them."

I was amazed by what had just been said. First, I did not comprehend how the story could have reached so far already. This is something I would never understand, but rumors have this way of traveling faster than men, and though it makes no sense, it seemed to be a universal rule. Second, this energetic ball of nerves had called Uncle "Mad-Cheng," and for the life of me, I could not imagine how he had earned this sobriquet. Those two men had obviously known each other for a very long time.

"They almost got me, though. Without this man here," Uncle went on, dropping his hand on Fat Ling's shoulder, "and the other folks of Fa Jia Po, I would be dead meat by now."

Fat Ling, blushing, adopted a *zuo yi* salute, but he barely got to clasp his fist with his hand before Deng's fell on them.

"You saved my brother," the short man said seriously. "No need for politeness between us." And it was like Fat Ling grew even taller again. "Without him, we would be lost." Something in his voice told me he hadn't meant it as a figure of speech, and Cheng Yuanzhi proved me right.

"He's already making a mess?"

"He's already doing nothing, you mean," Deng replied after a scoff. "Han Zhong is trying hard to get an actual decision out of him, but I gather this must feel like trying to start a furnace with your farts."

"Is that why you're waiting here, at the back of your men?" Uncle asked, smirking like a fiend.

"I'm not going there without you," Deng replied. "There is no telling I won't make our enemy's life easier by taking *his* head."

"All right," Uncle Cheng said. "Let's go see our dear leader together then. And I promise to stop you before you jump at him."

"And I'll stop you before you go wild again," Deng retorted.

The first of our folks passed by our sides and joined their fellow Yellow Turbans from Deng's group. Many of them knew those folks, and it was soon impossible to distinguish one group from the other.

"Is that him?" Deng Mao asked while I looked at the reunion between what I assumed to be two actual brothers. I thought he meant the leader they had spoken of, but when I turned his way again, I saw his finger pointed at me. "That's the eagle-eyed kid you spoke of?"

"More like pig-headed," Uncle Cheng replied as he fondled my hair, "but, yes, that's him. Liao Dun of Fa Jia Po. Dun, meet my brother-in-arms, Deng Mao."

I bowed my head and gave as perfect a *Zuo Yi* as I knew how to back then. "A pleasure to meet you, sir," I said, which got Deng Mao to bark.

"You call him uncle, but I'm *sir*?" he asked, looking truly cross. "You call me Uncle Deng, or you don't call me at all." When I looked up, I saw that Uncle Deng wasn't angry, it was just in his character to exaggerate everything. I liked him right away. "Come find me once we settle a little," he said after dropping his heavy hand on my back. "I got plenty of stories about this crazy old bear here."

"Be careful," Uncle Cheng told his comrade. "He'll never leave you alone once you acknowledge him." I attempted a kick in his shin in reply, but Uncle avoided it with a peal of heartfelt laughter.

"It's fine," Uncle Deng said as Cheng Yuanzhi pushed him forward. "Haven't had a servant since the army. I still can't believe this old goat got killed a week before the end of our enlistment. Did you know…" The rest of their conversation got lost in the noise of thousands of men shuffling aimlessly as we penetrated the mass of Deng Mao's followers.

"It seems you have a new uncle to worship, *Eagle-eye*," Fat Ling said, and he was right. This is also how I gained my nickname within the Yellow Turbans, Ying Yan, *Eagle-eye*, and that too I liked instantly. I did not see what it meant, but when I asked Deng Mao, he said that eagles have this stare that never rests, always intensely looking for the next prey or threat. I had never seen an eagle from up close, but when I finally saw one a year later, I remembered this conversation and understood exactly what he had meant. That eagle had intense eyes of golden brown, and this too offered a similarity between us.

Whatever the case, I was suddenly proud of this particularity people used to make fun of me about. And, as if inhabited by the spirit of this bird, I walked to the very front of our groups to take a good look at Wan, the capital of Nanyang and one of the five great cities of the empire. What I saw from the top of a low hill filled me with awe. Not so much the city, which sat like a wart on the plateau, but the sea of people crowding its southern side, a *li* or so from the ridiculously high wall.

The disorganization made our army look even bigger, but even then, Wan was clearly doomed. I heard unbelievable numbers about our army on that day. Some even claimed that half of the two million people living in Nanyang commandery had joined. In reality, we were far less than that, probably close to eighty thousand people, maybe a third of whom were fighters.

"Unbelievable," Uncle Cheng said, sounding more disgusted than impressed. "He hasn't even surrounded the city."

"Pah," Uncle Deng said. "Every time a new bunch of us shows up, a horseman leaves from the north gate without a care in the world." And just as he said so, I could indeed see a horse rider galloping the other way from the city. "I reckon we have a week before strong reinforcements arrive."

"What is he waiting for?" Uncle asked after spitting a thick gob toward Wan.

"Huang-Lao's return, or to grow balls maybe, I don't know," Deng Mao replied, sounding irritated.

"Let's ask him then," Uncle offered as we resumed our walk.

Soon we would meet Zhang Mancheng, the first of many inept war leaders I would serve in my life.

There is no nice way to describe Zhang Mancheng. Imagine a praying mantis wearing a lamellar of leather, standing with a back as straight as a bamboo pole, and you won't be far from the man as he was. In many ways, he looked like Fat Ling, but where my neighbor exuded his peasant simplicity, Mancheng was hard and haughty. His eyes were so slanted that you could barely find them, but when he looked at you, you could feel all his cold judgment. His mustache had been trimmed recently, and his beard consisted of a pointy patch down the chin, making him look very much like the government officials we were to fight.

"Glad you could join us, at last," Zhang Mancheng said when both my uncles reached the grove under which the Adepts had gathered. The Grand Adept clearly did not like staying under the sun.

I had been allowed to accompany the two of them, as was Fat Ling, but besides us were only Adepts of the Yellow Turbans, maybe thirty of them. I think there were about thirty-five counties in Nanyang back then, each of which would have an Adept, though some had probably met the fate of He Luo. There were also people coming from other commanderies, of course, including a great bunch of fighters from Jiangxia and Nan commandery.

"My apologies for being late," Cheng Yuanzhi said while saluting his superior, who simply waved it away as if it were of no concern. Of course, we were not late since all of this happened a month earlier than planned.

"And I see you bring elite warriors with you," Mancheng said, nodding in my direction. A few of them laughed at the jibe, while the rest remained quiet and looked away, marking a clear distinction between two groups among our commanding circle. I felt the heat quickly rise to my cheeks but remained quiet. Uncle Deng didn't.

"Well, at least *he* has taken part in a battle."

Zhang Mancheng's lips tightened at once, and if it wasn't for the shadow of the canopy over his head, I'm sure he would have turned red. Frankly, I did not know where to put myself.

"Eagle-eye here and this man Ling Jun have risen against the blue sky and proven to be good brothers, as all of us are here," Uncle Cheng said in an attempt at cooling the heat.

"And they will have many occasions to do so again," Mancheng said. It sounded almost like a threat. "Back to the matter at hand."

"Why have we not surrounded the city?" Cheng Yuanzhi asked as Zhang meant to turn back to his council of war.

"It is not necessary, that's all."

Deng Mao spat on the floor, not in anyone's direction, but his thoughts on the matter were clear.

"We are letting them dispatch riders—"

"Which works in our favor," Mancheng interrupted. Deng Mao and Cheng Yuanzhi shared a look of confusion, to which our leader replied with a long sigh. "Wan will fall at our whim. And when it does, we will have an easily defensible ground. The more soldiers they send at us, the easier it will be for our brothers in other provinces. They are, at worst, a week away. We will be ready." It has to be said in Zhang Mancheng's favor that he was extremely devoted to the cause. Some said he was the closest to our Grand Master, whom we called the General of Heaven at this point, in terms of healing power. He was educated, this much was certain, and he lived to see Zhang Jue leading the land. He was just not a very caring man, nor a warrior. Still, as excuses went, it wasn't a bad one, though it took five heartbeats for Uncle Deng to destroy it.

"Surely we can let a few of them out to warn their masters *after* we have taken the city."

"Have faith," Mancheng said.

"I do have faith… in the cause," Deng replied, meaning he had no faith in our current leader. Now Mancheng was getting angry, and his small eyes turned into two lines sharp as blades.

"See those thousands and thousands of fighters there," he said, taking a couple of steps toward my uncles and stretching his arm toward the mass of Yellow Turbans. "They will take that city in less time than you'd need to saddle a horse. Wan has five hundred men, at best, to defend it. We have over one hundred times that number."

"But do we have the ropes, the ladders, or any kind of missile to throw at the defenders while we storm the walls?" Deng Mao asked. Zhang Mancheng remained speechless for a few seconds, enough to know he had considered none of this.

"I'm sure we have ropes and ladders among our followers," he finally replied, which got a headshake from Uncle Deng.

"We need to surround the city to put pressure on them," Cheng Yuanzhi said. "If they see how doomed they are, they might even surrender, and—"

"Surrender?" Zhang Mancheng spat, his hand landing on his chest as if he'd been insulted. "We do not want *surrender*. We are here to make an example of Wan. Any dog of the Han within those walls will perish!"

"If you offer them no way out," Cheng went on, "you make sure the inhabitants of the city will fight against us as well, and suddenly we do not have five hundred foes but twice our number."

"All the more reason not to surround them then," Zhang Mancheng triumphantly said. "And I'm sure we can count on our brothers who live in Wan to open the gates or something for us." That was and will always be the problem with men of strong principles; they can't imagine that regular folks do not share their dedication.

"We could send them messages," a man from the group of Adepts said. He looked like a copy of Zhang Mancheng, though shorter and younger.

"With what?" growled Deng Mao. "We don't have arrows or bolts to waste. And it's not like many of them could read your message."

"This would be a good plan," Uncle Cheng said, walking to put himself slightly between the fuming Deng Mao and the equally vexed Grand Adept. "If we had time to sow discord in the city. Unfortunately, as our leader has explained earlier, we have a week at most."

Oh, this was smooth of him, using Mancheng's words against him. It did not please the man at all, so he did as incompetent leaders do when they feel threatened in their authority. He used it.

"We will not surround the city until it's time to launch the attack. This is what I decreed. Now, all of you can go back to your men and find ladders, ropes, and whatever else you deem necessary."

"When will the attack be?" Deng Mao asked.

"Soon," was all he received in answer. Mancheng then pivoted on his heels to show the conversation was over. The circle disbanded, again in two distinct and even groups.

"You heard the man," Deng Mao said as Cheng Yuanzhi shook his head at the approaching Adepts. They split into smaller groups immediately, understanding that it would be worse if they all came to him at once. Only one kept his course as we headed back to our people.

"Thanks for your intervention," Uncle Deng said sarcastically once we were out of earshot.

"I was tired from talking to that ass while you hid at the back of your men," the newcomer said, which got a chuckle from Uncle Cheng. I guessed he was the second man Cheng Yuanzhi had mentioned before, Han Zhong, and he too was a former soldier; this was obvious.

Han Zhong looked as if life had chewed him and spit him out, minus an ear, a few teeth, and a big patch of hair on his skull now marked by a long, oddly shaped scar. He would have been a handsome man. Instead, he was the scariest warrior I had met. In his case, it was a complete facade. Han Zhong, as I would learn, was the most patient of the trio, and a deeply caring man. Almost all his scars, Deng Mao once told me, had been inflicted at one point or another while he rescued some of his comrades.

I knew nothing of it then and tried really hard to both check his face and stop looking at him at the same time.

"I swear, he's going to get a lot of us killed for nothing," Han Zhong went on.

"Should we try to negotiate behind his back?" Deng Mao asked.

"Nah, it's only going to make things worse in the long run. I'm sorry for the people of Wan, but their fate has been sealed," Uncle Cheng replied. I did not get why he said so. Surely those who did not fight us would survive? How naïve I was back then.

"He seems... arrogant," Fat Ling said, speaking for the first time in a while.

"Arrogant?" Deng Mao spat before scoffing. "The man believes he farts higher than his ass." Farting seemed to be a measurement system in Deng's mind, and he often referred to it.

"And you'd know," Han Zhong said, "since your nose is basically at his ass level."

"Ha-ha," Deng retorted, "a joke on my height, how clever. Did you find your brain? Was it with your ear?"

"No, that I left at your mom's bedside last night," Han Zhong replied, which got Fat Ling and Uncle Cheng to burst out laughing.

There were a few exchanges of the sort between the two friends until Uncle Cheng grew tired of it and asked Han Zhong if he had news of the rebellion in the rest of the empire.

He did, and it was off to a great start.

Of course, the strongest blow had been dealt near Julu commandery in Ji province, where our leader, his brothers, and half of our members had gathered. This place being so far off, we had very few details about the exact situation, but we knew the region must have been flipped over in a matter of hours. Further north, in You province, our brothers had been fast and unstoppable; some even said they had killed the provincial inspector.

In Yu province, the one east of Nanyang commandery, the rebels were also doing their best to bring death to the blue sky. A few big cities had already fallen there, and according to Deng Mao, since the Grand Adept for that province was Bo Cai, we should pity the poor bastards on his path.

The world was moving fast, and the Han empire was seeing its last days. I had no doubt in my mind that the time of the Yellow Turbans drew near, and never again would I see a plow. We were in the *Chunfen* period of the year, the spring equinox, and swallows were twirling over our heads to fill their bellies after their long journey north.

Soon though, another kind of black bird would swarm over Wan, and they would not feed on bugs.

CHAPTER FOUR

North of Mianzhu, Yi province
11th month, 4th year of the Jingyuan era
of the Cao Wei empire (263)

I MUST COMMEND CHEN SHOU on his work as my scribe. He has not interrupted me once over the last three days of recounting my childhood. I could see on his face that the stories of a child, a son of a farmer at that, had presented a very limited interest, but even then, he has shown a great sense of restraint and dedication. We had paused only long enough for him to grind more ink and order some more tea, but nothing else during those few days on the march.

Our defeat still lingers like a bad dream in my mind, and I'm tempted to let the young man rot with his writing once in a while, but I must admit that I enjoy remembering those times when things were simpler, if not more agreeable.

When I woke this morning, shortly before my wagon left its spot, I was even tempted to go outside and see my beloved country one last time. But the shame still burns too strong, and the weather is too cold for those old bones.

Chen Shou joined me shortly after my morning meal, and we are to resume the tale of my life.

"May I ask a question?" he asks, and I have to fight my usual reply to this question, which is that *it was a question.* He may be a petulant, high-born fragile piece of work barely deserving the name of man, but he is the son of a friend, and a child of Shu Han, so I restrain myself.

"What is it?" I say.

"I'm just surprised a city as big as Wan only had a garrison of five hundred men or that you could travel from Xinye to Wan with no resistance," he says. Now I can't stop myself.

"I didn't hear a question," I say, smiling to myself.

"I meant—"

"You meant to say that you don't get why the government had not brought the battle to us earlier," I answer for him. He nods. A fair point, coming from the mind of a man born during the Three Kingdoms.

"The Han government was weak," I say, which gets his mouth to open wide. "I know, I have spent more than half of my life trying to revive it, but it was a weak dynasty at its end. And one of the main reasons for its weakness was its lack of army. Nowadays, it feels like everyone's brother and cousin is a soldier, but back then, there was almost no professional warrior within the borders. Sure, we had troops in the north to fight the Xianbei, the Qiang, and occasionally the Xiongnu, though those were relatively quiet then. But those were hardly the troops we have now. For a start, most of the soldiers were convicts, like Deng Mao, Cheng Yuanzhi and Han Zhong had been, and second, they had no experience of battles in our own land. So when the Yellow Turbans struck, no one was ready nearby to answer the challenge. And just like in Wan, the few soldiers maintaining the peace at the county and commandery level were not enough to stop us."

I can see the information carve itself in Chen Shou's brain. I bet he will write it down the second he is back in his own wagon.

"Why didn't they have a stronger army?" he asks after a click of the tongue.

"What do you think?" I answer. "They didn't trust their own people, that's why. When you have an army, it means you have trained men in your backyard once they retire. Trained men who know violence are always tempted to use it. As long as bandits were not trained for battle, they were easy to put down. They also didn't trust their war leaders. That's why we have this idiotic rule of relinquishing command every time a campaign is over. This way, no general feels like he is more than he actually is, with a loyal band of warriors behind his back. Which, in turn, means no one was ready to rally troops."

"Trust, huh?" Chen Shou says, mostly to himself.

"And money, I guess," I go on. "Maintaining an army is expensive. The Han government, despite its palaces and fanciness, was broke more often than none, and that was without an army to feed, equip, and pay. I don't think they could have done otherwise, to be honest."

Now Chen Shou looks more convinced. I still think the main reason was trust, but it was far from being the only one; that's true.

"But they did respond to the challenge?" he asks.

"Oh, that they did. It was still a few days and weeks from us when we arrived in Wan, but they sent men. Three armies to be exact, plus a shitload of volunteers forming their own militia."

I can see young Chen's eyes gleaming with pleasure. He knows his history and where this is heading. He will have to be patient, though.

"Of course, facing the high walls of Wan, all we cared about were those five hundred men manning the ramparts. And as we were about to learn, a few hundred trained and well-equipped men can do a lot of damage."

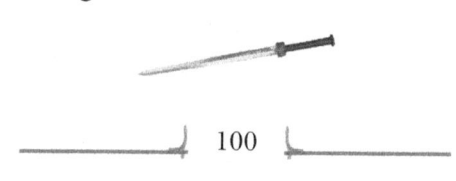

*Wan, Nanyang commandery,
2nd month of the 7th year of Guanghe era
(184), Han Dynasty.*

It took the better part of four days for people to make ladders and ropes to a number deemed sufficient by Uncle Cheng. Of course, no one had brought ladders with them, and ropes had to be readied for an assault. Javelins were made in great quantity from broken carts and bamboos, and while they were of terrible quality and could not pierce any armor, we hoped they would keep the heads of the soldiers down long enough for our warriors to climb the walls.

From an inventory of our military equipment, mostly stolen gear from the garrisons met on the way, three hundred crossbows were counted, with maybe twenty to thirty bolts per piece. I don't know how the sharing of those was decided, but ten of the bows went to the people from Xinye, and one was given to my father.

The crossbowmen practiced a little, but the number of lost bolts grew so fast that soon they were simply shooting blank. At least they learned how to pull the string and shoot without hurting themselves.

A delegation came to parley with Zhang Mancheng, offering a total surrender of the city if he agreed to leave the people in peace and the soldiers to flee, without their weapons, of course. It was a decent offer, which our Grand Adept refused right away. There would be no mercy.

Later, Deng Mao commented that Mancheng should have accepted, then killed the defenseless soldiers as they fled, which sounded cruel but would have saved a lot of our people's lives.

But since there was no agreement, it meant the assault would happen soon, and the atmosphere of the camp changed accordingly. Men grew nervous around the evening fires, and tempers became short. Several fights broke out, and the Adepts quickly had to make a few examples, something Uncle Cheng did not relish but acted on nonetheless. Thankfully, no one from Fa Jia Po made a scene, and all my folks remained safe from punishment.

Then, late on our fourth afternoon near Wan, just as we were feeling like things would remain as such for a while, criers came to each of the many camps spread south of the city and called for the fighters to ready themselves. I had not seen Uncle Cheng in the day, so I was as surprised as anyone else. My first reflex was to check my father, with whom I sat at that moment, the both of us inspecting the bolts for defects as if we knew what we were doing. He looked very serious, almost strong. I was both proud of him and worried sick. My sister was playing with the fletchings, but when she noticed my father standing up, she immediately started crying.

"Take care of Mihua," he said as he picked up the crossbows and rearranged the bolts in the bag that would be strapped to his shoulder. Then, he tightened the turban around his head, and I had to fight the tears as well.

"Be careful," I said as Father knelt down to look at us. He dropped his hand behind our heads. They were shaking hard.

"I don't want you to go," Mihua said through her sobbing.

"Me neither," he said, kissing her on the forehead. "But men sometimes have to go." He said the last looking at me, and for the first time in our lives, we understood each other.

He left to gather with the rest of the fighters, following the criers who had called the rally. Similar scenes were happening all over the place. Some men were crying, and some even looked as if they had just soiled themselves. Men had to drag their friends away from their families, and a few arguments broke out, but in less than a couple of minutes, they were gone. Thousands of yellow-scarved heads went bobbing toward the great walled city of Wan.

I felt worse than ever, not even being able to advance with the rest of the men, only knowing what was happening from the obstructed sight of the city. I had promised both my father and Uncle Cheng that I would go nowhere near the fighting. But I wished to at least observe the battle.

The sound of thousands upon thousands of men walking together in the same direction is enough to wake dragons. The earth seemed to shake as they advanced, and when the first lines stretched away from the camps, it was as if a forest of golden trees moved toward Wan. Somewhere within that forest of men were my father, Fat Ling, Uncle Deng, and Uncle Cheng. But not Zhang Mancheng, for the coward had decided long ago he wouldn't be part of the action but lead from the back, atop a mound from which he could see the whole fight.

From where I stood, holding my sister's hand, I could see our army spreading itself around the city, from south to north by the western side. The eastern side was covered by the Bai river and did not have enough ground to launch an attack. Years later, when I led my platoon of elite warriors, this is exactly where I would have chosen to go, but on that day, the eastern wall was left alone.

In a quarter of a *shi*, our army was covering the ground on three sides of the city, leaving just enough distance to discourage the defenders from using their artillery. The said distance had been slightly misjudged here and there, especially where the soldiers had mounted heavy crossbows, and the first of our brothers met their end before the assault was ordered.

Nothing happened for a very long time. Actually, nothing happened until the sun nearly settled for the night. I had spotted a man, maybe halfway to the walls from us, with a couple of yellow pennants in his hands. This must have been one of the flag bearers, I correctly assumed. I stared in his direction for a while, so focused that soon my eyes dried up. When I rubbed them, the flag-bearer raised his left hand, and less than thirty seconds later, the world became alive again.

"Dun-*gege!*" Mihua said, pulling on my sleeve. Unknowingly, I had taken a step.

"Stay here," I told her, and immediately the tears came out of her eyes again. She begged me to stay, thrashing the ground in her effort to physically keep me on my spot. But I couldn't. I had to see what was about to happen.

"Go with Grandma," I said, meaning our old neighbor, an old Liao, probably related to us somehow, who had always taken care of us when my father couldn't. Grandma Liao must have heard me, for she pulled my sister into her arms and *whooshed* me away. I could still hear Mihua crying for a while after I started running.

I say running, but I was mostly shuffling through the compact crowd of folks shifting left and right to get a better view. I took a few glimpses when possible as I advanced with the city on my right, and realized that only one side was assaulted, the western wall. Our army had not moved from either north or south.

Finally, after what felt like a battle, I emerged from our camp and ran through the nearest grove, then north again, until I reached the tree line. More people had gathered in front of me, so I climbed on the closest tree, scratching myself along the arm in the process. I found a spot on a thick branch, right on time to see the wave of fighters dashing from north and south to attack the wall. Our fighters on the western side were already climbing ladders and hurling javelins at the defenders. In their wake, I could spot a great number of unmoving bodies.

I was too far to hear the screams, but the memory of the ambush came, and it was like I was there myself, assaulting the city and cursing the foes manning the walls.

Somewhere within the pack of Yellow Turbans, Cheng Yuanzhi would be waving his blade for his men to keep pushing, and Deng Mao would be climbing a ladder, his eyes already searching for his first victim. I could imagine my father pointing his crossbow at the top of the wall, waiting for an unfortunate soldier to raise his head. Men were dying, blood was being spilled, and though my heart threatened to jump out of my chest, I wanted to be there.

It all seemed to take forever, and it surprised me to see the first fires being lit on the walls. Night would fall soon. The first men made it to the wall on the west side, only to be pushed back down into the yellow sea. A couple of torches swirled into the air before landing amidst one of the units attacking the south wall, then caught on something that had previously been thrown, and a great flame erupted suddenly. A circle of men formed away from the unlucky fighters as they burned down, and while a few meant to help them, they soon gave up and instead offered their brothers a quick death.

It looked like an army of ants assaulting a hill, and I can only imagine the despair with which the city soldiers fought on that day. More and more yellow heads made it to the top. There was a distinctive moment when all resistance seemed to vanish, and the men on the ladders increased the speed of their climbing. Then the walls were covered in our colors, and I breathed out at last. We had breached the walls; the victory was nearly ours. The feeling spread through the camps, and the thousands of followers shouted their joy in unison. Two women under the tree embraced and jumped like little girls, while an old man kept beating the ground with his cane, smiling his toothless grin at those around him.

Except that it wasn't over. At least the violence wasn't. The walls of the city served as a sound amplifier, and while I had heard few sounds from the battle, I clearly heard the screams from the people in Wan as they suffered the price of the soldiers' defeat. I remembered what Uncle Cheng had said, that those people were doomed, and now I understood what he had meant. Flames arose in the city, looking brighter with the growing night.

In a matter of minutes, every man in the army was over the wall, leaving only the dead behind. The southern side, besides the scorched mark where the fire had killed many of our men, had suffered less than the western one, and the northern one, which I could not see, even less. I would later learn that Zhang Mancheng's brilliant plan had been to use the setting sun to blind the defenders, which was why he had chosen that side for the first attack. When the enemy understood it, he thought, they would send more soldiers there, thus depleting the defenses north and south. Not a terrible plan, except, as Deng Mao gently put it, that with such a dense army as ours, it didn't matter if the enemy could see clearly or not. All it had done was to offer a packed target for trained crossbowmen.

Of course, my two uncles and their men had been chosen for this task, though I did not know it yet. Neither did I know that among the bodies lying lifelessly by the west wall of Wan was my father's.

It wasn't until well into the night that the city gates opened, and only because Zhang Mancheng came pounding on them, refusing to climb the ladders still littering the walls. Very few people were allowed in, and a growing sense of anxiety spread among the folks.

I went back to my sister when it became clear nothing would happen of the night and found her sleeping in Grandma's arms. I did not wake her. My legs buckled under me when I meant to sit, and while I tried to keep my eyes open, I promptly failed and accompanied my sister in the realm of dreams. There was a lot of movement during the night, and sleep came and went. I heard a few sudden cries, guessing that someone had learned of their man's fate. But almost no fighter came back, too busy they were looting the city and letting their different kinds of lusts go free.

When I woke up for real, it was because someone was shaking my shoulder.

"Dun," Fat Ling called, almost in a whisper. "Wake up."

I almost screamed when I saw his face. Fat Ling was covered in soot, blood, and other substances I could not identify. He had suffered a nasty cut under the eye, but according to him, that was all. He looked extremely tired, but also showed an emotion I did not recognize: guilt. Though at this instant, he looked more sorry than ashamed.

"Dun, I'm so sorry," he said and got no further.

Tears came before I fully understood what he meant, and when I did, they were accompanied by the most pitiful whimpering a boy can voice. My heart felt as if stabbed, and my throat hurt from this new sound I struggled to produce, something between hurling and shrieking. It woke my sister, and whether or not she knew what was happening, she accompanied me in my lamenting. Fat Ling remained with us, rocking us back and forth against his chest as we processed our father's death. Fat Ling was not a father figure like Uncle Cheng had become. In fact, until he had trained the folks of Fa Jia Po, I had not given him much thought. But he showed kindness on that day, and I will always be grateful to him for that.

When we finally calmed down a little, feeling more exhausted than ever, he apologized and said he had more people to talk to. Fa Jia Po had lost nine men.

"Wait," I said when he stood up. "Uncle Cheng?"

"He's fine," he answered with a gentle smile. "The three of them are busy trying to bring some calm to the city."

The rest of the morning was spent within a strange atmosphere of expectation as people waited for news of their loved ones. Once in a while, a woman would see a man come toward her and start crying before he had reached her. The great majority of our fighters had survived the battle, but to the few of us who had lost someone, it felt like a defeat.

I made my way toward Wan when I managed to gather the necessary courage. The dead had been laid in rows according to their original counties, and folks were walking around like ghosts, heads down as they searched for the face of their family member. First, I had to find the pile belonging to Xinye, and I did so because I spotted the old Fa woman kneeling with her head between her hands. She cried over her husband less than a week after losing her only son. I did not go to her, not knowing what I could say to lighten her pain.

About twenty men further, I recognized a neighbor who used to rent our ox for his plowing, an old friend of *Yeye* who should have been too old to find himself here. Then, three men down, I found my father. I don't know what I expected, but it wasn't that. His skin had turned pale, and his fingers were curled on themselves like dead spiders. He looked peaceful, unlike so many others who had passed away with an air of terror carved into their faces. The bolt that had taken his life was still embedded in his chest, very close to this great heart with which he had loved my sister, my mother, and me. Kneeling by his side after forcing some space between him and his closest companion, I held his hand, trying to force his fingers to open, and that is how I stayed while I apologized in my heart. I still think to this day he died because of me. Those with crossbows presented the primary targets, and though Uncle Cheng denied it, I was certain he had chosen my father to please me. Not to get him killed, of course, simply to turn my old man into a warrior in my eyes.

"I'm sorry," Uncle Cheng said behind me, his hand falling gently over my shoulder. "He was very brave, you know." I did not know, but I took his word for it.

When I turned to see him, I was glad to notice that Uncle Cheng looked mostly unhurt, besides the bruise growing dark around his right eye. He was tired though, and I thought he might collapse on the spot. His gaze moved left, then right, and I could see he fought the rage inside of him. Many of those who had died, died because of his feud with Zhang Mancheng, and even more, because our Grand Adept was a piece of shit who thought himself an expert because he had once read the classics on war. I was too tired to be angry at Zhang Mancheng, but that time would come.

"Can I stay a bit longer?" I asked when Uncle said he had to go.

"Take all the time you need," he answered. "If you want to see me, I'll be over there," he then said, pointing at an empty spot west of the city. I nodded in response, and he took a couple of steps. "And, Dun," he called, "if you still want, you can stay with me."

I thanked him and told him I still wanted it, though at this moment, the image of my sister popped into my head, and a wave of guilt filled me from head to toes. It brought new tears to my eyes, and Uncle Cheng left me with a last pat on the head.

After a while, I let go of my father's hand. His bag of bolts was stuck under his back, so I removed it, thinking that we would need them. When I searched through the bag, I noticed that two bolts were missing. Two shots, at best. This was how far in life my father had gone.

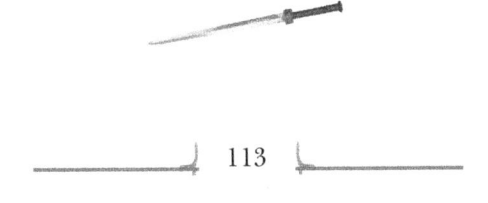

The place where Uncle Cheng had been headed after talking to me was the place chosen for the mass grave. We had lost a little over two thousand warriors, more than four to each soldier. This is what it means to fight without being ready.

For all his faults, Zhang Mancheng did right by the dead. He went to every mass grave and prayed at length for the fallen, which took him well into the evening. Some folks who had come from nearby villages took their dead back home, and I guess many of them never returned, disgusted with this war already.

A strange sense of calm anger filled me, and I did not know where to direct it. So, the next day, just as the non-combatants moved into the emptied city, I went to speak with Deng Mao and asked him to train me. He accepted right away, which greatly surprised me. Up to now, every step toward my warrior dream had been met with disapprobation. But as I was to learn, Deng Mao didn't give a dog's tail about how people wanted to spend their lives, even a kid. But if I was to become a warrior, I'd better do it right, as he said. I think he was just happy to have something to occupy his mind and keep him away from our Grand Adept. So he found a broken spear pole, broke it down even further, and handed me the remaining staff.

"A stick?" I asked, confused.

"Everything's a stick," he said, arms crossed over his powerful chest. "A spear is a stick with a pointy head, an ax is a stick with a flat blade, a sword is a—"

"I get it," I said. I didn't like it, but I knew I would get nowhere by letting him talk. So I assumed my best-looking fighting stance, stick held high over my head and aiming at his throat. He knocked it out of my hand with a slap I had not seen coming.

"That's much too soon for this kind of crap," he said. "You hold it close to your hip, pointing forward and up, like that." He demonstrated the stance, which looked rather silly. I could hit nothing from that position except a bird who would gently agree to impale itself on the tip of the blade.

"Then you strike like this," he said, just before thrusting with all his arm. I was amazed at the speed of his strike, but I was also doubtful.

"Isn't it better to go like this?" I asked, demonstrating what I thought was a great slash.

"Too soon for this kind of crap too," he said. "You want to kill the guy?" Uncle Deng asked. I did not know who he was talking about, but I said yes. "Then you thrust. Slashing looks good in front of the ladies, but you miss more than you hit. Thrusting gets the job done. And most weapons can thrust, but you can't hack with a spear. So thrust, boy, thrust."

So I did. I thrust that stick until my shoulder was too painful to even raise the stick anymore. I thrust until I couldn't lift my arm, and even then, Uncle Deng made me practice the same strike over and over again. When he finally let me stop, it was almost noon, and I gave serious doubts about my worth as a warrior.

"By my fat ass, you just don't tire!" he shouted, sounding as happy as I was exhausted. "No wonder Mad-Cheng won't let you go." The compliment gave me a new surge of energy, so I resumed a few strikes. Then we went to get a meal inside the city.

Wan was a ruin. Houses had turned black, and streets were littered with the dead, from dogs to soldiers. Our men were cleaning as best they could, but unlike our warriors, we just dumped the enemy soldiers in the river once their possessions had been removed. Zhang Mancheng agreed to give greater care to the dead civilians, and he at least had the decency to look at his feet while he passed down the streets of Wan. This was his doing. All those people could have been saved. I still did not understand why our men had basically destroyed the city, but according to Uncle Deng, it's just that men do crazy things while their blood runs hot, and nothing makes the blood hotter than battle. Pillaging would never be to my liking, but I would lie if I said I never partook in the deed, and if you want to keep your men content and loyal, you got to let them loose inside a defeated city once in a while.

We ate a light meal of rice, something I had rarely tasted before but loved, and what I assumed was dog meat, their carcasses littering the city for us to pick. Then we continued on our way to the palace of the administrator, and it's a good thing we went when we did, for Chu Gong was about to be executed.

It wasn't nearly as flashy as He Luo's death, but Zhang Mancheng gave a speech for the crowd to know this was not a barbarian act but justice. Chu Gong represented the evilness of the Han dynasty, especially since he led the Nanyang commandery, which had produced a great number of emperors and kings since the Liu line had killed the usurper Wang Man. I, and frankly, most of the Yellow Turbans present at the execution, could not give a rat's ass about the reasoning. We just wanted to see our oppressor die. Which he did with far less grace than He Luo had, screaming and cursing until the very moment the blade severed his head from his shoulders. In one swing, I should add. My anger dissipated a little from then on, though it might also have been the exhaustion of my training session.

"Our *leader*," Deng Mao told me shortly after Chu Gong's body was thrown down the river, "is going to give us some directives. You want to join?"

"I wouldn't miss it," I replied. "Mancheng making a decision is a rare event after all." I thought Deng Mao would unhinge his jaw when he laughed at that. I was pleased that I had amused a great warrior like him. It felt like being recognized as one too.

To no one's surprise, Zhang Mancheng claimed the palace of the administrator for himself and what was becoming his staff. The first of them was his shadow, the Adept who had suggested sending messages to the people of Wan, and whose name was Zhao Hong. Though he did not look like much, he was slightly less incompetent than Zhang Mancheng when it came to military organization.

He is the one who welcomed us as we passed the gates leading to the palace-turned-headquarters, and while not being friendlier than Mancheng would have been, he at least saluted Deng Mao with all due respect. Uncle Deng forced himself to return the politeness, but his heart was not in it.

"Our youngest recruit is always nearby," Zhao Hong said as our steps echoed on the path's stones going from the outer wall to the main building. This place, while having suffered some damage, was magnificent. Dragons and phoenixes were carved into the column supporting a tiled roof stretching over the path. The trees and grass looked too perfectly trimmed to be natural, and there was even a pond further down the garden.

"Eagle-eye here is our lucky charm," Deng Mao said before giving me a wink.

"Let's hope he stays around then," Zhao Hong replied, which forced Deng Mao to halt his walk and by extension, us too.

"You've heard something?" Uncle Deng asked, the tension rising instantly.

"Nothing you won't hear in a minute," the other answered.

"Are we leaving?"

"Some are," Zhao Hong replied, enjoying the air of mystery he was giving himself. Deng Mao did not enjoy it though, and I thought he might soon demonstrate his thrust on a living target. But before he did, a great clash rang from the mansion, followed by the voice of Uncle Cheng.

"This is ridiculous!"

We ran toward the commotion, just in time to see the great hall of the city in turmoil. Zhang Mancheng stood at its end, facing south. All the other Adepts had gathered in front of him in a tight pack, except for Cheng Yuanzhi. No one stood by his side, not even Han Zhong, but when we did, I could see the ire in his eyes. The white in them was quickly turning red as he checked Mancheng with ideas of murder.

"What is it?" Deng Mao asked, grabbing Cheng's wrist.

"This... idiot," he said, pointing an accusing finger at our Grand Adept, "had yet another amazing idea."

"Be careful how you speak, peasant!" Mancheng barked. "I am your leader and—"

"Or what?" Cheng pressed on. "You will put me and my men on the *Sidi* again?"

The *Sidi* is the death ground, the place that leaves you no other choice but to fight or die. Warriors fear it, and generals love it. As for me, for most of my life, I would call it home.

"Or you will share Chu Gong's fate!" Mancheng said, spittle shooting from his mouth. Uncle Cheng's nose wrinkled dangerously, like a snarling wolf. I don't think Mancheng ever knew how close he came to a premature death at that moment.

"Will someone, in the name of Huang-Lao, explain what's happening here?" asked Deng Mao, which somehow brought Cheng Yuanzhi away from his staring contest with the Grand Adept.

"Our leader wants to split us," Han Zhong said.

"What?" Deng asked, his stupor making his voice higher pitched. "Why?"

"Because we don't have enough food for such an army," Zhang Mancheng answered. This was true enough, and everyone knew it would quickly become a problem. We had hoped the city's granaries held enough grains for us to pursue our effort for a few weeks, but this was far from the case. Gathering what the people of Wan had "left," plus the alarmingly low level of the granaries, we could feed ourselves for a little less than two weeks.

"That's not why I'm considering unsheathing my sword again," Uncle Cheng said.

"Careful," I heard Deng Mao whisper to his friend.

"Tell us again what the two groups will do," Uncle Cheng asked Mancheng.

"Half of our fighters will take the road to Julu," Zhao Hong explained, drawing all the air from Deng Mao's lungs in a loud gasp.

"Why on earth would we go all the way to Julu?" Deng Mao asked, and this time it was Zhang Mancheng who answered.

According to his latest report, an imposing army was heading toward our Grand Master in Julu, where the first great battle of the war would be held. Furthermore, besides Wan and Runan, we had won no great victories, and many commanderies expected to rise in rebellion had remained silent when the time came. Sending half of us to Julu would serve two purposes: reinforcing our main base and forcing our brothers along the way to take action. Again, the idea was sound. The realization, however, would be complicated.

Julu was two thousand *li* away, or, as Uncle Cheng claimed, a month on the road, at the very best, which meant without baggage, a second pair of shoes per man, and a clear sky above our heads.

Zhang Mancheng joked he couldn't do much about the weather—he wasn't this kind of miracle worker. Only a couple of Adepts laughed. But he had ideas for the rest. One of them was for this army to find food on the march, something no officer or soldier enjoys. It is extremely difficult and worrisome to lead men without the promise of food. A logistic nightmare and a morale-burner.

"At least it temporarily solves the issue of food for the other group," Zhang Mancheng finished.

"Who will be doing what?" Deng Mao asked, his tone suggesting he could already see where this was going.

"Nothing," Cheng Yuanzhi replied for our leader.

"Not nothing," Mancheng went on. "We will fortify Wan, prepare our defenses, gather more supplies, and present a threat to the enemy. That is, until the battle in Julu is over, and our brothers march west, where we will gather and crush the Han government once and for all." His voice had risen as he spoke, but he found only head shakes when his eyes fell on his subordinates.

I think this was the first time I doubted our order.

The general expectation on the morrow of Wan battle had been that we would head straight to the imperial capital, Luoyang. This city was half the distance to Julu, straight north, with few obstacles on the way. Furthermore, we were the closest troop of Yellow Turbans to Luoyang and could end the war in one big swoop before the government had the time to gather a powerful army. It was as good as it could get, but it wasn't meant to be.

I saw Deng Mao's hand closing on the grip of his sword, and I was sure that next time, Zhang Mancheng would not allow weapons inside the headquarters. Except that there would be no next time, for Zhang Mancheng had kept the best part for the end.

"Let me guess who you're sending to Julu and who is to stay in Wan to sit with their thumbs up their asses," Deng Mao commented. And, of course, he was right. Cheng Yuanzhi would lead a total of ten thousand men, a little less than half of our fighting force, with Deng Mao as his second in command. Han Zhong, who had remained a little more circumspect in his dealing with the Grand Adept, would remain in Wan. None of the three looked happy about this plan.

"I can see no one better to join our General of Heaven in a timely manner," Mancheng said in a feigned tone of flattery.

"When do we go?" Cheng asked through his teeth. Mancheng pretended to think about it, but it was clearly an act.

"Tomorrow morning. You have the night to rest," he said, and if he expected some gratitude, he was dead wrong.

"One day to prepare for a two-thousand-*li* march," Uncle Cheng replied. "There will be no rest tonight, believe me."

"Well, the fight for justice requires sacrifices," Mancheng commented, looking anything but sorry. "You have your orders."

Cheng Yuanzhi forced a salute, then left. Deng Mao did not even bother. Their steps were loud as we left the hall, and I had to run to keep up with my two uncles.

I did my best to be helpful, but Uncle had been right. It turned out to be a brief, sleepless night.

One of the greatest challenges for Cheng Yuanzhi and Deng Mao was, unsurprisingly, to gather enough men. Of course, the men of Xinye and Anzhong, Deng Mao's county, were automatically included in the count, but even then, we were only four thousand fighters. A call for volunteers was shared within the city, and by the evening, we had an extra five thousand fighters. But as the night went by, many men left Wan and returned to their farms rather than facing a journey across half of the empire. So by the time we left, we were eight thousand and maybe four hundred men.

As we were to move as fast as possible, the families had to stay in Wan or go back to their homes. Many chose the former, if only because Wan had thick walls. This was the case of Grandma Liao's, and as such, Mihua's as well. She had run out of tears to shed after our father's death but still found some for me. I pretended to be a man and kept mine behind my eyes, but I still hugged her and promised I would be back after I avenged our dad, which made no sense since whatever soldier had killed him had met the same fate and was presently feeding the fish of the Bai River. Mihua did not care about such things. She was just a child abandoned by yet another member of her family. But I have never been great with children, even when I was one myself.

We left at noon the next day, from the northern gate, with only Han Zhong to see us off. Zhang Mancheng had "given" us ten horses, and nine of them went to men who claimed to know how to ride. The last one, to my great pleasure, was offered to me. In reality, it had been given to Deng Mao, probably as a last mean joke, for it was a short mare. But Uncle Deng laughed and bowed toward the palace, claiming as loud as possible that our Grand Adept was a great man for offering his lover to a departing subordinate. He then handed me the reins of the animal, and from that point on, she was renamed *Lover*. In the course of the next weeks, I would very often be told to go climb my *Lover*, or to make sure my *Lover* was pleased, bits of advice that made everyone laugh but me, if only because I did not understand the humor in them.

Uncles Cheng and Deng met one last time with Han Zhong before calling the march. I followed suit, but not before I shared a word with the scarred veteran. For the first time, I should add.

"Sir," I called, my voice weak with the fear he inspired me. I was, of course, not mounted on Lover, for I did not know how yet, so he towered over me, as most adults did. "My little sister is staying here," I said, looking at the ground. "I know you will be busy, but can you keep an eye on her, please, sir?"

"Hair to shoulder, same eyes as you, always munching on something?" he asked, giving me a perfect representation of my sister. I nodded, extremely impressed that he had noted a child among the pack of them. "I'll do better," Han

Zhong said. "I'll take care of her as if she were my own daughter."

I thanked him from the bottom of my heart, wondering if I should kowtow or something, but Uncle Deng's voice called me over the din of eight thousand and some men trampling the floor of Wan city.

I pulled on the reins of Lover, but it took Han Zhong to gently slap her croup for her to move.

"Wait," I said right after, "do you even have a daughter?"

"Me? By Huang-Lao, no. I can't stand children," he replied, and for a few seconds I waited for him to say something else, but he kept his stone face. Then it peeled off, and he left, laughing like a drunk. I wasn't sure if I had entrusted my baby sister to the right person, but it was all I could do at this point.

I passed through the northern gates of Wan, a horse trotting behind me, a yellow turban over my head, and a broken spear shaft in my belt. This was to be the greatest of adventures, and in a sense, it was. Just not the one I imagined.

CHAPTER FIVE

The first couple of days on the march, I was not allowed to ride Lover. Uncle Cheng claimed it was unfair for those who had to walk and that a true leader walked as much as his men if he could afford it. The argument was lost on me, for I had never formulated the idea of becoming a leader someday. The nine riders who had been chosen for their skills were sent on a scouting mission, three on both flanks and three ahead. According to Cheng Yuanzhi, neither they nor their horses took pleasure in riding, with all the back and forth it required. He also added that I needed strong legs if I wanted to become a warrior one day. That I could not argue, so I walked. But after two days, I felt like my legs were made of rock and would no longer carry me. I was just seven, after all. So I was allowed to ride on the third day, with Uncle Cheng accompanying me on one of the nine other horses for a little while, and the most amazing thing happened during that morning—I discovered how much I loved riding.

I was not only enjoying it immensely; I was good at it. I say this with as much humility as I can muster, I am a naturally gifted rider. Some people can shoot a bow in a matter of hours, others learn entire books from one read. *I* could ride a horse. With few explanations, I understood how to lead my horse and make her obey me. I was lucky that Lover was on the old side and thus quite docile, but even then, I quickly grasped the basics of equitation.

Uncle Cheng, clearly impressed, soon returned his horse to one of the nine riders, who then resumed his scouting mission, and on the next day, I accompanied a group of them. Then I had to walk again, not only because I enjoyed riding too much for my uncles' taste but also because my ass had gotten so sore that I could barely sit. Instead, whenever Uncle Deng or Cheng had some time to spare, they trained me while we walked. And since I had potential as a cavalryman, Deng Mao relented and agreed to teach me some of the basic slashing techniques, those being more useful when fighting from horseback.

"I'm not telling you to hack!" he yelled at me when, after half a *shi* of trying, I did not seem to get his point. "I told you to slash!"

"I'm trying!" I replied, feeling the ball of anger growing more and more.

My arms ached so much at this point that I was tempted to give up and learn how to shoot a crossbow instead. But I did not, and Uncle Cheng came to my rescue.

"Dun, have you ever seen a butcher cut some meat?" he asked. I told him I had not, so he found another example. "How about when your... folks saw some wood?" He had almost used the example of my father, but we both pretended it had not happened. This I had seen, of course. "How do they do it?"

"They go back and forth over the piece of wood," I replied, not getting where he was going at all.

"Is that all?" he asked. "Think hard."

I pictured my dad and my grandfather hunched over some branch or plank, looking down on it as the sweat prickled their eyes. The saw was not parallel to the ground but angled.

"They also force toward the floor," I said. Uncle Cheng gave me a wink, and the solution came soon after.

A good cutting technique requires the force to go in two directions, vertical and horizontal. Most warriors strike with a combination of backward and downward, which is the easiest way to go about it from horseback, but not exclusively. I even met a man whose technique used a forward movement like a thrust, accompanied by a slight upward angle. A move that leaves an opponent either dead or scared shitless, something I can vouch for personally.

Once I got the idea, I quickly pleased my instructor, which meant I was pleased with myself as well.

Marching is a boring affair, and I believe this is why Cheng Yuanzhi and Deng Mao did not begrudge schooling me in the art of fighting a couple of *shi* a day. But when we marched through the territories which had not rebelled as planned or had failed, the tension around our two Adepts was so strong that I kept to myself or went with the scouts.

Crossing Yu province, another strong bastion of the Yellow Turbans, proved a simple task. We found enough food or were given some by our brothers, but the moment we stepped into Yan, things changed.

Thankfully, we only had to go through a couple of commanderies, namely Dong and Chenliu, to reach Ji province, the center of our rebellion. But even considering the briefness of the crossing through Yan, I can't say any of us took pleasure in that week.

In my eyes, every forest was full of ambushing soldiers, every village wanted us dead, and every night would see us being attacked. I wasn't the only one feeling as such, or, more accurately, the talk around the fires made me see those things. We suffered a great desertion rate, though new fighters joined our ranks as we marched by. Wherever we went, folks knew of our imminent passage, and our brothers who had not rebelled but wanted to were pleased to join us. It meant that, again, we had families joining our ranks, and our progress slowed considerably. At least we did not struggle with food for a while since villages willingly offered what they could to avoid being raided. We did not, in fact, raid any village or hamlet, if only because we did not have the time for it. It did not sit well with some of the men who had already developed a taste for looting. So, Cheng Yuanzhi offered to raid the next city we came across. It was smart of him, for the next city happened to be a well-fortified place in the middle of Chenliu commandery. The locals warned us not to attack this place. Over one thousand men defended it, but the worst, they claimed, were not the soldiers but the man leading them. To listen to them, he was not only cruel; he was also cunning and resourceful. They put the fear of death in the heart of our most bloodthirsty fighters, and no one complained when Cheng Yuanzhi called for the march to continue with no stop.

We acted similarly with the next towns, pressed on by the rumors of powerful armies coming our way from every direction. There was a persistent rumor about a man they called the Tiger, who, while not being a noble, had gathered a few hundred loyal and savage warriors. They had met only victories against our brothers and pushed the frontline so close to us that soon the east of Yan province would see no yellow flags waving in the wind. Deng Mao wanted to veer east and tame that Tiger, but Cheng Yuanzhi refused to change our course, and before we could see anything of this man, whose real name was Sun Jian, we crossed the Huang He and entered Ji province.

So far, the march had not amazed me in terms of sight. The land of Yan and Yu provinces had been fairly disappointing, being either similar to my own county or so flat that your eyes could just not see the end of the horizon. But catching sight of the Yellow River, which we also call the Mother River, left me in awe, and I wasn't the only one. Up to that point, the Bai river flowing through Nanyang was the greatest waterway I had seen, and though I knew the Huang He, the Dajiang, and the Huai He had to be a lot bigger, I was not prepared for the greatness of their difference.

On that day, when we came to it, the Mother River was not particularly strong, it was just immense. I could not see the other side, and I wondered if maybe we had actually reached the sea. The locals promised a few rafts would meet us at the exact spot where they had led us, and after a nervous couple of *shi,* those embarkations glided to the bank on which Uncle Cheng waited. There were twelve rafts, each manned by three men. They could carry around thirty men per crossing, which meant they needed at least twenty-five crossings for each raft for the whole army of nine thousand men to land on the other side. It might not sound like much, but one crossing can take anywhere from twenty minutes to half a *shi*, and depending on the whims of the river, the crossing could take the raft a *li* or two further down, which meant a longer delay.

It took the rest of the day and a great part of the next morning for the ordeal to be completed, meaning that we spent the night split in two, with two-thirds of our men in Ji and the rest nervously waiting on the southern bank of the river. On my side, I must admit that my anxiety grew twofold when I stepped on the raft, and while the passers assured me it was as quiet as it could get, my hands never left the wooden floor of the barge. With more experience, I grew to be fine with boats and sailing, but I never enjoyed this mode of transportation, and that day, it left me livid for hours. Lover did not fare any better, shaking like a leaf by the time she landed, and I decided I would stick to horses as much as possible in the future.

The large group of passers left our group as richer men, and since they did not show any sign of being from our side of the war, it must have cost Uncle Cheng a little fortune. He assured me the money was a departing gift from Zhang Mancheng. One the Grand Adept probably had yet to figure out.

From then on, we were in Yellow Turbans territory, and we could stop watching over our shoulders. The morale improved, and since we were too far from our home province, the desertion stopped. I have often noticed that men fight better either close to home or far from it, but there is a certain distance, maybe between two hundred and six hundred *li*, where soldiers' morale is easily going down. The attraction of home never really fades, and when the risks of a journey back are not strong enough, the most willing ones act on it. We had passed this limit when we crossed the Huang He.

Surprisingly, however, food became more of an issue. We were months away from harvesting, and the seedlings were barely sprouting from the ground. It didn't take an expert eye to realize a lot of the fields had also not been properly sown.

Our brothers and sisters, while all willing to welcome us and direct us toward Julu, had no food to share, and since we belonged to the same camp, we could not realistically shake the grains out of them.

It's a strange thought coming from the son of a farmer, but Ji gave me an odd impression of poverty. The ground was drier and poorer, to the point that we could walk for half a day without seeing as much as a thicket. But even in the way people walked and talked, it felt like the bottom of society. I am not judging the people of that province, they were as educated and polite as any I've met, but they had an air of resignation I hadn't experienced before. You could not believe, looking at them, that we were toppling an empire and bringing justice back to the land.

I couldn't complain, though. Cheng Yuanzhi, pressed on by Uncle Deng, pulled rank a few times and got us a house for the night. We were now at the very end of the *Guyu* term, meaning summer was nearly upon us, and judging by the dryness of the air and the scorching heat, summer was coming early in this part of the empire. Sleeping under the sky was not a burden, but I was still happy when, after a month on the road, I got to spend a night with a roof over my head.

I don't think the men begrudged me the pleasure, nor did they mind Uncle Cheng using his rank. Oh, I'm certain a few grumblers voiced their opinion on the topic—an army wouldn't be one without them, but Uncle was well-loved by the men, and I had become everyone's son or nephew along the road. Whenever they saw me trotting joyously on the back of Lover, they cheered and claimed that no one could get the drop on us since Eagle-eye protected the flank. I believe the entire troop knew my nickname, while only a few could tell you my real *mingzi*. It was fine by me then, but it made my life slightly more complicated a few days later, when we arrived in Julu commandery.

We knew we had reached the commandery when the land changed from a plain to a cluster of rocky hills, then to low mountains. And if I thought the south of Ji to be desolate, it looked like heaven compared to Julu. Those mountains were nothing but rocks and dust, with only a few leafless shrubs to mark the land. Everything was in shades of yellow, beige, and brown. The last few years had apparently been cursed with droughts, and I could easily believe it, but even then, I couldn't picture this land lush with vegetation.

Our leaders, the three Zhang brothers, who were from this commandery, had established their camp at the center of a maze of mountains. I think they might have done so to increase the mystic feeling of their work at first, but as natural defenses went, it wasn't bad. Not only did it require excellent knowledge of the area to find it, but it was also easily defensible. There was just one big flaw in this choice; it was hardly habitable. And since a war was fought from there, it was very much inhabited indeed. From the first gate, manned by a group of maybe one hundred warriors, to the center of what could be called the camp, we had to walk for more than a *shi*. And in this lapse of time, I saw more people in one place than I ever would in my life. It was hard to find a piece of dirt without a group of people standing or sitting on it. People crammed every hole or recess in the mountains to avoid the sun. There was only little movement, as if they were all waiting for something, like those lizards who can remain still for hours under a rock. Uncle Cheng did not look positive as we struggled through the crowd of observers on our horses, and Deng Mao's mouth hung wide open more often than none. Things had changed since their last visit, and not for the better.

For obvious reasons, our army had not been allowed in, so only thirteen of us walked to the center of the maze: Cheng Yuanzhi, Deng Mao, Fat Ling, the nine riders, two of whom had to walk, and I. The men had been left under the command of Old Mi, and I felt an odd sense of pride thinking that from the folks of Fa Jia Po, one was basically commanding an army of nine thousand, while two others would meet Zhang Jue.

I was more nervous than ever, the feeling made worse by the persistent, empty stare of the onlookers. Zhang Jue, our General of Heaven, was as legendary as a man can be while still being alive. Not only were his healing powers famous, but even his person was supposed to be of another caliber than regular men. He was rumored to be over eight *chi* tall, with earlobes falling down to his shoulders. People said his eyes could see the truth in your mind, while his voice could tame thunders and storms.

We reached a part of the maze that was empty of people, except for a group of strong-looking warriors standing in line around a large square stage made of wood. Those men carried dagger-axes, wore armor like those of professional soldiers, and kept their stares straight ahead, even when we walked by their sides. From my horse, I could see that a large piece of fabric covered the stage, though being cut into a circle, it did not completely hide it. We dismounted right after the stage, leaving our horses in the care of boys barely older than I was.

The mountain right in front of the stage was taller than the others, and no one stepped on it, making it look naked. But the most surprising thing about it was the great hole facing the stage. It did not look like a cave, for its shape was too perfect, but its size made me doubt its human origin. Ten men would need to stand next to each other, arms stretched, to reach both sides of this entrance, and the same distance applied for the height.

YELLOW SKY REVOLT

I cracked my neck as I observed the roof of rock as we passed under it and nearly bumped into Uncle Deng's back when we stopped. I only didn't because he dropped to his knees so fast that it caught my attention. Not just him, but Uncle Cheng too was kowtowing. Fat Ling and the other riders reacted faster than I did and followed our Adepts' example. I went down a couple of heartbeats later.

There was a man in front of us. The darkness of the grotto prevented me from seeing him clearly, but the faint light from the torches hanging on the sides allowed me to notice the rich clothes of golden silk adorning him and the crown of straw on top of his head. His eyes looked very dark and cold under his thick brows, though it might have been because of the grotto's lack of light. His thin lips, however, were not a trick of the light. I doubted he was the General of Heaven, for he was not as tall as I'd heard, but maybe the stories had been exaggerated. I dared not look up from the moment my forehead touched the floor, so this was as much as I could see of this man at that point.

"Cheng Yuanzhi and Deng Mao, Adepts of Xinye and Anzhong counties in Nanyang commandery, are here with nine thousand men, upon the orders of Grand Adept Zhang Mancheng," Uncle Cheng said in a rapid, perfunctory tone.

"Ah," the man replied, with a tone suggesting he had been expecting something of the sort. "Welcome, brothers, you may rise," he went on with the warmth of a winter morning. We did not stand up, but following my uncle's example, sat straighter on our knees. The floor was not flat or even, and the sharp rock hurt my knees. "You must be tired," he said. "But the council of war will be held shortly, and you will be expected to give your report then."

"Should we give our report to the Grand Master first?" Uncle Cheng asked.

"My brother is... indisposed," the man replied. So this was either Zhang Bao, General of Earth, or Zhang Liang, General of the People. "He's been riddled with dreams," he then pressed on to explain our lord's indisposition. Dreams, especially when experienced by saints, are powerful portents. And for a man like Zhang Jue, powerful dreams could only mean an omen.

"Dreams?" Deng Mao asked right after the general gestured for us to stand at last.

"Our leader dreams of great things for the Yellow Turbans, but to assure those visions, he has to sacrifice all the pleasure of the earth from himself, and his body needs more rest than the rest of us do." He shook his head pitifully as he spoke, as if his brother's pain was now his own. This Zhang brother appeared sincere in his affliction, and I was left in awe at our leader's devotion to the cause. "Last night," he went on, "the General of Heaven dreamt of a bright, golden eagle landing on this very mountain. When he woke from the dream, he said the eagle was a sign of heaven's favor."

My stomach twisted on itself as I arrogantly thought that the eagle could be me. I stopped myself from saying anything, but I was obviously not the only one to entertain this idea. I felt the eyes of my companions on me, and a brief silence fell, something that did not go unnoticed by our general.

"What is it?" he asked.

"I think you might want to bring us to your brother after all," Uncle Deng said.

We did not meet Zhang Jue, at least not then. Zhang Bao, for that was who we'd met in the holy cave of the Way of the Great Peace, had welcomed the news of my foreseen presence with a limited interest. I would soon find out why, but at that moment, I felt insulted by his callousness.

He promised to tell his elder brother when he woke up, but to listen to him, this was not as important as the council meeting about to take place. So we left the cave. I had gone maybe ten *bu* inside, so I didn't know for sure what could be found there. From what I could see after my eyes got used to the darkness, it went perhaps a hundred steps further, and besides a couple of alcoves dug in the rock itself, it felt empty. The place smelled like incense, and I could easily imagine the grotto full of pilgrims and devotees before the war started. Altogether, I was glad to exit the cave. My head was spinning because of the smell, and my knees hurt pretty bad. I've never enjoyed enclosed spaces, and this one proved no different.

So we went out, and the General of Earth led us to a neighboring mountain without a grotto, but with a cove in which stood a kind of tent. No one was allowed to approach the tent but the authorized Adepts and, to my surprise, me. Uncle Cheng first told me to stay out with Fat Ling and the nine, but Zhang Bao insisted that I should be present and be introduced to our war leaders. His desire went against the feeling he had given me earlier on, but I let it pass. I must say that Zhang Bao did not give me a great impression. Not one as bad as Zhang Mancheng, but something in his demeanor did not reflect what I expected of the three brothers. I think it was the way he walked through the crowd of his followers that I particularly disliked, hands behind his back and staring straight ahead. He certainly did nothing wrong, so I can't say why I felt an unease by his side, but it was present.

One of the guards opened the tent's flap to let the four of us in, and we were welcomed with a collective sigh of relief. The room, if we could call it that, smelled like a peasant's house at the end of a hot summer day, and clearly, the council had cooked in the tent long enough for a lingering smell of fart to hang low. This would be the first of many war councils I'd attend in my life, and it was an impressive one, at least in the number of people attending it.

There must have been over twenty people sitting around a long table of solid wood, each with a guard or aide standing behind them. A cup of clay rested in front of each sitting man, with a pitcher for every three men, but I saw no food whatsoever. Those with swords had dropped them against the table, while those with longer weapons had handed them to their second. Maps were laid over the table and on the walls, none of them looking more than a few days old, and some, those at the center, were covered with pebbles of yellow and gray. I did not read back then, but I guessed the map with all the yellow pebbles represented our current locations. There were no gray pebbles near it.

No one spoke from the moment we stepped in, but the tension was palpable. When I raised my eyes from my inspection of the map, I realized a good number of the men present were staring at me, and I felt suddenly embarrassed.

"Why are we always the last ones to join?" Deng Mao asked in a whisper.

Throughout my life, I attended many a war council where attendees looked out of place. This was not one of them. In fact, besides Zhang Bao and a few obviously educated men, everyone present had the look of a warrior. A third of the table, on the right side, was empty of guests; this is where Zhang Bao invited us to sit. By right, Deng Mao should not have been allowed to take a seat since he was only a second in command. But as there were some empty spots, he took one, the closest to the end, while I remained standing between my two uncles. Zhang Bao took the spot at the top. On the other side sat his brother, Zhang Liang. They looked very much alike, with the exception that Liang's belly was round where his brother's was flat. He also looked friendlier, if only a little.

"Now that everyone is here," he said as he stood, "we may begin this council."

It took a few more seconds for the last ones to stop staring at me, and from that moment, I felt a bit more at ease.

It was hot in there, and to be honest, it was actually quite dull for a child, so after a few minutes of listening to the different Adepts giving an account of their districts, I dozed off a little. I popped out of my reveries whenever a new voice spoke and tried listening, but would eventually fail.

From what I gathered, this was a regular council, the likes of which happened every other day since the beginning of the rebellion. Those men were, for the most part, Adepts or Grand Adepts of the Way, but few had seen any action. They relied on messengers to know the situation, which made Uncle Cheng and Deng a bit of heroes among the council. Cheng Yuanzhi was actually the first to speak, being the last to arrive, and many heads went from arrogant glares to respectful nods by the time he was done. He had not only spoken of the battle of Wan, but of the situation we'd witnessed and rumors we'd come across on the way.

"This is consistent with what we've heard," Zhang Liang said from the other side of the table. "You've done well in Wan, brother Cheng, you too, brother Deng, and on coming here as fast as you did." I wasn't so sure about the last point, since it had taken us a week longer than expected at first, but if our General of Earth deemed it so, it must have been good enough.

Cheng Yuanzhi sat down again, and the next in line spoke. As I said, I did not follow everything, but what I learned can be summed up in a few points.

First, the Yellow Turbans were being reorganized into divisions of ten thousand men. Cheng Yuanzhi was officially named a division leader, and Deng Mao his grand leader, second in command. To the nine thousand who had come with us were added another thousand, and Uncle named his army the Golden Eagle division. I was touched, but since at this moment of the council, no one had heard about me, the point was lost on them.

We also got a clearer picture of the overall situation. In one month, the rebellion had taken over the entire Ji province, most of You province in the north, and great cities and commanderies in the west, namely Wan, Runan, and Yingchuan. According to Zhang Bao's reports, You province was the part seeing the most action, and already some sort of counterattack was being organized with the support of local militia. No reaction had been accounted for around Nanyang and Yu province, but it was only a matter of time. As proof that the Han government was preparing their response, Emperor Ling had named his brother-in-law, He Jin, known as the butcher, as general-in-chief. His byname came from his ancestry, not from any kind of cruelty on his part, but it wasn't reassuring. In turn, He Jin had appointed three generals to organize as many armies. This was as much as we knew about the enemy's reaction then.

However, to listen to the various reports, the most pressing enemy wasn't the Han government but the lack of food. Triggering the rebellion a couple of months early put us in a tight spot. By scraping every bit of grains, we could last until harvest season, but it would be done through deprivation and hunger. And since the men had been taken away from the fields too soon, there wouldn't be enough resources for the next year. Which is why division leaders received a new directive. Any town or village encountered had to be sacked down to the last unhusked grain of wheat, whether friendly to the cause or not. It proved a hugely unpopular decision, even more so since many of our leaders came from the surrounding areas, but something had to be done about the supply issue. And we were fighting for the people after all. It was only normal that they sacrificed a little, or so said Zhang Liang.

The lack of food and the reorganization of the rebellion were the reasons for the next item, the dispatching of the divisions among the territory under the Turbans' control. This is where it became complicated for us. Cheng Yuanzhi and two other division leaders were ordered to defend You province against the aggressive militia resisting us. More specifically, we were assigned the defense of Zhuo commandery, the closest one to Julu. We were to go further north, though the trip wasn't nearly as far as what we'd done so far, which was a relief. But where things got heated was when we understood that no reinforcements would be sent west. Deng Mao went through his cup of wine in a matter of seconds, which calmed his nerves for a few precious minutes as the generals moved on to the next point of the council. Then he could take it no longer and interrupted Zhang Liang halfway through a sentence, which did not please the general in the slightest.

"How about Nanyang and Yu?" he asked, his tone as neutral as possible.

"Just as your Grand Adept has told you, they will resist until we press on and come to their aid," Zhang Bao answered.

"Which could take months," Uncle Deng went on. "They are isolated down there, with just as much food as we have here, if not less by now."

"Do you doubt your Grand Adept?" Zhang Liang asked.

"Yes," Deng Mao answered without pause, which got a few gasps from the assistance.

"We do not doubt his loyalty to the cause," Uncle Cheng said, coming to his friend's help. "But Wan is just one city. Should one of the three armies you mentioned earlier be directed towards it, they won't be able to resist for more than a few weeks, at best." A pain in my chest burst suddenly as I thought of my little sister. From what I could gather, Wan was not a priority for us, and being the furthest place from our center of command, it would be the last to be helped. For the first and not the last time, I wondered if I should not have taken her with us. I was also sickened by how little thought they gave to a place my father and thousands of others had given their lives for.

"Bo Cai will help them," said a man sitting two spots from Zhang Bao. "You know the old bugger. If he hears our brothers are in a tough spot, he'll rush to their help and kill whoever stands between him and his mission."

"That's if he's not too busy with his own fighting. The enemy will not give up Runan so easily," another said. Runan was an important fief of the empire, and many rich, powerful men came from that place. Not least of them, the Yuan clan, who had produced many ministers and excellencies over the centuries. The man who had spoken was named Liu Pi, and he would play a part in the early years of the drama of the Three Kingdoms, as well as in my life. At this point, I was mostly amazed by the size of his biceps and the two missing fingers on his left hand. He knew what he was talking about since he too was from Runan.

"We need to secure our base before sending men all over the land," another said, a voice like that of a snake, though he reminded me more of a weasel, and this is exactly what he proved to be in the long run. His name was Bian Xi, a young, dubious-looking man from Ji province. He sat next to Liu Pi, and the dislike of both men for each other was hard to miss. Since I had found Liu Pi to look like a decent man, I immediately sided with him in my mind.

The conversation went on like this for a while. Half of us wanted to press the offensive while the rebellion was hot and the enemy disorganized; the other half objected for a solidification of our base and a focus of our effort on securing more resources for the next offensive. And since the two generals and, according to them, our Grand Master agreed on the latter idea, this is what we were ordered to do. We would leave in two days' time, which was only slightly better than what Zhang Mancheng had given us.

No one seemed surprised by Zhang Jue's absence, besides my two uncles, and I assumed the General of Heaven rarely attended those councils in person. For a moment there, I started doubting his implication in the rebellion, if not his existence. But then Zhang Bao brought up the last point on the agenda.

"Tomorrow morning, from the sacred square, our great leader will address the people. He has some omen to deliver, including one regarding the young man standing here. I can assure you, you will want to hear those words and share them with your men. You are thus required to attend the address." I blushed when the whole room turned their attention my way, and it took Deng Mao to slap my back for me to bow respectfully twice. Once toward Zhang Bao, once toward his brother. It only came to me then that Zhang Bao had declared Zhang Jue's intention to speak of me without having asked the man first. Then again, maybe this was how the three brothers worked, with complete trust in each other.

Nothing else was said on the topic, and after offering the assistance a last chance to speak, which no one took, we were dismissed.

It was getting dark when we stepped out of the makeshift tent, and I felt more tired than ever. Fat Ling and the others had gone from the place where we had left them, but when my eyes got used to the growing darkness, I recognized my neighbor and some of the nine men among a group of old folks sitting around a fire.

"That was interesting," Uncle Cheng said, his hand on my shoulder inviting me to keep moving.

"That's a way to put it," Deng Mao replied, not sounding enthused at all. "I'm not looking forward to telling the men we're leaving in two nights."

"Me neither," Cheng Yuanzhi replied. "Let's focus on the fact that we probably got an extra day thanks to our eaglet here," he went on, giving me a friendly wink.

"Our lucky charm indeed," Deng Mao commented.

"Am I going to have to do anything?" I asked, my nerves starting to betray me.

"No idea," they both replied. "And I don't know who does," Cheng Yuanzhi said.

"It's kind of the theme here," someone else said from behind us. When I turned around, I was not surprised to see Liu Pi, his bulky arms extended in front of his chest as he saluted us. He gave us his name, which none of us knew before, and we returned the politeness.

"You came from Runan?" Uncle Cheng asked.

"A week ago," Liu Pi answered. "And just like the two of you, I can't say I'm impressed by the way things have changed around here." He spoke loud, especially considering the nature of his words, but such was the nature of Liu Pi; he just did not care. Uncle Cheng did though and asked if there was a place to share some wine in peace around here.

Liu Pi invited us to his private quarters, a word he used with sarcasm. Thankfully for me though, Uncle Cheng ordered all of us back to our division, the Golden Eagle, to rest for the night. Deng Mao wanted to accompany the two men, but since we couldn't find our way without him, he stayed with us. It proved a blessing, for when we finally reached our group, they had only been served water, and it took all my uncle's authority to get some porridge brought to the nine thousand of us.

I had dozed off on my horse on the way back, so I had regained a bit of energy. Just enough to stay awake until Cheng Yuanzhi came back, still scratching his head from the events of the day or from his conversation with Liu Pi. When he saw I was not yet sleeping, he came next to me and asked how I was feeling. I told him I was nervous about the next morning.

"Nothing to worry about," he said. "You'll only be introduced by the most powerful man in the world to a crowd of a few dozens of thousands of people." I cursed and tried to punch him in the shoulder, but he deflected my blow while laughing. I was now worried sick, but what really took the sleep out of me was what he whispered next.

"If only he can make it."

CHAPTER SIX

I WOKE WITH THE SUN, or more accurately, with the light drizzle accompanying the rising sun. Those drops lowered the heaviness of the climate a little, and it was altogether a welcome sign. Not enough to turn the ground to mud, it still kept the dust at bay while we made our way back to the stage in front of the holy cave. To gain some time, we ate on the way, and since Zhang Jue was to speak, everyone was allowed to join. But after a few minutes, many of our men gave up. They all wanted to hear the Grand Master of the Way, but it was just impossible to cram so many people into such a tight, already crowded space. Devotees and pilgrims had come all night long, filling the roads until they seemed about to burst. How they knew Zhang Jue would make an appearance, I do not know, but they knew.

Not everyone would hear the general's words, so criers were spreading among the folks. You could spot them for their Taoist robes and because they stood alone, facing the other way around.

The previous day's atmosphere had been quiet and heavy, but now it was electric, like the few minutes before the first lightning bolt. I kept shifting left and right as Lover peacefully followed the horses of Cheng Yuanzhi and Deng Mao. At first, I thought it would be impossible for horses to make their way through the masses, but then I found out that without them, we would never have made it. It was mid-morning by the time we exited the crowd and climbed down from our mounts.

Huge flags flew with the wind from the four corners of the stage, each carrying a different symbol. I recognized the one for "yellow" and the characters for the *jiazi* of the new sixty-year cycle we had entered three months ago. Besides those flags, the only thing visible on the great square was a small table of dark wood and a big flat bowl of clay at its center.

Zhang Liang came toward us from a group of young men looking like priests as well, and I realized he was shorter than his brother.

"So the eagle has landed," he said with a warm smile for me, his hands rubbing each other like a merchant about to strike a deal.

"And is a bit nervous," Uncle Cheng said.

"No need to be," Liang said, brushing the idea with a wave of the hand. "Just stand there, by the table's side, and wait for my brother to begin the ceremony. Once he calls for you, join him and just follow his instructions. It won't take long. You'll be back down before you know it. Now, however, I'm afraid we need to remove that filthy shirt." And before I could say anything, a couple of young priests were peeling the shirt from my back. I meant to protest because it had been the garment given to me by Uncle Cheng back in Xiangyang. I felt even more embarrassed now that I stood bare chested, but Deng Mao infused me with confidence when he declared that my training had started to show. Before I had the time to reply anything, a loud bang of a drum resonated, immediately quieting the thousands upon thousands of voices chirping. The rubble of bodies shifting their attention in the same direction replaced the sounds of voices, but it too died down almost immediately.

"Quick!" Zhang Liang said as he pushed me up the small stairs leading to the stage. I was about to call Cheng Yuanzhi for help, but the two young priests who had stripped me down formed a barrier behind me, and my two uncles were grinning like fiends as I climbed the last steps.

While looking on my right, toward the entrance of the cave, from where more notes of drums, *bo* cymbals, and some wind instruments I did not recognize were being played, I made my way to the table. I was so focused on the cave that I bumped into the corner of the table and let out a curse while a few thousand people laughed at me. I am smiling now, thinking about what I must have looked like, but I was absolutely mortified, about to cry and run away, never to be seen again.

Thankfully, their attention soon shifted to the cave, from where Zhang Jue emerged. Walking slowly, to the beating rhythm, our General of Heaven was most impressive. He wore a complete *shenyi* set of robes and sashes made from golden silk, a high *liang guan* hat, but of the kind I had never seen before, higher and wider. It looked to me like a hand trying to reach the sky. But contrary to anything else I had seen, he wore his hair loose under the hat. His beard reached down to his sternum, and even from afar, I could spot the gray in it. More surprising still was the knife in his left hand and the thin rope in his right. The rope was tensing in front of him, and then a goat kid stepped obediently on the stage. Behind the Grand Master came the musicians, along with servants pulling the cart carrying the drums and a few more bending over as they spilled some white powder from bags of linen. I would later learn this was salt, and the idea had not even crossed my mind because I could not imagine anyone wasting good salt on the floor like that. Those two servants split when they reached the stage and went around it, forcing the spectators to take a few steps back so as not to walk over the forming circle of salt. When they were done, they retreated to the cave, and Zhang Jue, who had stopped at the bottom of the stairs, now resumed his walk. His head appeared higher and higher as he reached the stage, and though I don't think he was eight *chi* tall, he could not have been far.

I forced my eyes down when he shot a glance at me, for the first time noticing the yellow triangle sewn from the edges of the white circle carpet. A triangle within a circle within a square, our most sacred symbol. The goat kid was trembling by the time it reached the table, and I pitied it, knowing of its fate.

"You may raise your head," Zhang Jue said, his voice soft and low.

I looked up at him and almost gasped in shock.

A lot of what had happened since the day before made sense now, from the secretive attitude of Zhang Bao, to Uncle Cheng's last comment when he came back during the night. Even the way those servants had pushed the line of spectators with that circle of salt had a purpose beyond its ritualistic nature. No one was supposed to see Zhang Jue from up close, for it was obvious our General of Heaven was nothing but a dead man walking.

From a distance, the illusion was perfect. With a heavy layer of makeup, what I now assumed to be a wig, and long robes to cover his frail body, you could not imagine how desolate he truly was. But a couple of steps away from him, as I now stood, the mirage vanished. Like a fart in the wind, Uncle Deng would say.

His eyes were more yellow than white, with red veins crisscrossing all the way to his irises. They, in turn, had grayed, like those of the dead men I had seen by Wan's wall. No makeup could conceal the darkness surrounding those sick eyes, nor the sweat pearling on his forehead as if he'd stood under the rain.

Zhang Jue dropped the knife on the table in a slow, majestic gesture hiding the fact that he could hold it no longer, and I caught a glimpse of his bony fingers and thin wrists. The blue of his veins looked incredibly pronounced, but he brought the long sleeve over his arms before anyone else noticed. Considering the height of the stage, I don't think there was any risk of that happening anyway. I searched for Uncle Cheng in the crowd, and when I found him, he shook his head meaningfully in my direction. He knew and wanted me to keep it together. I finally closed my hanging mouth just as Zhang Jue spoke.

"Brothers! Sisters of the Way of the Great Peace!" he called in a surprisingly powerful voice. The criers relayed the words, but I don't know how far they went, immediately drowning in the chaos of cheers from an adoring crowd of several thousand people. You can't imagine what it feels like when so many people gathered in a tight, resonating location shout together. I almost dropped to my knees under the pressure, and I did cover my ears. Zhang Jue chuckled at my reaction.

"Our time draws near!" he said and again had to wait for the shouting to stop. It went faster this time, the people's voices quieting after he raised both his hands. "Yesterday, I received an omen in my dreams!" He had to speak slowly to make sure the criers could relay his words. "I dreamt of a golden eagle landing on this very mountain," he went on, pointing his shaking hand toward the mountain behind him. "With a voice coming straight from Huang-Lao, the eagle told me the war would be over soon. It told me the prophecy of the *jiazi* would soon come true, and the time of the blue sky has reached its end."

A wave of cheers responded to Zhang Jue, spreading across the mountains as the words were spoken again and again.

"And not half a day later, all the way from Nanyang commandery in Jing province, came this young man, whom they call Eagle-eye." The collective gasp of the crowd chilled my blood. I could feel their thousands of stares pointed at me, and never before did I feel such an intense heat rising along my spine. "This young man," Zhang Jue said again, dropping his hand on my shoulder as he spoke, "has witnessed the fall of Wan with his own eyes and has crossed the land to tell us of our brothers' glorious victory. In doing so, he made my dream come true. He is *our* golden eagle and will lead us to victory!"

Nearly eighty years later, the memory still makes my skin prickle. The way the people responded to his enthusiasm left me in awe. And when finally they calmed down, I realized many of them were crying.

"I will bless him, and wherever he goes, our army will be invincible," Zhang Jue said as he drew the knife above his head. Then, in a lower voice, he said, "Can you place it on the table?" He was talking about the kid, and I understood he did not have the strength to do so himself, so I obeyed as well as possible, though my heart wasn't in it. The little white goat made a pitiful sound as I dropped it under his right hand. "Try to keep it steady."

My pity for the little beast increased even more when Zhang Jue brought his shaking, feeble hand to its throat. Yet he cut through in one clear motion, and after a few seconds of thrashing, it fell on its knees and died. The bowl filled with blood in a few seconds. Zhang Jue, with grace, accompanied the goat and let it lie on its side, then picked up the bowl and walked around the table. I followed him.

He made me face him as we stood in front of a silent crowd and left his hand on my shoulder as he knelt down. I guessed it looked all fine from down the stage, but up there, I struggled with his weight, for Zhang Jue had to use me for support. He dropped a bit of blood but otherwise made it look natural. I almost knelt as well, but quickly understood it would have made his gesture pointless, so now I stared right back into his face. He had gentle eyes, despite the sickness, and his smile was genuine. I think I would have worshiped him as well if I had met Zhang Jue in health, and who knows how the future events would have unfolded. But there was no denying the man stood at the doorstep of his own demise.

"That's our secret," he said in a whisper, as if reading my mind. I nodded, and I only betrayed this secret when I had to, though that's a story for later. I'm not counting my talks on the topic with Uncle Cheng, of course.

Zhang Jue dipped the first two fingers of his right hand in the bowl of warm blood, then traced a line from my forehead to my chin, then took some more and applied the liquid over my lips. He closed his eyes and mumbled something incomprehensible. Then stood again, dropped his right hand over my head, called on heaven to watch over me, and splashed the remaining blood toward the crowd. The throw had been feeble, and only a few followers received the sacred liquid, but they immediately erupted into a frenzy.

It all went very fast, and as soon as Zhang Jue faced them again, the crowd rose into another chorus of deafening cheers. I had not heard him, but Zhang Bao was standing behind me, and I only knew of his presence when he placed a robe of silk over my shoulders. I had never worn anything made of this material, and it felt like a cold, soothing cloud was enveloping me. The robe was covered with golden phoenixes and was far too big for me.

"Time to get down," he whispered in my ears just as Zhang Jue recited our creed, *death to the blue sky, the time of the yellow sky is near*. No matter what, I thought, it would rise without its founder.

From the moment I walked on stage to the moment I came down from it, less than five minutes had passed, but I was exhausted, and it wasn't over. Just before I stepped toward Uncle Cheng, who was drowning behind a row of maddened devotees, Zhang Bao removed the robe he had just placed there, telling me they would tear it to pieces. I believed him, and he promised to give it back to me later on, which he never did. I had owned a garment of silk for less than two minutes and had already developed a taste for it. So when Uncle Cheng bought yet another shirt for me, a regular one this time, it felt coarse and dirty.

I was keenly aware of the great honor I had just been given, and if it hadn't been clear enough, the adoring crowd shaking me in every direction as we waited for them to disperse made it plain. And yet, my newly found knowledge of our leader's situation left a bitter taste in my mouth. Not only would our revolution lose its founder soon, I also understood how much of the Way was an illusion. The worst was that Zhang Jue truly gave me the feeling of a good man deserving to be followed.

One interesting effect of the ceremony came with the great number of warriors who volunteered to join our division. Before the day ended, Cheng Yuanzhi was given an agreement to include an extra two thousand men to his division, meaning that he was elevated to Grand Division Leader. I don't know what it meant for him officially, but unofficially, it gave him the right to haggle from two thousand people eager to join the invincible Golden Eagle.

Liu Pi came to see us off, as did Zhang Liang. The former promised to keep an ear open on the events in the west, and the latter reminded us of our two missions: gather more food and keep the enemy from penetrating Ji province. If we could, we were to completely annihilate them, but giving time for the rebellion to get stronger was the first objective. We knew nothing of our enemy besides its reputation as a ragged band of independent militia under the command of leaders acting on their own initiative. But we knew their numbers would not match ours, and neither could their passion. At least this is what Zhang Liang reminded the men as we took our leave.

I guess I remained too quiet for Cheng Yuanzhi's taste, for half a day later, he pulled my horse aside and asked me what was wrong.

"It's just that—" I said, not finishing my thought.

"That our Grand Master is dying," he finished for me.

"Not just that," I went on. "It's all an illusion. All of this. The Way of the Great Peace, the Yellow Turbans, our plan to remove the Han and bring justice back to the land."

"Hey," Uncle Cheng snapped. "I don't know where you got this impression, but it ain't true."

"How can we follow a healer that can't heal himself?" I asked, for that was the part that bothered me the most.

"Things are more complicated than that, Dun. Zhang Jue can't save himself because his power can't be used on himself. And since no one is as powerful, it just means his disease can't be cured."

"How do you heal people?" I asked. Until then, I had never cared much about the healing magic of the Way, but I needed something to hook my waning faith to. A bit of enchantment to see that behind the illusion still lingered an actual miracle. I would be sorely disappointed.

"Water," he said after a long sigh, "it's just water."

"Sacred water?" I asked.

"Regular water. And some words."

This is how I got a glimpse into the "mysterious" art of the Way. Those initiated would bring water to the ill, pretending to purify it first with some mysterious incantations or powder, whatever worked. Then, after the person in need of healing drank it, a conversation followed. The sick had to repent, to unburden their guilt by speaking of the worst deeds he or she had ever committed. Then and only then would the water heal them, on the condition that the person believed in the water's power and had honestly repented. I called it a dog fart, which made Uncle laugh. I couldn't believe talking about one's faults could heal anything, to which Uncle explained that so much was unknown about the way the human mind and body worked. The Way of the Great Peace believed guilt to be one of the strongest illnesses affecting individuals. Though a necessary one. Clearing one's sense of guilt was like unclogging a river and seeing the liberated water run free and pristine.

The second reason I could not simply take his word for it was that I could not picture Deng Mao engaging with folks about their guilt and past wrongdoings. Cheng Yuanzhi laughed at that too and told me I would be surprised. And I was indeed surprised when on that evening Uncle Deng told me it was time for me to confess.

He proved me wrong, not only because Deng Mao was a great conversationalist, far from the rough image he wore like a second skin, but also because it did heal me. I wasn't sick like so many of our pilgrims but was suffering from a certain form of sadness no boy of seven is supposed to hold. I won't relate in detail what I told him, only that there were a few mentions of my father and my sister. But also about my mother, which surprised me more than it did him. By the time he was done with me, I had cried more than ever before, and it felt great. A new sense of purpose took over me. Or rather, my purpose had come back. In the end, I found out through Deng Mao's patient healing that the Way's supposed magic mattered very little.

What did matter was the good we were bringing to our brothers and sisters. Simple folks, for the first time in our long history, had a chance to see some improvement in their lives, and that was worth a few lies. My faith never completely recovered, but in a way, I was now more of a Yellow Turban than before, for I was now part of a great secret and would guide our men to victory as their fake charm of invincibility.

CHAPTER SEVEN

Zhuo commandery, You province,
6th month of the 7th year of Guanghe era
(184), Han Dynasty.

For the next two months, Zhuo commandery was our home, and it was not a comfy one. Summer in this part of the land was just an unending, scorching day. Even the night offered no respite from the heat. Locals claimed it was not a drought, but it sure felt like one.

I was not to be pitied, for I was given more water than I knew what to do with, along with other gifts such as meat, eggs, shoes, and many other things our camp followers could spare. They all wanted the protection of the Golden Eagle for their sons or husbands in the coming fights. I wanted to refuse, but Deng Mao insisted I oblige them, if only to share their offering with the men. Even Lover was so well-fed that she gained weight in those days.

And all I had to do in return was to parade in front of the division before a battle began and wave a yellow flag as high as possible. Sure enough, we won every fight we engaged in, but those were ridiculously unbalanced battles. We dwarfed any of the militia facing us, those being as badly equipped and organized as we were, and never numbering over a few hundred, at best. The only reason they accepted the fight was to protect their villages or towns.

Even then, scavenging any house, farm, or hamlet we stumbled upon, food was always an issue. The men never went to a handicapping level of hunger, but the same cannot be said of the followers, which made their offerings even more difficult to accept. We always remained as close as possible to rivers and lakes for water, so at least we never really struggled with thirst.

There was a town, whose name I forgot, where an interesting event happened. I was just riding my mare in front of our battle-hungry division when the gates opened. A man rode to us, waving a white flag for us to know he came in peace, ready to surrender. This, in itself, wasn't rare, save for the fact that he was riding a donkey. Uncle Cheng was right behind me, and usually, this was when I would vanish within the group of the closest warriors. But this time he told me to stay and talk to the man. I was used to obeying him and gently kicked my horse to face the coming representative of the town.

"Where is your leader?" the man asked, not hiding his displeasure at being here. He was rather short, though it was hard to judge from the back of a donkey. His clothes marked him as some kind of merchant, but his choice of mount told me he wasn't a successful one. The most surprising, however, was the sword hanging from his belt. It was a simple yet well-crafted *jian* sword, the kind typically adorned by officers, and maybe this was what the man had been once. It looked shorter than the ones I had seen so far, increasing my impression of the man being more on the short side.

"He's in front of you," I said as loud as possible, straightening my back. I heard the snort from Uncle Cheng behind me and had to fight a smirk.

"Don't play with me, boy," the man said, bringing his donkey a little closer and already looking past me.

"One more step and I unleash those men on your town," I said, using my best impression of Uncle Cheng's commanding voice. It did the trick, and the man pulled on the mane of his donkey. Oh, he was pissed, and for a second, I wondered if he would ignore my threat and grab me by the neck. But he did no such thing and waited a few seconds before speaking again.

"Are you really leading this army?" he asked, frowning his bushy eyebrows as if trying to peer into my head.

"I guide them," I said, squaring my shoulders to an exaggerated degree. "What do you want, old man?" He wasn't that old, but for a child, every grown-up is old, and I wanted to humiliate him a little. It was puerile of me, but I was enjoying myself, and since we had taken a fair number of such places, I knew how things were supposed to go.

"*We* want you to get out of here," he replied. "Leave us in peace. We have nothing for you."

I told him they had food and wine. The look on his face when a child told him he wanted their wine was worth my weight in grain. I should have stopped there. It was all very unfair to the poor man; he had no choice but to agree to whatever we asked of him, or we would take it anyway. But I did as children do, and adults too; when given a bit of power, I used it.

"And your shoes," I said.

"My shoes?" he asked, looking at his feet, which were covered with good but worn-out leather shoes. I could see he did not want to part from them.

"Not just yours," I said, "all of theirs."

Deng Mao scoffed really hard when I said so, and I was sure Uncle Cheng was throwing him his most murderous gaze, for this scene resulted from a conversation from the previous day. Deng Mao had been complaining that so many of our men needed new shoes, we would soon be unable to walk more than twenty *li* a day. To which Cheng Yuanzhi replied they could make sandals out of straw or grass. Uncle Deng accused him of being made of the same wood as Zhang Mancheng if he thought the men would accept that idea and that *just maybe* he had spent too much time on his horse and could no longer share the distress of his fellow warriors. That's when Deng Mao offered to clear the next town of their shoes, which Cheng Yuanzhi had forbidden him to do. But he had given me no such orders.

"And why not my wife while you are at it?" the man barked. Finally, I thought, he was taking me seriously and not looking over my shoulder for another sign of authority among us.

"She's free to join us if she wants," I said, which raised another chorus of laughter behind me. "But from you, I'll just take the sword."

This is how I gained my first blade. The man had taken good care of it, though its age showed through a few cracks, and the sheath would have to be entirely remade, according to Uncle Deng.

We left this small town barefoot, with just enough food to last until the harvest. At least they kept their lives, and in a sense, it was because of me, though the donkey-man would not see it that way. This was not always the case. Some chose to resist.

Despite Zhang Liang's orders, looting towns and villages wasn't our main purpose and happened either out of necessity or opportunity. Our chase of the different local militia took us all over the commandery and sometimes further. More often than not, our enemies refused the battle, for good reasons, and disbanded or ran away. Those with horses we did not pursue, but the others were at the mercy of the Golden Eagle division, and many never saw their home again.

When the battle became inevitable, or when the enemy was fool enough to come after us, a tradition I did not fully understand took place. They would send their best warrior to challenge one of ours to a duel. Deng Mao had accepted the first challenge and had won in less than two bouts. The enemy had all but crumbled upon their champion's defeat and did the worst thing possible in battle; they ran away. There was no stopping our men when that happened, the bloodlust turning them into hounds pursuing a fleeing hare. And since men don't run as fast when they keep checking behind them, very few survived.

Cheng Yuanzhi accepted the second a few days later. He also won, though his opponent had been some kind of heavy brute armed with a battle-ax.

I don't know who was the most surprised when Uncle plunged his blade into the big man's guts, him or my uncle. Contrary to Deng Mao, Uncle Cheng did not think himself to be such a great warrior. He was just a veteran who had survived a good number of battles and had formed life-saving habits. Whatever his humility said, he won three more such duels and had been the last one to accept a challenge.

On average, battles happened once or twice a week. In between, we were always on the move, always pursuing the rumor of a militia, only taking the time to bury our dead and treat those who could be. The wounded who could travel were sent back to Julu. The others, I am glad I did not know of their fate.

It wasn't much, but every fight claimed lives on our side too, and though the men cheered, our two leaders did not seem to partake in the joy of victory, at least when away from prying eyes.

Two weeks after we took the shoe-town, as we called it, this is how I overheard my uncles talking under the cover of Cheng's flimsy tent. I was bringing Uncle Cheng a bowl of soup but stopped myself right before I elbowed the flap open.

"How far?" Deng Mao was asking.

"About four days, if they're still there," Cheng replied. Something in my uncle's voice made me wait in my spot.

"And otherwise? We abandon Zhuo?" Deng Mao asked. Now I knew something was wrong.

"What else? We're the last ones in You province, Julu is about to be surrounded, and our supplies are melting faster than we can gather them."

"What did you just say?" I asked, not able to keep it any longer. I stormed inside, two bowls of fuming soup in my hands. One was supposed to be for me, but I had lost my appetite.

"Dun, damn it, come closer," Deng Mao said, waving me in as if me standing in the door would make his words fly to everyone's ears.

"What's happening to the others and to Julu?" I asked as I gave them the bowls. They exchanged a look only two old friends can share, and Deng Mao shrugged, as if to say I was knee-deep in the same shit, anyway.

"You can't tell anyone about it," Uncle Cheng made me promise. "Not even Fat Ling or the folks from Fa Jia Po." Again, I promised, and it's a good thing he made me swear twice because I was tempted once I heard the truth.

What was happening was terrible for our cause. Among the three divisions sent to You province, only ours still existed. The two others had been swept away in a matter of days. When I asked how on earth it was possible, thinking of the ease with which we had won every battle so far, Uncle simply told me that the militia of the other commanderies in You province had gathered under a Han colonel named Zou Jing. Though according to the rumors, another was actually leading. They proved a formidable opponent for our brothers, and now most of the province was gone from our grasp.

As for Julu commandery and Ji province, one of the three armies sent by the government, under the command of the newly appointed General of the Household of the North, Lu Zhi, had won great victories against our divisions and was now threatening our base.

If we did nothing, as Cheng Yuanzhi explained, our division would soon be separated from our command center at best or surrounded at worst.

This was terrible. How could we be losing the war while everything moved so well here? And what about those hundreds of thousands of people counting on us in Julu? I was so hung up on the idea that we were losing both Ji and You that I did not ask the most important question of all. But Uncle Cheng beat me to it.

"That's not all," he said, and the look on his face told me something even worse had happened.

Zhang Mancheng had been killed. In itself, it wasn't such bad news, but this was how Uncle brought up the situation in Wan. Another of the three imperial generals sent from Luoyang, Zhu

Jun, had brought the fight to Jing province and surrounded Wan. From what we knew, this Zhu Jun was also accompanied by the officials of Jing province, as well as this famous Sun Jian Tiger we had heard about. How they managed to lure Zhang Mancheng from the safety of the city was a mystery, but the Grand Leader had gotten himself killed. The city was now under the authority of Zhao Hong, Mancheng's lackey, and the siege was going on. At least it had been when the messenger left a couple of weeks ago.

I could so clearly see a picture of my baby sister, crying in the arms of old Grandma Liao, the city in flames around them, that I almost burst into tears. But I had too much rage as well, and it overtook my sorrow.

"How did they do that?" I asked. "Wasn't this Tiger far east? Runan was in between, no?" I wasn't sure I got the geography of the land right, but it turned out I did. Except that a last piece of news had to be shared.

Runan and all of Yu province had fallen. This was where the brunt of the Han counterattack had happened. In a classic blow, like in a game of *weiqi*, they had severed our effort in the middle, thus creating a gap between our forces. Not only this Zhu Jun, but the third general, Huangfu Song, had collaborated in the effort to destroy our forces in Yu.

Bo Cai, our most feared warrior, was dead, and no one seemed to know what had happened to Liu Pi. The two imperial generals had then split, and while Zhu Jun attacked Wan, Huangfu Song was fighting our forces in the south of Ji province. At least *he* seemed to struggle more than the others, if only because he had to cross the defended Yellow River.

The rebellion was facing its strongest challenge yet, and it was failing. As far as I could see, we were the only division still knowing a semblance of victory, and that was only because this Zou Jing had kept us for last on his kill-list.

"What do we do?" I asked.

"Apparently, nothing," Deng Mao said without masking his sarcasm while crossing his arms on his chest.

"Not nothing," Cheng Yuanzhi retorted. "We keep defending Zhuo and destroy this Zou Jing and his militia, who, according to our intel, are four days away."

"Or we could go back to Julu and regroup," Deng Mao offered, which made Cheng Yuanzhi sigh.

"We received no such order," Uncle Cheng said.

"Maybe the messengers just didn't make it to us," Deng Mao replied through his teeth.

"Not an excuse to leave our post," said Uncle Cheng, his hand waving the idea away.

"This isn't the army, Yuanzhi!" Deng Mao barked as he stood up in anger.

"But you're still under my command," Cheng Yuanzhi replied, kicking his stool back as he too stood up.

They just stared at each other, like two rams about to butt heads. Deng Mao was breathing hard through his nose, and I thought he would charge, but he was the first to relent. His fists opened, he closed his eyes, and the tension went down a notch.

"I'll go get some fresh air. If this is fine with you, *leader*," Deng Mao said, and I really wished he hadn't used that tone at the end.

"You should get out, yes," Uncle Cheng replied. Deng Mao left, and it was like the air returned to the tent. Uncle apologized for the spilled soup, something I couldn't care less about. Somehow, I now understood those children whose parents quarrel.

"Do you think my sister is fine?" I asked once my nerves returned.

"She's with Han Zhong," he replied, shoving a few slices of boiled radishes in his mouth. "She's safer than we are." My thoughts went to the scarred warrior we had left in Wan, and I sent a silent prayer that he was keeping his word and protecting Mihua as if she was his own daughter.

I did not stay long after that, choosing the simple company of my horse, something I did more and more often in those days. Sometimes, when the tension around Cheng Yuanzhi was getting too strong, I would either take a walk with Lover, or meet with the folks from Fa Jia hill, but with what I now knew, I couldn't do the latter. Who knew what they would have done if they learned of their families' situation?

Sleep came hard, and dawn much too fast. The morning sun brought another hot, cloudless summer day, and with it, the solution to the problem of our next step. A messenger rode all the way to Cheng's tent. His horse was foaming at the mouth, and his eyes were livid with exhaustion. The man had pushed it as hard as the beast could take. I ran behind, as did all those who had witnessed the man's haste.

I had spent the night with Lover, something that always made the men laugh to no end, so I had a long way to run before I reached Uncle Cheng. When I did, I had to elbow my way through a group of a few dozen fighters and emerged just in time to see Cheng Yuanzhi climbing over a cart and calling for silence.

"Everyone, pack your things. We're heading south. Take only what you absolutely need. This will be a forced march. We're moving in a quarter of a *shi*."

For a second I thought the messenger carried an order from our leaders in Julu, but as I was about to find out, his provenance and purpose were very different. Zou Jing had decided to spare us and instead attack the northern front of our base commandery, which no one was protecting.

A forced march is the most taxing way to move an army, especially for one as untrained as ours. It's not just the body that suffers, but the mind as well. Not knowing if the commander is going to call the halt with the setting sun, as would usually be the case, is surprisingly draining. The same goes with all those small habits warriors get used to, like a hot meal, the camp fortifications, or even the simple joy of a section fire. Of course, the Yellow Turbans did not build fortifications on the march, and there was no such thing as a platoon or a section. Still, after four days of an impossible rhythm, the men had even lost the energy to grumble, which is never a good sign.

The camp followers had fallen behind on the first day, and for the few of us who had family there, the temptation to leave must have been strong, especially since everyone seemed to know what we were running after by then. For those whose loved ones had stayed in Julu, however, we were never going fast enough.

The Yellow Turbans' base in Julu was south and slightly west of Zhuo commandery, where we had spent the last two months. By going straight south, Cheng Yuanzhi hoped we would intercept the army of this Zou Jing since they had started on our east and had left a day before us, at best. So far, no sign of their presence had been spotted, so all there was to do was follow the plan. Best-case scenario, we would fall on their rear. In the worst case, we would make it to Julu with just a slight delay, hopefully still early enough to catch them before they could try anything.

I don't know who was the worst to be around, Uncle Cheng for the shortness of his temper or Uncle Deng because he had been right and gladly reminded his superior any chance he got. They only spoke to each other when they had to and sometimes used me to deliver messages, which I happily did because it meant less time with either of them.

Halfway through the middle of the fifth afternoon, we finally spotted the cloud of dust marking the presence of our enemy, straight ahead of us. We were getting closer to Julu, though we would still have to march for two days at this speed. The land was getting mountainous again, just enough to get a better impression of distance. This militia, which had destroyed two of our divisions, was perhaps ten *li* ahead. We would be on them in two *shi*. Uncle Cheng kept checking behind, worrying over our own cloud of dust, but this could not be helped. We were not trying to surprise our foes, just to catch and destroy them.

"Dun," Uncle Cheng called from ahead, shouting over the sound of his horse's hooves hitting the ground and the din of over eight thousand men jogging. I pressed my horse, though it didn't need much of a push. I gave him a warm smile when I reached Cheng's level, but his frown did not give up. "When we get to them, I want you to go behind our forces. No *golden eagle* today, understood?"

"What if the fight doesn't start right away?" I asked.

"Then you may come ahead, but at the first sign of fighting, you get back. And, Dun, if we lose today, you just keep going. You try to make it back to Julu to tell the Zhang brothers of our defeat, but you don't stay. Go back to Jing if you can, find your sister, and keep a low profile."

Now it was my turn to frown. Not once had Uncle Cheng spoken of our defeat before, at least with me, and never before had I thought for a second of leaving him. I told him I would abandon no one, and he cuffed me behind the head. Once again, I had not seen it coming. At least he was smiling now.

"I'm not telling you to stop fighting," he said. "Just to keep it for another time."

"I won't need to," I replied. "We have Mad-Cheng and Deng Mao in our ranks. No one can beat us."

He laughed, but I could feel it was forced.

I stayed with him for another half a *shi*, until the distance with the enemy thinned to a couple of *li*, then he waved me to the back of the line. Just as I steered to the left and allowed Lover to slow down, Uncle Deng ran past me, his dagger-ax bouncing on his shoulder with each step. He made a point of not riding while most of the men had to run, but his puffed cheeks and sweat-covered skin showed his exhaustion. He still gave me a wink, and then he was gone.

We did not march in line or anything in the Yellow Turbans, so our eight thousand men passed by in uneven groups. I refused to go all the way back, where the weak, the stragglers, and the cowards ran, so I kicked Lover to resume our march once two-thirds of the division had passed and stayed on our left flank.

As it turned out, all of this had been for nothing, for we intercepted the enemy half a *shi* before sundown, trapping them between us and the dead end of a ravine running between two mountains. They could have scattered over the mountains, but chose to mount a defense, and by the time I trotted back to the front of the line, we were facing a wall of soldiers with shields and spears going from one side of the ravine to the next. I can't say how many they were exactly, but if I had to guess, I'd say a little below seven hundred. They looked more professional than all those we had defeated so far, but even then, their numbers did not threaten us. I reasoned that maybe after destroying two of our divisions, this was all that was left of this militia.

Four men stood in front of the wall of shields, and one of them had to be Zou Jing. I assumed it was the one with the best armor, riding a horse as black as the night.

Deng Mao was grinning when I pushed my horse back toward my two uncles, riding next to each other for the first time in days. Uncle Deng was back on his horse, probably because he was the one to engage in a duel. If it came to that.

"What do you think?" Deng Mao asked.

"I thought they'd be more," Uncle Cheng replied.

"I guess our brothers killed most of them," Uncle Deng went on, echoing my own theory.

"You don't have to accept their challenge," Cheng Yuanzhi said. "They're trapped and will fight to the end, anyway."

Uncle Deng scoffed. "We have a reputation to maintain," he said. "And someone seems to disagree with you."

He pointed his dagger-ax ahead, and sure enough, one of the four riders was advancing in our direction, waving a great spear over his head for us to know he did not mean peace. He wore a simple armor of leather and no helmet, but the strangest thing about him was the tip of his spear, which looked as if undulated instead of straight-edged. He was no great rider, but he did his best to keep his horse steady while he bellowed his challenge a hundred steps from us. His voice was strong enough to be heard from such a distance. Strong and deep.

This fighter was young, probably around eighteen years old, though his voluminous muscles, his short, dense beard, and his vocabulary suggested otherwise. I won't go into details, but there were many mentions of our mothers, fathers, and ancestors in his challenge. He promised us many good things for our wives and to let our bodies rot under the sun. At first, it was all good and fun, but the part about the ancestors truly angered Uncle Deng, and his horse was picking up on this, skipping on the side and tossing its head every time Uncle Deng clicked his tongue.

Then, without rushing, Deng Mao kicked his horse, and the beast walked on toward the challenger. Immediately, our men cheered for their champion, screaming his name and calling for the death of the blue sky. Uncle Deng kept his dagger-ax low, close to the ground and dragging behind as not to be seen by his opponent. The young challenger did something peculiar; he dismounted, then slapped his horse back to their ranks. Even a bad horse rider would remain on his mount to fight a duel, if only not to put himself below his opponent. But this man chose to be on foot, either because he did not trust his horse-riding skill or because he was confident in his fighting capacity from the ground.

Deng Mao's horse moved to a trot, and my heart matched it. He changed his grip in response to the man's unusual tactic, bringing his weapon to his shoulder level, arm stretched and parallel to the ground. The dagger-ax bobbed up and down in rhythm with the horse's steps. Uncle brought it higher still, ready to bolt it down on the unfortunate young man.

Then, over the brouhaha of our men, I heard a shout from the other side. It must have been the young man, but since I could not see him behind Uncle Deng's horse, I could not say for sure. He had a mighty roar, even considering the echo of the ravine. And before it died down, in the blink of an eye, Deng Mao flew away from his stallion, unsaddled, and pushed backward a few steps from the young man. I could not comprehend what I was witnessing. One second, Uncle Deng was about to strike; the next he was landing flat on his back, his horse pursuing his run by himself. Silence fell in a heartbeat.

It's only when the dust settled a little that I saw that the young man was now unarmed. And as I focused, I could see the great serpent spear jutting from Uncle Deng's chest like the pole of a flag. I felt very cold inside. My mind refused to acknowledge what had just happened. It refused to register that Deng Mao had been defeated by a man twice younger.

I wasn't the only one in shock. All our men behind me were mumbling, cursing in whispers, and wondering what to do.

The worst seemed to be Uncle Cheng, who clung to his horse's reins, his mouth agape. He was shaking. His mouth opened and closed like a dying fish, but no sound came out.

The young challenger nonchalantly covered the space to Deng Mao. His hands found the pole of his spear, which he removed in one big pull. Uncle Deng gave no reaction, besides his body slightly lifting from the ground before the spear came out. Then the young man spat on my uncle's face, and that woke up Cheng Yuanzhi.

I heard the scrape of his blade leaving its sheath a second before he pointed it forward. His eyes filled with rage, his jaws tensed, and I could even see some foam at the corner of his lips. This, I assumed, was Mad-Cheng. He called the charge, and his horse sprang forward right away. Less than a second later, the men followed him, but to my great shame, I didn't.

All around me, men were rushing toward our fallen leader to kill his victor and all those behind him, but I was panicking. It was one of those moments that happen fast but move slowly in one's mind.

Uncle Cheng was a few steps in front of everyone, though the faster runner came close. The young warrior turned around and dashed back toward his comrades, but he would never make it in time on foot. One of the three officers from the militia seemed to understand it, for just as the wall of shields came marching toward us, he kicked his horse. I will never forget this officer, for even then, he was remarkable. He was tall and strong, with long, muscular limbs. His beard, very dark in contrast with the light gray of his horse's coat, went down over his throat, and his sideburns fell down to his shoulders. They flew behind him as he pressed his horse on, and I could see he had chosen Uncle Cheng as his target.

I remember screaming Cheng's name but could not even hear my voice over the sound of eight thousand men charging.

With a strange sense of stillness, I saw on both sides of the ravine the soldiers of the militia popping from their cover and aiming their hundreds of crossbows at our packed army.

Again, I called Uncle Cheng's name, for he had not seen the ambush yet and kept his crazed, vengeful charge.

The young warrior ran past his comrade, just as the horsed officer raised his own weapon, another unique one made of a long pole ending in a crescent blade. My heart froze when I realized Uncle was about to engage this man with only a *jian* sword, which was not a great weapon to use from horseback.

The first bolts from the crossbow were released, almost all at once, making a distinctive mechanical *twang*. One of them hit a man right next to me, and his scream, combined with his fall, scared Lover, who then sprang forward along the charge.

I grabbed and pulled the reins, but my mare would not listen, panicking as much, if not more, than I was. I raised my head again, calling for my uncle to help me, but his name died in my throat, just as I saw the bearded warrior bringing his crescent halberd in a perfect swing. Its course went uninterrupted, even when it sliced through Uncle Cheng's neck.

Our leader's head flew from his body, followed by a gush of red.

I did not try to stop Lover this time. In fact, I did nothing. In less than a minute, I had lost Uncle Deng Mao and Cheng Yuanzhi, who had been more of a father figure than my own father had been. I wasn't just paralyzed by the shock, it also made me oblivious to the world around me.

I felt more than I saw the wave of our attack falter. And while many of our brothers kept pushing, even more tried to run back, away from the death trap we had fallen into. Bolts were raining on us, picking us up one by one with ease. The confusion of the men retreating prevented the others from moving on, meaning that our front line soon disintegrated under the coordinated effort of a fairly well-trained militia.

I saw Old-Mi falling down with a bolt through the neck, his eyes showing the surprise of his demise. I don't know why he looked like that; we were all going to die. Why would any of us make it alive if great men like Deng Mao and Cheng Yuanzhi hadn't?

Finally, my horse could no longer move, pressed on all sides by panicking Yellow Turbans. But she kept thrashing with her hooves, biting anyone who came too close, and soon enough, it was like the sea of yellow vanished in front of our eyes as our brothers decided unanimously that we had lost and rushed the other way around. This gave another surge of energy to our foes, who charged after our forces with more vigor. For the first time, we were the ones being pursued.

Not me though, for I had yet to regain my senses.

So, when the bearded warrior pushed his horse in my direction, it was only through some basic reflex that I brought my arms in front of my eyes and waited for death in complete darkness. I heard the clamor of the militiamen as they killed our fighters, then the hooves of the warrior coming closer with great speed. Lover neighed with fear. A fraction of a second later, she buckled under the weight of the white horse shouldering her with speed. I opened my eyes as I fell, just long enough to keep a mental image of the man who had killed my beloved uncle. The back of my head hit the ground, and everything went dark again, and quiet.

This is how I met Guan Yu.

CHAPTER EIGHT

*Julu commandery, Ji province,
6th month of the 7th year of Guanghe era
(184), Han Dynasty.*

I MEANT TO OPEN MY EYES but only felt pain, especially where my head had landed on the rocky ground of the ravine. At least I wasn't dead. The world was spinning around me, though I could not yet see anything, and I tried to lift my head but found that it was already up. There was something under my ass, as if I still sat on the saddle, and I could barely feel the side of my face. I wanted to say something but could not hear my voice, and instead heard a low echo. Then I passed out again.

When I woke for the second time, at least the second time that I remember, it was night, and though the spinning had not stopped, I could open my eyes this time. It took me a few minutes before I got used to the darkness, during which I realized that all around me were the bodies of my fellow Yellow Turbans. Some were sleeping, some others wept, but none spoke. So when Fat Ling did, it was like he was shouting.

"Are you with us this time?" he asked, and I blinked in pain when I turned my head to see him. An echo of a similar question popped into my mind. This had been another life ago, in the backyard of an inn in Xiangyang, back when so many people I knew still lived.

Fat Ling looked, for the most part, unhurt, but something was gone from his eyes. Hope, I guess.

"This time?" I asked, my voice resonating inside my head.

"Last time you didn't make any sense," he said. "It seems better now."

"You carried me?" I asked, now understanding that when I last awakened, it was his arms I felt under my butt and his chest against my cheek.

"I did," he replied, "though that was two days ago."

"Two days?" I asked, sitting straighter in surprise and regretting it right away. The spin sped up, and for a second, I thought I would throw up.

"The battle was three days ago," he went on, and as he dropped his elbow on a bar made of bamboo, I realized we were sitting inside a cage. We were also not alone, for on every side of the cage were patrolling soldiers.

"Where are we?" I asked.

"We're back home," he answered. By home, he meant the base of our rebellion in Julu, or at least not too far off. "You look pale. Keep your head down, and when you feel better, I'll tell you everything."

I accepted, already feeling my vision tunneling. I lay down, helped by Fat Ling's hand.

"And, Dun, I'm sorry for Cheng Yuanzhi."

"Me too," I said. And despite the image of his head flying in the air, I fell asleep in less time than it takes to say "defeat."

I woke late the next morning and felt like I could finally focus long enough to hear the story of our last battle and its consequences.

It had been a massacre. Once both our leaders got killed, and under the pressure of the ambush, our men ran away, but only a few managed to. Those crossbowmen were good, and at least now we knew how this militia had destroyed two divisions before us; with cunning and crossbows. Our men resisted with more vigor when they realized they could not flee, and for a few minutes, it looked as if the battle could be turned around, but the unstopping rain of bolts, coupled with the effect of those two officers as they kept fighting and killing, was too much for our last fighters. They surrendered, dropping their weapons and falling to their knees. By then there were only a few hundred survivors. We had just experienced what the difference in training and equipment could do, even though we had fought a militia and not an actual army. By all accounts, we should have been dispatched to a quick death, but one of the officers argued against it, and Zou Jing spared us. But did not let us go, of course.

The prisoners, in chains two by two at the feet, walked all the way to Julu, where the militia gathered with the army under Lu Zhi, one of the three generals sent by the Han government. There, we had been split into groups of one hundred, corralled in those bamboo cages to serve some purpose later on. The said cages had been assembled over pits dug up to waist level, meaning that even if we wanted to, we could hardly threaten our captors.

My only comfort came from being roped to Fat Ling. As far as I could see, we were the only two from Fa Jia Po in this cage, and I wondered how many had survived altogether.

Ling knew very little about the situation of the rebellion, and I told him more than he told me. From what he had gathered, this Lu Zhi commanded nearly fifteen thousand professional soldiers, plus an even greater number of militia and auxiliaries from the northern tribes. But those soldiers now faced the full strength of the Yellow Turbans' forces, in their own territory of ravines, mountains, and caves. It seemed our brothers were giving as much as they got, and the soldiers looked no more optimistic than we were.

I wanted to ask about the man who had killed Uncle Cheng, but the memory of his death, and of the last year in his company, was like a punch in the guts. All of a sudden, I burst into tears. I was finally dealing with his death, and it left me weak for the day. Whether Fat Ling understood or not, he left me alone, as did our brothers in the cage.

Sorrow then made way for anger. Pushing my fear inside, I relieved the last moment of the battle, drawing the clearest image of my uncle's killer from memory. Before I had covered my eyes, I had seen him up close. He had been shouting, deforming his face with the thrill of the fight, but I would recognize him anywhere. He would be hard to miss. The skin of his face had a dark red taint, and his eyebrows were thick and well-drawn. Contrary to what I had believed from afar, he was also very young, probably in his early twenties, but his bearing could have belonged to a man twice that age. Though he must have been of humble origins, he sat with grace and nobility over his gray horse. And if not for his remarkable appearance, his weapon of choice would help me find him, for I had never seen or heard of a man using a halberd of this type. It looked as if he had mounted a broad sword on top of a spear pole, and it must have been both heavy and clumsy, yet he used it with skill. But that would not save him.

One day, I told myself, I would find that man and remove *his* head from his shoulders. He was my enemy. He had taken the person who meant the most to me, and he would pay for it. It was a vain hope, seeing that I was a prisoner of war, on the losing side, but I could not imagine this would be my end for one second. Later on, this hope would vanish, but at this point, it kept me safe.

"That's funny," Fat Ling said, interrupting me from my thoughts of vengeance.

"What is?" I asked, slightly crossed by his choice of words.

"For us, the war finished the way it started, in an ambush." He was right, and I had not considered it. I refrained from saying that we had been on the wrong side of the last one, otherwise, we would be with our brothers in the mountains.

"What do we do now?" I asked.

Fat Ling gave me a sorry look. "We do nothing," he said slowly. "We stay quiet, obey their orders, and hope they either spare us when the war ends or that the Yellow Turbans pull some miracle and free us."

I called him a coward, which he didn't like. I was being unfair. Few people had earned the respect due to a warrior more than Fat Ling. But instead of cuffing or cursing me, he said the only thing that could have made me feel worse.

"Don't you want to see your sister again?"

So I stayed quiet, obeyed their orders, and bided my time.

I did not keep track of time, but those were awful days. Long afternoons under the sun, with no shadow to protect us, followed each other as we worked at the whims of our captors. We dug cesspits, built fences, cleared paths for the arrival of more soldiers, and performed many more tasks reserved for the slaves and convicts. I guessed we were a bit of both, and the enemy did not care about letting a child do this kind of labor. At least, when out of the cage, I could try to gather some information about the war and about the men who had defeated us.

My original impression had been right; the battle for Julu had reached a stalemate. Every attempt at infiltrating the maze was met with fury, and the army leader seemed reluctant to proceed without a better plan. General Lu Zhi seemed to favor the idea of a siege, thinking that with so many mouths to feed, our forces could not keep going for much longer. It wasn't a bad idea, but that was without counting on the resilience of our brothers and sisters.

Even through my restless anger, I felt a hint of respect for this General Lu Zhi, who, despite his age, seemed to be everywhere. He was a gray-haired man, well in his sixties, and obviously built for brushes and ink more than war, but this did not stop him from leading efficiently. During his time in charge of the army surrounding Julu, there were very few mass graves dug, and we never went famished. His soldiers treated us with disdain, of course, and made examples of the more belligerent among us, but we were never humiliated or punished without cause.

I think this was one of the reasons for his demotion. He wasn't ruthless enough to get results. And the man who came to replace him one day during the seventh month of the year was his complete opposite. From the moment I set my eyes on him, I knew our lives, no matter how pitiful then, would get much worse. His name was Dong Zhuo. A name cursed for the ages because of his later actions, but back then he was an officer from the northern frontier who had covered himself in glory during our last campaign against the Qiang tribes, and he had traveled all the way from the northwest corner of the Great Han to fight against us.

My vision of Dong Zhuo might be distorted by future events, but I remember him as an ugly, fat man, well in his forties, if not more, and with vicious yet clever eyes. A eunuch accompanied him, or at least that's what some men in the cage said, and a platoon of guards who shoved Lu Zhi in a small cage fit on a cart. Though the irony pleased us greatly, it didn't take long for our misfortune to become clear to us.

Dong Zhuo took pleasure in making us work from morning till one of us collapsed under the heat or the exhaustion. This, in turn, gave him an excuse to make an example from our lot, and our numbers in the cage dwindled almost by the day. I was only lucky that our ranks had a fair number of elderlies with less energy than the young boy I was, which did not stop me from waking every day thinking it would be my last.

Our food and water rations were cut in half from the first day of his leadership, and within one week, we started being fed from a couple of wood buckets filled with dry grains. I wonder how many of us realized those were the same buckets we shat in and how many chose to ignore it. This was far from the only humiliation falling on us day in, day out. They beat me on a weekly basis, though never enough to make me invalid for the day's forced labor, and I heard tales of men being stripped naked and flogged for the entertainment of our new general.

After one month under Dong Zhuo's harsh captivity, there was a commotion not too far off from my cage, and this was when I finally saw the target of my hatred, the bearded warrior. He and two other men, one being the young man who had killed Deng Mao, were arguing with the general, and it sounded more than just a little heated. The youngest of the three, with the serpent-spear, was particularly agitated and aggressive, going as far as pointing his finger in the chest of Dong Zhuo. The general shouted at him to *"get back to the cesspit" he called home before he executed him*, and it took the best efforts of the two others to keep the younger one from pushing his luck. I wished they would let him. No matter what would have happened next, one of our enemies would perish, and this would be our first victory in ages. But the bearded warrior and the other one, who acted as if he led the two champions, took the young fighter away, leaving a fuming Dong Zhuo to pace all the way to his tent in hot fury.

Less than a *shi* later, the trio of officers that had defeated us two months ago rode past our cage, followed by their original militia, or what was left of it at least, and all I could do as the man I hated the most in the world left, was to spit under his horse's hooves.

On the same day, soldiers came to our cage and selected a group of ten men among the most fragile. Fat Ling shoved me behind his back so that they would not spot me, and I'm as sure as one can be that he saved my life that day. The ten left, pressed on by the spears of as many soldiers, and none of them ever came back. Our guess was that Dong Zhuo had used them as hostages to parade in front of our brothers protecting the maze, then killed them one by one in an attempt at negotiating.

Those were miserable times, made worse by the fragility of our bodies and the diseases ravaging our already shrinking numbers. From the one hundred men put in the cage by Lu Zhi, we were now down to perhaps forty, and I could not believe I was one of the survivors. I can only explain it for two reasons. First, Fat Ling, along with many other brave men of the Golden Eagle division, protected me to the best of their capabilities. I'm certain none of them would have given their lives for me, but if they could hide me, give me some shadow with their own body, or simply sing a song to lift my spirit, they did so. Some of the soldiers, mostly those from Lu Zhi's original division, also seemed to miss seeing me when they had to choose workers among us, and I hope none of them got in trouble for that.

And second, I still had purpose.

Keeping a specific goal in mind can do miracles. When everyone breaks, the man with a purpose lives on. More than food, having some kind of ambition keeps us strong, focused, and safe from insanity or depression. And my goal was clear. I would live on to avenge Uncle Cheng and would never feel satisfied until I saw the light leaving the bearded warrior's eyes. This was my last thought at night and my first at dawn. I broke every rock I was told to with this idea in mind, cleared the bucket of shit, carried stones, and dug more holes in the ground, all the time imagining this moment, over and over again.

I can't really explain why I was so angry at this man, while Deng Mao's killer meant little. Of course, I had a stronger rapport with Uncle Cheng, but I also think it is because he had beheaded him. Deng Mao had a clean death, and frankly, I could only respect the young challenger for having boldly thrown his spear. Had he missed, especially without his horse nearby, he was as good as dead. But Cheng's fate was a humiliation, one I would see repaid.

Among the many dark thoughts I entertained at night upon revisiting our defeat, the greatest concerned the status of my uncles' relation when they died. They had been friends for many years, like true brothers, really, and I don't doubt they had plenty of arguments during their friendship. But they had always stayed close and resumed a spirit of good comradery. Not this time, though. They died not speaking to each other. And if I had one regret about the whole affair, it's not having mended the gap before their untimely death. Surely this was the only thing I, and only I, could have done.

Then, one day, I believe as we reached *Qiufen*, the autumn equinox, a delegation approached Dong Zhuo's tent, and though I could not hear what they said, I could see the general was not happy. Shortly after the delegation came, Dong Zhuo welcomed another officer at the gates of the camp, bowing low before he gave his staff of authority to the new commander of the army in this region. Before the day was over, Dong Zhuo left camp aboard a chariot, followed by a long stream of cavalrymen from his auxiliaries of barbarians. We cheered loudly when we understood the monster was gone for good, and though I believe he would have deserved the same humiliation as Lu Zhi, the most important was that he would no longer mistreat us.

The third and last general playing the role of our captor was Huangfu Song, one of the original three generals sent to destroy the Yellow Turbans. He had taken part in the obliteration of our forces in Runan, and though he had struggled in the south of Ji province, he had apparently overcome our brothers there as well.

I barely ever saw him, for the man seemed to live in his command tent, but his officers were always active. Leading an army is never a sinecure, even if, like Huangfu Song chose to, its only task consisted of besieging an enemy force. It takes an inhuman capacity for organization, a great head for numbers, and some instinct to delegate the hundreds of decisions required daily. And as much as I know, General Huangfu Song excelled in the three, particularly in the delegating part. His officers all shared an air of capability, but none more so than the handsome colonel they called Cao Cao.

We were now deep into autumn, but the days remained hot for longer than usual, so we had to suffer some of the worst thunderstorms I would ever experience. The bolts of lightning crossing between the surrounding mountains would have been a sight to behold if we were not so afraid that one might hit us. To make matters worse, the rain accompanying the thunder was turning the inside of our pits into mud baths. Nights were getting colder, but at least daytime was less insufferable.

I guess our captors were running out of tasks for us to accomplish, for we got less time out of the cages from the moment Huangfu Song was put in charge. He never fed us much, but neither did he mistreat us. I think he was content in forgetting about our existence, and we were glad to oblige him by not seeking his attention.

During those autumn days, I managed to befriend one of our guards. I only knew his family name, Guo, a soldier of about thirty years and altogether a nice man. He had three kids, and I believe this is why he accepted to chat with me while so many others simply hit me back to my spot—that and boredom.

Sieges are boring for most soldiers, especially when no artillery is involved, and the camp is already well set like it was then. Soldiers fall into the boredom of routine, and bad habits form during those times.

Soldier Guo kept his back to me when we spoke, so I rarely saw his face, but those were the happiest moments of my time in the cage. By then, we had spent nearly four months in the pit, and this was the first time we learned of the situation in the empire.

Only two pockets of resistance remained for our cause. The first in Julu, where no battle had been fought for weeks, and in Wan, where war raged on.

Fat Ling and I listened intently to Guo's report on the fight there, and it was with mixed feelings that we learned of the fall of Wan.

Zhu Jun's army had finally gotten over the wall of Wan, the first of the assailants to make it above being this Sun Jian Tiger we had heard so much about. The fighting had been terrible, no side giving an inch to the other, and in the chaos, Zhao Hong got killed. But just as it seemed the city was lost, Han Zhong, the scarred Adept, had led a fierce resistance and pushed the invaders back to their camp. Wan had fallen for a few minutes before the Yellow Turbans took it back. And now our brothers were led by a competent man, who also happened to be my sister's guardian.

Guo had come with Huangfu Song, all the way from the city named Chenliu, in Chenliu commandery, Yan province. When I said I had never heard of the place, Fat Ling reminded me we had passed next to the city on our way from Nanyang. He was talking of the walled city the locals had urged us to stay away from, for the man leading it was a ruthless, cunning bastard who scared the shit out of every living soul who dared to cross him.

"Yep," Guo said, pride in his voice. "That would be our Colonel Cao Cao."

This is the first time I heard the name of the greatest man that lived in my time, though at that point, his fame was yet to be made. I had assumed the leader of that city to be some kind of demon, more monster than man, while in fact, he was a handsome, noble-looking officer in the prime of his life. If one didn't know of Huangfu Song's presence, he would assume Cao Cao led the army, for he was everywhere.

Guo could speak for an entire *shi* about his colonel, always with a mixture of love and fear, and with obvious pride in calling him his leader. I must say I grew fond of this Cao Cao, even though I had never even spoken to him.

He was the grandson of a eunuch, something I could not understand until I was told that his father had been adopted. His blood family was the famous Xiahou, descendants of the great Xiahou Ying who had served under the founding emperor Liu Bang, but the Cao clan was more powerful nowadays, and Cao Cao used all this power to bring himself up in the world. His first claim to fame came from a post he had been given in his youth as captain of the Northern Gates of Luoyang, the empire's capital. While in his early twenties then, he had made himself known for his harsh respect for the law and his disregard for people's status. He had, according to the stories told by soldier Guo, caught an uncle of a powerful eunuch as the man tried to pass the gates after curfew and ordered a flogging, under which this uncle died. We in the cage liked this story very much, and our respect for the man increased. Following that stunt, Cao Cao was sent away from the capital with some assignment that looked like a promotion on paper but turned out to be everything but. He left his new post and bided his time in Chenliu. Then, because of his fierce reputation or because he bribed the right persons, he was given the title of Colonel of Cavalry and allowed to gather a regiment of one thousand men from his commandery. While most regiments such as this were composed of untrained men, Cao Cao had turned them into competent soldiers in a couple of months. They would not rival the professional armies fighting at the border, but to us, they were like gods of war with their lamellar of steel and solid weapons.

Two young officers, his cousins from the Xiahou clan, always accompanied Cao Cao. The resemblance between the three was evident, but the two others did not match their leader in terms of physical appearance. Cao Cao had a natural charm, enhanced by his perfect posture, long strides, and eyes that missed nothing. He wore no helmet, but the sword hanging at his hip was the work of a master smith. Of his cousins, one always looked as if about to go to battle, with a helmet mounted with two long feathers, while the other seemed ready for his next meal, no matter the time of the day. The first walked with a heavy gait, a never resting frown between the eyes, while the second grinned more often than none, and his laughter carried far and wide.

I wanted to know more about those two, for they looked like competent officers as well, but soldier Guo was sent to another post, and I couldn't shake the feeling he had been punished for his blabbering. The soldier replacing him never even opened his mouth, except for threatening us if we did not shut ours.

For nearly two months, nothing worth mentioning happened besides a few men falling ill in our cage. Winter had begun, and it came with a sudden icy wind that left us shivering all day long. When too many of us went down with some kind of cold, they gave us blankets. We asked for a fire, but this was met with refusal, probably for fear of what we would do with it. Their fear was misplaced. There were too few of us to try anything, and we were both too weak and too resigned to rebel anymore. I still do not know why they kept us alive. Maybe Huangfu Song meant to add our numbers to those he would capture at the end of the siege, giving him something to boast about upon his triumphal return to the capital, but it seemed like a waste of grain for such a poor result.

Whatever the case, he would have no resistance from us—we were just waiting for the end of the war. A bunch of breathing dead, submissive to the fate they would grant us.

Then, one day, this Cao Cao and his two Xiahou cousins walked by our cage, and for the first time, I could hear their conversation.

"They eat their dead?" the usually joyous one asked.

"That's the only way I can explain it," the other replied. "Cousin, what do you think?"

"That would certainly explain how they can still fight," Cao Cao said, his chin stuck between two fingers. His voice was sharp, like the edge of a *dao* sword.

"Wait," the first said, catching Cao Cao's elbow and forcing him to stop, "there are two hundred thousand of them, according to our spies. They can't just survive on dead meat."

Until then, I had never considered that the Yellow Turbans had spies in their ranks, but as I would learn later, we had plenty, even in our command center.

"I didn't say they only eat that," the second replied. "They probably have mushrooms in those caves, maybe some chicken. I don't know."

"That's beside the point," Cao Cao said, looking slightly annoyed. "What I really want to know is—"

"Why do they keep fighting?" the first cousin said.

"Exactly. They must know they cannot win, and they have no hope for reinforcement. We offered terms, but they refused. I can't understand them." It truly seemed to bother him. Not understanding, I mean.

"They still have hope," the first one said, "though I guess they would call it faith."

"In what?" the second asked, his anger rising fast. "That scumbag Zhang Jue? Fanatics," he went on, spitting a rich gob of saliva toward our cage. "If I catch him—*when* I catch him!—I'll make sure he regrets having ever thought to foment a rebellion."

"You'll never catch him alive."

I don't know who was the most surprised, this Xiahou officer or me for having spoken. The words had come out of my mouth before I realized it, and if I hadn't spoken, my life would have turned very different.

"Shut up, peasant," this Xiahou said, raising his hand as if about to strike me, even though we were separated by bars of bamboo.

"What do you mean?" Cao Cao asked, and it took me a moment to realize he was speaking to me. From his vantage position, he looked threatening, like a cat observing a mouse, so I answered.

"As I said, you'll never catch him alive."

"Why not *alive?*" he insisted, and it was like he could read my mind. I swallowed hard and broke my promise to Zhang Jue. My instinct warned me to answer honestly if I wanted to survive this conversation.

"Because Zhang Jue is dead," I said. The cage stirred like a kennel when it's time to feed the dogs.

"How would you know?" the officer said, kicking some dirt in my face.

"Young man," Cao Cao said as he knelt to my level, "be very careful about what you say. There is no joking in the army." Again, I felt like I was a plaything in his palm. His choice of words was perfect.

"I met him," I explained, "from up close. And he was more dead than alive. There is no way he still lives. But his brothers were keeping the illusion of his strength going. They might still be pretending."

Cao Cao twisted left and right to his cousins for their impressions. The second shrugged as if it mattered little. The first tilted his head as if to say it was doubtful. They had spies in our camp; of course, they would not simply believe the words of a boy who's been taken five months ago.

"The General of Heaven has blessed this child in front of thousands of our brothers and sisters in the early summer," Fat Ling intervened, standing up and forcing me to do as much. "Ask any prisoner you have here. I can guarantee none of us has approached Zhang Jue closer than him, at least not for a very long time." He could not know any of that, but Fat Ling's gamble paid off.

"Guard," Cao Cao called without taking his eyes from me, "take these two to my tent."

I cannot describe the pleasure of being freed from the shackles at my ankle. Fat Ling shared the joy, looking very much as if about to cry with relief. We grinned at each other as if we were free. This was far from the case, and the butt end of a spear reminded Fat Ling that we were not out of the cage for a stroll but were expected.

Our four guards did not speak as they took us to their colonel's tent, which showed the difference between the commanding style of Cao Cao compared to Dong Zhuo or even the disgraced Lu Zhi. Two soldiers manned the tent door, but I noticed they kept a distance of two or three steps from said tent, as if to stay out of earshot.

They must have expected us, for immediately, one of them pushed the flap open, and we resumed our advance. By the time the leader of our escort reported our arrival, I had gotten used to the change of light. Cao Cao liked to stay in relative darkness, and his tent was lit with only a couple of lamps and the sun passing through the fabric of the walls.

The man liked his comfort; that much was certain. He sat behind a heavy table, on a chair from the same exotic wood, with a tiger skin behind his back. A screen of lacquered wood hid one side of the tent, and I guessed the colonel's bed would be on the other side.

The angry Xiahou stood with his arms crossed over his chest, looking at me as if I had been sculpted from dung and smelled as such, the latter part being true, of course. The other one sat on a simple stool across Cao Cao, though he turned around to face us when we entered. There was also a small desk in the corner, with a discreet old man scanning through a roll of wooden slips. This man, Cao Cao's secretary, paid no attention to us and only stopped his reading to pick up his brush and take some notes on another set of wooden slips.

"Thank you, that will be all," Cao Cao said dismissively. The four soldiers bowed, the secretary stood, and they all left as one. What followed was one of the most important conversations of my life.

"So," the colonel said, "you claim Zhang Jue is dead?"

"I did not see him dead, but yes, I think he's been dead for a long time," I replied. My mouth went dry after the first sentence.

"You have nothing to fear," Cao Cao said, reading through me again.

"Unless you lie," the angry one commented. I decided then that I did not like that man; I don't think many people did.

"Which he won't," Fat Ling said.

"Are you the boy's father?" Cao Cao asked.

"A neighbor, *xiaowei*," Fat Ling replied, returning a perfect military salute.

"And a former soldier I see," Cao Cao said as he sat back a little. "Take a seat," he offered politely, though it sounded more like an order. The sitting Xiahou pulled another stool from under the table and set it an arm-length from him. Then this officer pulled on a fuming pitcher, poured some *mijiu* inside a bronze cup, and handed it to Fat Ling, who looked as baffled as you can imagine. This cup was probably worth a peasant's yearly income, and the wine even more. With trembling hands, Fat Ling took the cup to his lips, and a tear fell from his left eye. The officer poured some more of the rice wine while his brother or cousin clicked his tongue nervously.

"Thank you, sir," Fat Ling said. Cao Cao brushed it off as if it was of no concern, then returned his attention to me. I had kept my back as straight as possible, not wanting to show any weakness.

"Tell me, in detail, what happened when you met Zhang Jue," he then ordered me. I told the story of my blessing with all the little details I could remember, down to the breath of our General of Heaven smelling like mold. Whenever I spoke of the ritual, the older Xiahou, or at least the one I assumed to be older, puffed and scoffed. This was all a waste of time to him, but the two others listened more carefully. I went as far as saying that Zhang Jue had reminded me of my grandfather on the eve of his passing.

"That's hardly proof," the older Xiahou said.

"Have a little faith, Yuanrang," the other replied in a mocking tone.

Yuanrang was the officer's *zi,* not his real name. I knew people of power, or rich merchants and the likes, received this courtesy name with their cap of manhood. Their meaning conveyed a particular moral characteristic of the young man, some ancestry, or simply the order with which he was born into his family. They tended to be very pompous, and we simple folks scoffed at those names, but it was disrespectful to call someone of power by anything other than this courtesy name, especially if he was older. I never really liked this idea of *zi*, not even when I received one.

"A few people knew it," I went on. "His brothers, some of his priests, and even some of our leaders."

"Some leaders?" Cao Cao asked.

"He didn't say so to me, but Liu Pi of Runan knew," I answered.

"Liu Pi," the younger Xiahou repeated with an exaggerated shiver. "That was a tough bastard," he went on while pouring himself a cup of *mijiu*.

"He's dead?" I asked, maybe a little too fast.

"Not yet," Yuanrang replied, smirking. I understood that Liu Pi had escaped, otherwise they would know about Zhang Jue already. "Why did *you* meet all those men?" he then asked, and since Cao Cao said nothing to the question, I assumed he too wanted to know. So I explained where I came from, what Cheng Yuanzhi had been to me, and what I represented for the Yellow Turbans, or at least for our division.

"Is this true?" Cao Cao asked Fat Ling once I was done.

My neighbor, his cheeks turning slightly red by then, nodded, then said, "He is our Golden Eagle, and he took our fear away before battle."

Cao Cao sat forward and leaned on his elbow, bringing his hands together, his two index fingers reaching for his lower lip. If I thought he could read me before, the intense gaze he now shot made me feel naked.

"You met several of those... Adepts?" he asked, though he already knew I had. "And thousands of Turbans saw you when you were blessed, and then as you battled in the north?"

"Mengde?" Yuanrang asked after I confirmed it, using Cao Cao's own *zi*. He knew his cousin and where this was going, though he did not seem to like it.

"What else can you do?" Cao Cao asked, ignoring his officer.

"I can ride," I immediately replied. "And I know how to use a sword." I wanted to say I had a sword until our last battle, but the story of its acquisition could only hurt me, so I kept the point to myself. As for Lover, I never saw her again, and I doubt she made it out alive of the ambush.

"You want to become a warrior?" the colonel asked.

"I want to become a soldier," I replied.

"You chose the wrong side then," Yuanrang said. I chose to ignore him as well.

A few drops of rain fell on the walls of the tent. Before it turned to a typical winter downpour, the three cousins exchanged a few glances, speaking through their eyes rather than with words. Yuanrang rolled his eyes, giving Cao Cao and the other the time to smile at each other.

"Another stray for you?" the young Xiahou asked his cousin.

"Maybe," Cao Cao answered cunningly. "Young man, I have a choice to give you." Suddenly, I was a *young man* again. "You gave us some useful information, and it deserves a reward. I will grant you freedom. Should you choose, you can go back to your hometown and live your life in peace."

"Or?" I asked. My mind was reeling with what had just been said. The idea that I would no longer stay in that cursed cage felt like balm on wounds. But I did my best to hide it.

"Or you can serve me," Cao Cao answered. To be honest, I was about to say yes, but it's a good thing Fat Ling beat me to it.

"Doing what?" he asked before adding a "sir."

"Do you know of the imperial university?" he asked me. This was one of Cao Cao's favorite forms of conversation, answering a question with another, seemingly unrelated question. Everyone knew of the university. It was a school like we had in most commanderies, where sons of nobles and powerful men learned the classics and probably some other things a peasant does not need. The imperial university had fallen into a state of disgrace over the past few decades but still provided the greatest level of education in the empire. Frankly, it sounded like an awful place where young boys were turned into scholars, the last thing I wanted for myself.

"I can't read," I replied.

"You will learn," Cao Cao said. "Though not at the university, of course. I only ask because I am building something of a school myself. Call it a training ground if you will. Young men such as yourself are invited to join, by me, or on rare occasions by some of my most trusted subordinates, and those who accept will be taught everything from reading, writing, mathematics," he explained. Again, I did not feel enthused. "And—" he continued, bringing his signature smirk to his lips, "other matters such as strategy, battle formation, weaponry, archery, cavalry—" He let the last word hang in the air, judging my reaction to it. I failed to suppress a smile. He had touched the right chord and knew it. "As well as some other points. I am still working on the curriculum."

"I don't understand," I said. "How is that serving you?"

"Good question," he answered. "In exchange for those years of education and the elevation it will bring to you in life, you will swear loyalty to me and serve me in whatever capacity I deem acceptable, according to your skills. I call it a fair trade, but, as I said, it is your choice."

My mind filled itself with questions and thoughts, most of which involved mental images of myself standing in an army, surrounded by well-equipped comrades, and possibly even from the back of a horse.

"Why me?" I asked, interrupting my own reveries with the most urgent question I could think of.

"I am, I believe, a great judge of character," Cao Cao replied. "And I can spot the bearing of a fine soldier in you. Of course, whatever you become is your responsibility. I give you the tools; you build your future."

As long as it is under your flag, I thought but did not say.

There was more, even a child could see it, but I did not press the point. Who was I to doubt the claims of a man such as Cao Cao? He must have sensed my doubts though, for he kept talking.

"I also believe that the world as we know it is ending," he said. The surprise must have showed on my face—this was something I had heard the Yellow Turbans say many, many times. I did not expect the same idea from a colonel in the Han army. "Don't make this face, young man. I am not saying I believe in the *jiazi* or Huang-Lao, only in cause and consequences. What you have started this year will have repercussions leading the empire to chaos, eventually. When that happens, those who are ready will triumph and bring an end to the turmoil, and I intend to be ready. You will be a part of my grand plan."

Somehow it did not sound like I had a choice anymore, which did not matter because I was sold on the idea. Not the empire-saving horseshit, just the part of elevating myself and fighting in the chaos of our own making. Truthfully, I did not think of my sister then, and I did not believe

I would ever see her again in this life at that point. But even if I had, the life of a farmer was still the most depressing choice a person could make, and nothing would make me get back to it.

"I have two conditions," I said, which made this Yuanrang puff louder than before.

"You little dog," he called me, ready to strike me down with the flat of his hand. Cao Cao stopped him by extending his.

"Tell me," he said, looking amused.

"First, you let Fat Ling here go free. No more cage for him either," I said, and I swear I saw new tears in my neighbor's eyes.

"What is your name?" Cao Cao asked as he picked the brush on the side of his table. "Not Fat Ling, I assume."

"No, sir," Ling answered, "I am Ling Jun, from Fa Jia Po, Xinye county, Nanyang commandery."

The colonel then wrote a series of characters on a few bamboo slips. I could not believe anyone could write so fast or so beautifully. Even now that I am at the dusk of my life, Cao Cao had some of the best calligraphy I ever saw. Back then, I could not distinguish between good and bad ink writing, but Cao Cao's amazed me immediately.

"Congratulations, Ling Jun of Xinye," he said as he rolled the slips and handed them to my neighbor. "You are now a free man. You can stay with us and travel back to Chenliu when the time comes; then you are on your own."

"Thank you, sir," Fat Ling replied, tugging the roll against his chest.

Later, Cao Cao told me he would have freed Fat Ling anyway, if only because he could not let him back in the cage after what he had heard in this tent. Now the man was bound to him in gratitude, and I am certain he never spoke of what happened there to anyone.

"What's the second condition?" Cao Cao asked, returning his attention back to me. I only realized then that he had accepted the first without knowing the second, which was clever of him. Fat Ling's freedom was now his hostage, and he could refuse me the second condition; I would still have to accept his deal.

"There is a man," I said, "who I want to kill."

The younger Xiahou whistled, impressed, and even this Yuanrang chuckled.

"Go on," Cao Cao said.

"He killed Cheng Yuanzhi, and I will avenge him someday. When I find out who he is, you'll let me kill him."

"I cannot help you commit a crime," Cao Cao said.

"But you can help me find who he is," I replied. My hands were sweating in my fists, and I could feel the tips of my nails digging into the skin of my palms. I had to hurt myself to stay strong for Uncle Cheng.

"We will deny we knew of your intentions," he then said, meaning he and his two cousins.

"That's fair," I replied. "And I promise to do all I can not to get caught and remain in your service." I saw the bump from his tongue going from one cheek to the other inside his mouth as he thought about it.

"We have a deal then?" he asked, standing up.

"We do," I replied, taking a couple of steps forward and bowing as Fat Ling had done earlier.

"Great," Yuanrang said, throwing his arms in the air. "Another stray puppy."

"What is your name, young man?" Cao Cao asked.

"My name is Liao Dun," I answered, which made the young Xiahou laugh with a bark, while the other groaned.

"You must be kidding," Yuanrang said.

"That's his given name," the younger one explained, his thumb pointing at Yuanrang. If my meeting with Xiahou Dun had been an omen, I should have listened to it and run away, but I'm glad I didn't, for the following years of my life would be the pinnacle on which I became the man I am today. Still, I did not like sharing a name with *that* man.

"Since you two are clearly connected," Cao Cao said, chuckling, "you won't mind taking this one into your home, cousin?"

"Why?" Xiahou Dun asked, not happy at the idea.

"My wife will kill me if I bring her yet another orphan of war," Cao Cao replied.

"Fair enough," Xiahou Dun said, relenting faster than I thought he would. Was this woman so scary that she could cower two such powerful men?

I did not like the idea of living with this perpetually frowning, bitter man, but after five or six months in a cage, I pictured his home as heaven.

"An oath requires wine and sacrifices. Here comes the wine," the other Xiahou, whose name I would learn was Yuan, said as he filled two other cups with some rice wine. The first he gave to Cao Cao, the second to me, and I had to check with Fat Ling to know if it was all right for me to drink. I had never even tasted *mijiu* before. He nodded. I extended my arms in Cao Cao's direction, then brought the wine to my lips, emptying its contents in one straight gulp as I had seen men do.

My head spun all of a sudden, and I felt very warm as the liquid burned down to the bottom of my throat. I opened my eyes, turned around, ran to the door, and threw up like never before.

"And here comes the sacrifice!" I heard Xiahou Yuan say before roaring one of his great, thunderous laughs.

Three days after I pledged my life to Cao Cao, the army attacked the base of the Yellow Turbans and routed them out. Six months of siege ended with a great slaughter. Zhang Liang, the eldest of the two remaining Zhang brothers, was killed in the action, while Zhang Bao, along with what was left of the rebellion, escaped toward the east. I can't say for sure, but it would be an amazing coincidence if those events happened with no relation to my delivering the news of Zhang Jue's death. I never learned the truth of the matter, but knowing Cao Cao as I know him now, I guess he spread the rumor of Zhang Jue's death in the Turbans' camp and forced some of them to inquire about the General of Heaven. If his agents within had any skill, they would have turned the rebels against each other before the army came to finish the job.

When the base fell, with thousands upon thousands of rebels caught, mostly children, women, and elders, the cave was searched, and Zhang Jue's body was discovered. According to Xiahou Yuan, whom I was quickly learning to appreciate, the founder of the Way had died a few months back. He was not the only one. Piles of bodies had been left behind. Many had died of some disease, and those were the ones waiting to be burned. We heard stories of cannibalism, murder, plagues, and more horrendous tales. So, by the time the siege ended, I think a good half of the rebels were actually glad to have lost.

I don't know the actual numbers, but Huangfu Song told the court he had captured a hundred thousand people and killed thirty thousand more. I don't believe those numbers, simply because had he kept so many folks alive, they would have been able to overcome their captors somehow. He executed many men of fighting age, which made my lord furious, though in his cold kind of fury. Something about *who would farm the fields in the coming years?*

At this point, I had become callous to the fate of the people of the Way. We'd been more dead than alive for months, and half of the rebellion had been spent in a near state of defeat.

Fat Ling left shortly after the siege ended. I wanted him to stay as long as possible, but he could not. The sight of men we had known for half a year, still rotting in their cage, did not sit well with him. The idea of being seen as a traitor by the prisoners probably also helped his decision. He promised to check on my sister if he could and to keep her safe until I came for her, but I held no illusion. By some extraordinary twist of fate, Wan fell, for good this time, a day or two from Julu's defeat. Han Zhong was executed by General Zhu Jun, and from what we heard, no one survived the second sack of the city. I shed tears for Mihua, but not nearly as much as she deserved. Now I had truly lost everyone and could only rebuild from the ground up.

I never wandered far from the colonel's tent. For the same reason Fat Ling had left, I could not show myself walking freely within the ranks of tents and prisoners' pits. I was allowed to stay in the section tent of a small unit of soldiers, which, upon my request, was that of Soldier Guo, whose given name was Wen. His unit of five men had lost one during the fight in Runan, so they had enough space for a child, and Guo Wen seemed happy enough for my company, as I was for his.

Not that we stayed for a long time, anyway.

It took two weeks to clean up the maze and organize the departure of so many prisoners. Many were simply sent back to their hometown with a promise never to rise against the Han, while others were ordered to move north, close to the border with our aggressive neighbors, in order to help with the recolonization effort. Of course, this all happened after soldiers committed many atrocious acts, and the women suffered the most, as usual.

Meanwhile, General Huangfu Song pursued Zhang Bao and surrounded him in Guangzong commandery near Julu. He did not send for Cao Cao and actually dismissed him. This might sound harsh, but in those days, an officer only kept his title until the campaign was over, which, as far as my lord was concerned, was the case. The general simply did not want to share the glory with the ambitious colonel, and he would bring an end to the war by himself.

Zhang Bao fell a month after his brother, thus ending the uprising of the Yellow Turbans, but by this time, we were about to reach Chenliu, where my new life would begin.

PART TWO

ORPHANS OF WAR

CHAPTER NINE

*Chenliu, Chenliu commandery,
3rd month of the 1st year
of Zhongping era (185), Han Dynasty*

EMPEROR LING NAMED THE NEW ERA *Zhongping—pacification achieved*—and in many regards, it did feel like there was peace. Some pockets of rebellion remained active here and there but were stomped on as soon as they sprouted from the ground. Some lords even pardoned the rebels on their lands and integrated their forces into their own, creating hybrid armies of peasants ready to take arms for the benefit of their benefactors. Cao Cao, at this point, did no such thing. He wasn't powerful enough to support an army of this magnitude and held no official post. Technically, he was simply a lord living in Chenliu, with a non-official command of the city.

We barely arrived in Chenliu when he was sent to Ji'nan kingdom in Qing province to quell the last remnants of the Yellow Turbans' wave as a temporary chancellor of the Ji'nan kingdom. This meant that whichever scion of the imperial Liu clan was in charge of the so-called kingdom could stay in his ivory tower while my lord did the work. He took most of his men with him, along with Xiahou Yuan and a younger cousin of his from the Cao clan named Cao Ren. Sadly, it left Chenliu under the responsibility of Xiahou Dun, the sour young officer.

Though I heard of other orphans of war living in the city, most of them staying inside the mansion of my lord, I did not meet many during the first few months, for I was the only one living within Xiahou Dun's domain. Compared to the houses I had lived in or visited so far, his was a palace. It was three stories high, with a yard even larger than the house and a wall marking the limit of the domain on four sides, which was within an enclosed district inhabited by the members of the Xiahou and Cao clans in Chenliu. Originally, the Cao and Xiahou came from Qiao commandery, five hundred *li* to the east, but since it is frowned upon to establish any kind of power near one's hometown, Cao Cao took it upon himself to relocate to Chenliu. The city was close enough to Luoyang to remain connected with the center of power while far enough to avoid the government's gaze.

Since Lord Cao left Chenliu, his school project did not kick off immediately. So, for the first part of the year, I was more of a servant than anything else. This was a part of the deal that my lord had avoided when he first mentioned it, but he never said I would be lodged, nourished, and taken care of for free. And Xiahou Dun made sure I knew my place within his house as often as possible.

At first, he, or rather his wife, Lady Cao, a cousin of Cao Cao, and a woman as bitter, if not more, than her husband, made me serve within the main building. Quickly enough, she grew tired of yelling at me for my clumsiness and lack of manners, and since Xiahou Dun was not always there to beat me with his thin cane of bamboo, she sent me to work outside. I think she never imagined how much it pleased me. For people born in comfort, the exterior world is a chore or a punishment. For me, it was a liberation. That I dreaded a future of farming did not mean I wanted to live within walls and mop the floors of a palace-sized house. Even better, as far as I was concerned, she sent me to work in the district's stable.

The stable served several members of the clans, which meant somewhere between twenty and thirty horses lived there, minus those who currently accompanied their owners to Ji'nan. I was only allowed to take care of the three belonging to Xiahou Dun, but even then, it was heaven. Two of them were bay-colored stallions, high of shoulders, heads always held high with pride but with the nastiest tempers ever. The third was a six-year-old chestnut mare, as gentle as you can find for a beast that age. She was a beauty. I never had enough of talking to her as I brushed her. As if she could understand me, her ears and eyes were always searching for me as I spoke. I might be biased, but I think I only saw a handful of more beautiful horses in my life. Xiahou Dun used the two others to hunt but would choose the latter for long-distance trips. He called her Chestnut, a name as unimaginative as the man himself, so I called her Brown Wings. She didn't deserve the name, for she wasn't the fastest horse ever, but I just wanted her to have a name worthy of the greatest steeds.

Of course, when I was first shoved into the stable, I knew very little about horse-caring. I had taken little care of Lover, and she had been happy simply grazing in peace as long as I took her to a source of water once a day. But war horses apparently need a lot more attention. Not just them, but their gear is also supposed to be treated with more care than you would a child. Not that they paid special attention when mounting. Xiahou Dun was a brute with his horses, and I often had to treat the wounds from his whip. This is something else

I shared with those animals—I knew how much he could hurt us.

Those things I learned from the stable master, an old, one-handed man named Xin Ping, a veteran of many wars, though, as he liked to remind me, he was never a soldier, just a stable hand—a joke he found funny to no end. I liked Xin Ping, though he took a few days to warm up to me. He loved horses as much as I did, and his only regret was not being able to mount as well as he used to. In fact, he did not ride anymore at all, being in his late fifties, with a bad back and weak legs from too many days on the march. But when it came to caring for them, Xin Ping was a master. He knew absolutely everything, from the type of food to privilege for each horse, to the way to mend broken leather and, of course, the best remedies for basic wounds and tired hooves.

It took me a whole week to get used to his northwestern Liang accent, but from then on, I could listen to him *shi* after *shi* as he mentioned cavalry regiments, the odd treatments he'd seen used on horses, or the way barbarians from the north would shoot while riding, and not just crossbows but actual bows. It all sounded fantastic, and despite the results of war on his body, I envied him a little for having experienced so much.

Xin Ping, however, was as lazy as it gets, which means I worked even more than I should have. But with only three animals to take care of, it wasn't a chore to begin with, anyway. The second I slacked off a little, I could be sure to hear his old, broken voice from the other side of the stable.

"Chun! Come here, boy!" he'd say, every time with the same intonation.

My name had been changed to Chun from the moment we left Julu. I had no say in the matter. Xiahou Dun simply refused that a stray kid like me, a former Yellow Turban at that, be called like him. Especially since I was to live in his house. I never really cared about my name, so when Lord Cao asked if I minded the change, I said I didn't. It was actually a good time for an official change since everything else was shifting in my life.

The name "Chun" was Cao Cao's idea. He showed me how to write the character "Dun," which I had never learned before, then how to change it to "Chun" by removing the part of the character meaning "small" and adding the one for "water" instead. I told him I was glad to leave the "small" part to his cousin, which made him chuckle. So I became Liao Chun, servant of the Xiahou domain in Chenliu.

And just like I knew Xin Ping's words by heart, I could guess his request before I stepped into the stall of the horse he was currently taking care of.

"Would you mind shoveling that nag's shit for me? It's my back. I don't think I can do it myself," he said, making a scene of patting the bottom of his back as if it pained him too greatly.

"I don't know, old man, if I get caught in another horse's stall than those of lord Xiahou, I'll be flogged," I replied, which was true enough.

"No one will see you. Come on, just a few shovels. And I'll let you ride one of your lord's." This was usually how it ended. It was like a game between us. I'd get to ride, even though just in the corral, and Xin Ping got one less chore. Those horses needed the exercise, anyway. The first time, he had meant it as a punishment, and I played along, but he could see I didn't mind shoveling manure that much. Once you're used to shoveling ox's dung, horse manure isn't that bad. And no one else accepted to ride the two stallions.

Besides being around horses all day long, the other benefit of my new position was that I rarely met the lady anymore. The smell of horses bothered her. So I was confined to the servants' quarters, and if the lady thought it was a punishment, she was also wrong. Those quarters, even shared with eight to ten people, had more room than my old house in Fa Jia hills.

There were no children here, but two years later, Lady Cao would pop their firstborn, then the second almost right away, and Xiahou Dun had a third one from his concubine. All three turned out to be real pricks.

From Cao Cao's generation, only he had children when I arrived in Chenliu, and I only met them in the third month of that year, when finally I was allowed out of the corner of the district on an errand to my lord's house.

Xiahou Dun was gone for a hunt and had lent his two other horses to his guests, so there was not much to do in the stable. And since he had taken many servants with him, there were few choices left for this errand. I had washed the day before, my clothes were clean, and Lady Cao, probably in one of those gestures designed to gain favors from the lady of the upper class, sent me to deliver some dry tea cakes, something I had never heard of, let alone eaten. The smell, as I carried the package wrapped in a richly decorated square of silk, dug a pit in my stomach. Later, I remembered this smell and realized it wasn't the tea whose flavor had awakened my senses but the peels of orange mixed with it.

I knew where Cao Cao's mansion stood, and it was hard to miss, being the tallest building in town besides the palace. It was situated north of the district, right before the palace used by the inspector of the province when on tour. I walked for ten minutes before reaching the outer gates of the mansion.

I don't know why the gates of every mansion were guarded since we were already within a protected district, but when I reached Cao Cao's domain, I had to inform the two guards of my purpose. They didn't seem to care much anyway, but they were professional and let me pass. After the outer door, while on the path of stones leading to the main building, I had a glimpse of my lord's domain, and the difference with Xiahou Dun's showed clearly.

The place where I lived was simple, direct, and frankly boring, with well-trimmed trees lining up the walls, classic ornaments for the fires at night, and square stones set in a straight line paving the way. Cao Cao's place, however, was both quirky and inspiring. Nothing was straight, but everything was working to the best of its nature. Trees were not forced into certain shapes; they simply grew the way they were supposed to, which did not stop them from being magnificent. The stones of the path were not squared and looked as if they'd been dropped randomly, but this was an illusion. One never had to make an effort to step on the next, as if the path had been designed specifically for the visitor. A myriad of other details I missed on that first errand could be found all over the mansion, and over the years, it became a game for me to spot them. Going to my lord's domain was like taking a stroll through his mind. Nothing was forced, but everything had a purpose.

Lord Cao Cao would never use a hare to do a tiger's job, but he made sure to choose the best tiger possible.

This is also the first time I met another of my fellow orphans of war. I did not speak with him, but I saw him down the path—a young boy around my age, raking the sand and pebbles of the garden without passion. He was too far for me to discern him in detail, but he was obviously a former Turban, or the son of one. The boy looked completely out of place, with his disheveled hair, slumped shoulders, and mouth hanging open. I wouldn't have been surprised if he came from a place like Fa Jia Po. Swallowing the will to wave at him as I would have back home, I pressed on and reached the main door of the mansion.

As people did at Xiahou Dun's, I used the ring set against the wood of the door to knock, and less than ten heartbeats later, it opened. A woman of middle age welcomed me with little warmth, and it took me a second to remember why I was here.

"Lady Cao, the wife of master Xiahou Dun, sends this gift for the lady of the house," I said, repeating the words hammered into me by my master's wife. There were several Lady Cao in the district, so I had to specify which one sent me.

"Wait here," she told me after inspecting the package in my hands. She left, walking with small, quick steps as if trying to find the perfect balance between walking and running.

It was customary, at least in our district, when a delivery was made from one lady to another or between lords, that the actual recipient received the package. Too many times in our history, people had been poisoned or insulted by someone claiming to represent an important person. When the recipient received the package, it made things easier in case of a trial.

This is precisely why my heart beat like a war drum at that instant. Lady Ding, Cao Cao's wife, had the reputation of being the meanest woman in the city, if not in the empire. I remembered how both my lord and my master had dropped the argument of who would welcome me when she had been mentioned. Even though I had never met her, I was terrified.

From what I had been told, Cao Cao used to have a consort, Lady Liu, whom he loved very much. But since he had already married Lady Ding, and since this woman's family held a lot more power, she remained his wife. That didn't mean she liked her husband's attention for his consort, and even less the fact that the woman bore him three children in as many years, while she could not seem to keep one up to birth. Even if the last of the three had been a girl, it was too much for Lady Ding, who then had her rival poisoned. Of course, nothing could be proven, which only helped to enforce Lady Ding's reputation. And if she could get Cao Cao's favorite concubine killed with no repercussions, what would she do to a powerless orphan?

The only thing positive I heard about Lady Ding was the attention she gave her husband's children. Once their mother removed, she took over and raised them as her own. At least this is what people claimed.

"What do you want?" said a young boy who had appeared from behind a folding screen on the left side of the hall. I assumed he was Cao Ang, my lord's firstborn, for he looked about my age, and I immediately hated him. He eyed me from head to toe as if judging a mule and clearly found me lacking. His hand was stained with fresh ink, so I guessed he had been practicing calligraphy when I knocked at the door.

"Lady Cao sent me to deliver this to Lady Ding," I said, not masking what I thought of his arrogance.

"I know at least five Lady Cao," he said, and even though we were about the same height, I could see deep up his nose. "Tell me which one sent you, or I'll have my guards kick you out."

"The wife of Xiahou Dun," I replied.

"That's *master* Xiahou Dun for you," he continued, just as two other boys left the cover of the screen and stood behind him. One of the two would be Cao Shuo, his little brother, who looked very much like Ang but had less cleverness in the eyes. They both looked the spitting image of their father without his natural charm. The third was maybe a year older than I, but from the way he stood behind, he seemed to obey Cao Ang. His name, which I did not know then, was Cao Anmin, the son of Cao Cao's dead brother.

"*Master* Xiahou Dun's wife, Lady Cao, sends this package to Lady Ding," I said through my teeth. Every inch of my body ached to punch this little weasel in the teeth, but I knew what kind of trouble I would get into.

"What's in it?" Cao Ang asked, nodding toward the package with his chin.

"Tea cakes," I answered.

"Show me," he said, not waiting for my reply before he shot his right arm toward the package and grabbed it. He was fast; I will give him that. Before I could react, the two others stepped up, and I especially feared the bigger one, who was a *cun* taller than me and broader in the shoulders.

Cao Ang worked on the knot of the package and inspected the inside.

"Something's wrong," he claimed, "one is missing."

How could he know that? I wondered. I never said anything about the number of cakes in the package, which I didn't know myself. And I had certainly not taken any out myself. He smiled, a venomous smirk full of complaisance, and I understood what he was about to do too late. Before I could react, he fished one cake from the package and stuffed it inside his robe. I tried to jump at him, only wanting to get the cake back before the lady appeared, but Cao Anmin shoved me back to my spot with ease. I heard the footsteps of the lady coming from the left side, and while she approached, Ang tied the knot back and threw the package against my chest.

"Mother!" he shouted. The footsteps slightly increased in speed. I was screwed. The only thing I noticed in my favor was the mark of ink Cao Ang had left on the silk of the package.

"What is this commotion?" she asked as she appeared from behind the screen. Her appearance sucked the air from me. She was malice incarnated.

Lady Ding was tall, thin, with lips pinched so tight you could not pass a grain of rice through them. Her eyes reminded me of an old woman from my hometown, who everyone claimed could perform some black magic to hurt people. She wore elegant clothes of silk, a beautiful hairpin of gold shaped like a phoenix, and accessories of jade, but somehow she looked as if wearing mourning garments. She wasn't pretty, so I assumed her family held a great deal of power or money. Cao Cao was a woman's man, I betray no secret here, and besides the Lady Ding, I never saw him with anyone but a beauty.

I shook to my core when she darted her chicken-like gaze in my eyes.

"Lady Cao sent you a gift of cakes, but this peasant ate one; I saw him!" Cao Ang said, throwing his finger in my direction. "Isn't it right?" he asked his two lackeys, who both nodded.

"It's not true!" I shouted. "He's lying!" I don't think I could have said anything worse. She took two more steps and back slapped me, making a sound like a whip. I had never been hurt so badly from a slap before.

"Silence, you little filth," she barked. "If my son saw you, this is what happened. Which Lady Cao sent you?"

"Uncle Xiahou's wife," Can Shuo replied when I remained silent.

"Why on earth did she send a... maggot to deliver, what? Cakes?" she asked, taking the package from my hands and opening it in haste.

"Master Xiahou Dun went on a hunt," I replied, working really hard to fight the beginning of a sob. "He took most of our servants with him."

"So what? She couldn't come herself?" the lady asked, and I knew then that I would not win this argument. She would find fault, no matter what. Now, as I said, I hated Lady Cao as much as her husband, but this was not her fault, and I have always reacted to an unjust accusation.

"My lady sent the cleanest of her servants at the moment," I said. "I'm sorry not to be to your liking." It's not what I said but the tone I had used that made the lady behave as if I had spat in her face.

"You insolent... maggot!" she said. "I will have you flogged for that!"

I was going to apologize, maybe even bow or kowtow. I knew those people liked it. But then I saw the way Cao Ang grinned and scoffed behind his mother's back, and I could no longer contain myself. Not even his cousin could stop me as I bolted toward my new enemy, a fist raised in the air.

"What did you think would happen?" Xiahou Dun said as he walked around me. I only wore my pants, and the night's chill made my skin prickle.

That and the fear of what was about to happen. I had learned my lesson and kept my mouth shut. Nothing I could say would help. "Stealing from the package you were supposed to deliver—"

"I didn't!" I said, cursing myself for speaking despite knowing better. The kick got me right into the ribs, and as I was lying on the belly, arms in front, there was nothing to protect me. Xiahou Dun resumed his circling walk.

"Then you attacked the son of your lord, the firstborn at that." As he spoke, he walked over the fingers of my right hand, but I did not scream. I knew he would do that. He always did.

"I'm sorry," I said through my tears.

"But the worst," he went on as if I had not spoken, "is that you shamed my esteemed wife. And both ladies asked me to lay it hard on you." There was no regret in his voice.

From what I gathered as I had waited for my punishment by the servants' latrine, Xiahou Dun had performed badly during the hunt. Then again, I don't think he ever caught anything during the past three months. If I was in a good enough state the next day, I would probably have a lot of healing to do with the horse he'd been using.

"It's that bastard of Cao Ang," I said. "He stole the cake and put it on me." I expected the strike to come right away; I had just insulted his nephew after all. But surprisingly, nothing came. "There was even some ink from his hand on the wrapping."

"Listen to me, boy," he said after a sigh. Even if I had changed my name to please him, he never called me Chun. "For what it's worth, I believe you." My mind reeled with the slim hope that maybe I had said something to get myself out of this. Could it be that Xiahou Dun hated his nephew as much as he did everyone else? "Cao Ang is even worse than his father used to be, and believe me, Mengde was a brat. But the thing is," he went on, and just then, he caressed the bottom of my exposed feet with the tip of his cane. I shivered and sobbed. "Ang is Cao Cao's son, while you're the bottom of the shit barrel." And with this, he whipped my feet so hard that I let a scream out. He always started with the feet. It doesn't leave marks, and it hurts for days after a beating. No one pinned us down. If we moved, he would hit longer, so we endured the pain.

The truth about Xiahou Dun came during the first few months I spent under his roof. He was a bad warrior and hurting those weaker gave him pleasure. He might very well be one of the fiercest-looking men I ever met, but it was all a facade. The man dressed like a warrior, cursed like one, and behaved like a veteran of many wars, but he could no more fight than most scholars. In fact, I often noticed that the more a man poses as a warrior, the less he is one. True fighters were more like his cousin, Xiahou Yuan, with a heavy belly, a great laugh, and an appreciation of life and its pleasures. When you might die in the next few weeks, you learn to enjoy the little things.

But for all his masked weaknesses, Xiahou Dun was a genius when it came to administration and organization. Cao Cao's affairs ran smoothly under his control, and nothing worthy of note happened until my lord returned three months later.

I was never sent back on an errand to Cao Cao's place while he was not there and just bought my time, spending as much of it as I could in the stable and developing a deep hatred for Cao Ang, whom I considered my rival for life. I did not want to hurt him, at least not like I wanted the bearded warrior. But I wanted to humiliate him. And the occasion came, though I had nothing to do with it.

Lord Cao Cao came back during the hottest days of the summer, roughly a year after Cheng Yuanzhi's death, and he did not look happy. The story claimed he had done a great work of putting down any flame or rebellion in Ji'nan but somehow had overdone it by destroying a few temples to local gods, thus angering the region's people. Sure, they would no longer rebel against the Han government, but they almost killed him for his blasphemy.

I only knew of his presence because more horses were sheltered in the stable, which made Xin Ping's life very busy for a few days, and which also meant I shoveled a lot of shit during that time.

Then, one day, perhaps a week after his return, I was summoned by a servant to Cao Cao's estate, and my heart froze. I hadn't been beaten for a month, and even Lady Cao could find nothing to say about my behavior. The only thing I could think of was the story of the tea cakes, and I assumed Cao Ang or Lady Ding had spewed their poison in my lord's ear. So, to say that I was afraid as I walked behind this servant would be a euphemism.

There was a certain tension in the air as I passed the outer gate of the Cao's domain. I saw no one along the path leading to the house this time. The doors were open, as if the building was ready to swallow me down, and I thought this would be the last time I felt the sun on my face. The servant only took a couple of steps, then opened his arm to the left for me to keep moving by myself. I could hear my heart beat against my chest. There was no screen this time, so I could directly see my lord, sitting straight on a chair, Xiahou Dun in the same position by his side, while in front of them kneeled my nemesis. Cao Ang was alone, his shoulders slumped and his breathing broken with sobbing.

"Liao Chun, come here," my lord said, waving me to stand next to his son. Cao Cao looked tired but still very strong. It was the first time I saw him in complete civilian clothes, and somehow he looked all the more fearsome for it. Not even the emperor could look more dignified. I stood next to Cao Ang, his face a pitiful mess of snot and tears, which pleased me more than I dared to show. I was about to kneel after I bowed to lord Cao, then to my master, but my lord told me to keep standing.

"Chun, I want to apologize for my son's behavior," Cao Cao said, and I could not have been more surprised if he told me I was made his secretary.

"There is no need to apologize," I said, choosing not to feign ignorance on the topic of the conversation. Cao Cao was no fool, and I knew very little about the correct etiquette back then, not that it changed much later on, anyway. Of course, I was supposed to shake in pretended fear and claim that I did not know what his son had done to deserve an apology, but that was dog fart, and I think my lord appreciated me being straightforward.

"There is," he replied. "Being born into a powerful family does not make one powerful. Respect comes from actions, not blood." All of this he said for his son's benefit, but I was touched as well. "You got wrongfully treated because of my son's actions. This wrongdoing deserves a response, which is why I have called for you." So far, Xiahou Dun had not reacted, which told me he was not surprised by any of this.

"Chun," Cao Cao said. "You will hit my son once."

"What?" both Ang and I asked, equally baffled.

"Sir, I cannot," I said. There was no way I would make it for very long here if I struck Cao Ang. It might have been at his father's request, but neither Ang nor his poisonous mother would see it that way.

"Father, you must be joking," Cao Ang said, standing up at the same time.

"Ang-*er*, you will stay quiet," Cao Cao said. He had not raised his voice, but the menace could not be clearer. "Chun, this is an order, and I assure you nothing will happen to you for obeying." He could not know this, but an order is an order, and many of them get soldiers killed after all. "And you are not doing this for yourself, but for my son's benefit. Ang-*er*, take it as a lesson and learn. You are no better than the way you treat your lesser men. Mistreat them, and they will abandon you when you need them the most."

Ang remained quiet, but I knew he would not learn this lesson the way his father wanted him to. Frankly, I was stuck. I could disobey my lord and refuse, which might earn me a bit of credit with Ang, though I doubted it, or I could obey and make an enemy for life. As I got older, I often wondered if I could have found a way out of it, for example, by asking for a similar punishment or maybe by pretending to strike. But I was very immature then, so I chose to get a little pleasure from it.

I hit Cao Ang as hard as I could, just as he turned his face toward me. I hit him with my open hand, something less painful but more humiliating than a fist. And the way his face froze with shock will remain with me until the day I die. I saw tears in his eyes, of pain and rage, but he was smart enough to remain quiet.

"Will that be all, Father?" he asked, shaking like a leaf.

"Did you learn?" Cao Cao asked.

"Yes, Father, I learned," Ang replied, his hand holding his reddening cheek. I spent all my focus on not smiling, but I admit it was my greatest moment in a very long time.

"You may go then," Cao Cao said, waving his son away. Cao Ang left and managed not to look at me, something I would not have been able to do. But I knew I would suffer the consequence of this at some point.

"Yuanrang, I will see you later," Cao Cao then said, and this time Xiahou Dun looked surprised. It did not last long, but when he stood up, I could hear his fists tightening around the arms of his chair.

"I'll finish my report then," Xiahou Dun said. He left too. Cao Cao waited until the footsteps of his cousin could not be heard before he spoke again.

"He does not like you very much," my lord said.

"Who does he like?" I asked, which made Cao Cao sigh deeply.

"You need to learn to keep your thoughts to yourself. This mouth is going to get you in trouble." If Cao Cao ever said something prophetic, it was then.

"Sorry," I replied honestly.

"Come with me," he then said, standing up and taking the first step toward the door at the same time.

Nothing more was said until we left the domain. We walked a little while longer, toward the stable, I thought. As soon as we had stepped out, Cao Cao's stride became more relaxed, which, in turn, soothed my mind a little.

"Do you know who told me about Cao Ang's action?" he asked.

I did not. Nor could I imagine one person wishing me well in Chenliu so far.

"Yuanrang did," he answered. You could have knocked me down with a flick, so strong was my surprise. Cao Cao chuckled from the face I made. "He is tough, my cousin, and the past months could not have been easy for you."

"I have seen worse," I lied. Self-pity would get me nowhere, I thought, but acting as a soldier might.

"But he does not like to be made a fool of, and when my wife used him to punish you, he felt insulted. He could not get back at her, though she deserves it, so he went after my son, who also deserved it anyway."

Cao Cao had openly told me what he thought of his wife, and this, more than the rest, baffled me. I think he understood my surprise.

"Never tell anyone I said all of this," he said. I promised I would not, and until today I kept my promise. "Do you know why I value Yuanrang despite his flaws?" he asked, something I had often wondered.

"You trust him to watch your back," I replied.

"Very good," Cao Cao replied. We turned left, confirming my assumption that we were walking toward the stable. "Trust is the hardest thing to find and is even harder to give. You don't need to love the men at your side, but you need to know how much you can trust them. As you are now, you cannot trust my son, and he won't trust you. One day you might have to, and much will depend on it." I was drinking up my lord's words. He spoke difficult ideas with simple words, something only a handful of educated men could do.

"I don't know if I ever will be able to," I replied.

"You will grow, both of you. And since you are going to study together, you will have a lot of time to mend the gap." I did not like the idea of spending more time with Cao Ang or his two minions, but I was also impatient to start studying.

We penetrated the yard where some horses were being trained by Xin Ping and a couple of assistants who came back with Cao Cao's regiment. Technically, they had disbanded when entering Chenliu, but all of them lived close enough that they could be recalled in less than a day. Cao Cao invited Xin Ping to keep the training going with a gesture of his hand, and we continued toward the stalls. When we penetrated the open building, I did as I always did and clicked my tongue before reaching the three horses belonging to Xiahou Dun. They reacted as usual and turned around to face away from the wall and toward us, peering as much as possible so that I could pat their muzzles. I didn't act as such to brag, this was just what I always did, but Cao Cao was clearly impressed, especially when he saw how obediently the biggest stallion dropped his head in my hand.

"Their master might not have much love for you, but they do," Lord Cao said, himself taking some time to pat the big bay horse. I was about to say that all it took was a bit of affection, but his advice was still fresh, and I kept the thought behind my teeth. Cao Cao saw it, of course, and smiled back at me.

"They are wonderful animals," I simply said. "Though Brown Wings has something special, and I admit I take better care of her."

"Brown Wings?" he asked quizzically.

"Sorry, I meant Chestnut," I said, correcting myself.

"*Chestnut,*" Cao Cao said as he rolled his eyes. I laughed inside, and it felt amazing. "Come here a second," he said, taking us away from the three horses, who must have wondered why they did not even receive a good scrubbing. We stepped to the last stall, which had been empty all those months, but now welcomed the black mare Cao Cao mounted. She was another beautiful beast, taller than Brown Wings and not as gentle, but very obedient. Cao Cao barely whistled when she stood on all four and turned around to him.

"What do you think of her?" he asked. I don't know if I was supposed to, but I caressed her muzzle as well, then let my hand move to her neck and shoulder. She was powerful, and I said as much. "What else?" he asked.

I was still far from being an expert, so I took a guess.

"She's heavy," I replied, meaning that she was expecting a foal. Cao Cao patted my shoulder to tell me I was right.

"She did well during those months in Ji'nan and before against… in Julu," Cao Cao said. I was touched that he did not mention the Yellow Turbans. "But frankly, it was a bit much for her, and I feared she might go lame. I still have much to do in the coming months, a lot of roads ahead, but not with Moon Shadow, I'm afraid." I was quite distressed to know that Cao Cao would not stay but said nothing of the sort, of course.

"Do you think Brown Wings would suit me?" he asked, though I knew it was not really a question.

"She'll serve you well," I replied. In the back of my mind, I was pleased to know Cao Cao would take his cousin's horse, and there was nothing he could do about it. At least, I thought, she would not get beaten by an incompetent rider.

"From now on," he went on, "you will also take care of my horses, and you are to pay special attention to Moon Shadow." There was no hiding my grin then.

When he joined us, Xin Ping pleased me even more by saying that at least I would stop lazing around, which was as good as a compliment I could get from him. Cao Cao laughed at the comment and left us both in the stable, but not before reminding me to get ready for a tough regimen once school started, which he said should be within the next few days. I was left wondering how I could possibly attend this famous school project while also taking care of more horses, but the answer would come fairly simply—I would sleep less.

In any case, contrary to what he had declared, school did not start right away. Cao Cao left a couple of days after I hit his son, this time for Luoyang, the capital, and did not come back for another two months, meaning that my daily life of fear and hopelessness resumed.

One day after he came back, I was invited to the first of many, many classes.

CHAPTER TEN

Fu county, Yi province
11th month, 4th year of the Jingyuan era
of the Cao Wei empire (263)

CHEN SHOU HAS MISSED his recording session for the past two days. He sent me messages to claim he was ill, but I know what it is really about—he's pissed—or maybe disappointed.

I called him a traitor for the way he folded to our new masters while I was the one who grew up with them. He doesn't understand how much can happen in a lifetime, or that I was born with nothing and would have followed anyone who promised a brighter future. And Cao Cao was far from being *anyone*. He was brilliant to the point that it blinded you, and without him, I would have simply vanished.

Nevertheless, I am no less a traitor than Chen Shou. Those I betrayed, I did out of conviction, not in a vain search of glory or comfort at least, but to a pedant youth such as my young writer is, it doesn't make a difference.

We've been stuck in Fu County for three days now, blocked by the season's rains. I could have told them this was going to be the case, but I'd be damned if I helped any of those scoundrels take me away from my home.

Yes, there was a time I followed the Cao clan. A lifetime ago. But those were not the same men. *They* were worthy of my service. Their descendants, not so much.

But this story is not going to write itself. So, for the first time in ages, I will work the inkstone and pick up the brush. Even the years did not manage to remove the Han characters drilled into me by my teachers in Chenliu, and among many things, I owe them for that.

*Chenliu, Chenliu commandery,
8th month of the 1st year of Zhongping era
(185), Han Dynasty*

Nearly a year after I first met lord Cao Cao, I made my way to the southernmost building of the district where most of the Cao and Xiahou clans lived in Chenliu. Of course, there were more than just two families inhabiting the neighborhood, but most, if not all, were related one way or another to Cao Cao.

After eight months stuck between the house I lived in and the stable, I was finally going to visit more of Chenliu, and just this would have made the day an exciting one. Chenliu was not a great city, in size or population. It was far smaller than Xiangyang or Wan, but of the first, I had only visited a portion, and I entered the second when it was more ruin than livable. But those two Nanyang cities lacked something compared to Chenliu, the Cao clan.

Cao Teng, Cao Cao's grandfather, had not only been one of the most powerful eunuchs of his time, but had also been the confidant of two emperors, meaning that he died a very, very wealthy man. While his son, Cao Song, had a tendency to waste that money with no sense of long-term strategy, the grandson proved a remarkable investor, capable of attracting merchants, scholars, and landlords of wealth around him. So when Cao Cao moved his base to Chenliu, the city flourished in a matter of months.

It showed in the quality of the architecture, and the novelty of the designs, down to the tiles of the roofs, showing patterns unique to the city. There might have been an official leader of Chenliu, but I never knew who he was, and I do not doubt many people of Chenliu believed Cao Cao was in fact appointed by the Han government. Even the inspector of Yan province, when visiting the city, first stopped by Lord Cao's mansion.

I was still technically within the Cao's district, meaning that I had yet to discover a big chunk of Chenliu, but I saw more on the short walk from Xiahou's domain to the school than in the past eight months, and I wasn't the only one. I saw several kids of different ages strolling through the streets, heads turning left and right as if on their first visit to Chenliu. Most walked by two or three, while I remained alone. I knew they were my fellow Yellow Turbans, those orphans of war rescued by Cao Cao himself.

The other children, those who walked as if the land under their feet was made of rotting eggshells, were the sons of the powerful men living in Chenliu or other places related to the Cao clan.

We all moved toward the same place—a simple building of one floor, with a large, non-decorated courtyard enclosed in a four-sided wall. The door was on the side rather than in the middle, and only two children could enter at the same time. Seeing that I was alone as I approached the building, I meant to be discreet, but this was not to be. I had not even stepped through the door when a hand fell heavily on my shoulder. I had spent the last night worrying over my eventual meeting with Cao Ang, wondering what kind of vengeance he had cooked up in his sick mind. So when someone touched me, I nearly jumped out of my skin.

"I know you!" a boy shouted enthusiastically from behind me. He recognized me faster than I did him, but here was the boy who I had seen sweeping the courtyard of Lord Cao on the fateful day of the tea cakes. He looked far more alert than on that day, and a great smile spread from ear to ear. "You're the boy who slapped master Cao," he said, and I don't know what surprised me the most, that he knew about that or that he called Cao Ang *master*.

Immediately, the other children around us interrupted their conversations and stopped moving. All heads turned toward me, and I felt my cheeks flame with heat in a couple of breaths.

"You must be confused," I said, as loud as possible, but just then, Cao Ang pushed through the unmoving crowd, giving me the shoulder as he did. Nothing could have better proved that I was who this boy had said I was. The whispers started right away. I had not even passed the entrance of our school and already had a reputation, all thanks to another lost child of the rebellion.

"Nah," he said, "I remember you. I thought you was dead! Didn't see you after that." He spoke incredibly loud, which made me wonder if he was maybe a bit deaf, while in reality, he was simply a peasant. "My name's Zhou Cang," he said, giving me the worst salute I had ever seen. There was something refreshing in Cang's presence, and while I should have been mad, I had to like him. Contrary to me, the war had not changed him, though he must have suffered as well. Honesty was written on his face, and hard work flowed through his veins. Zhou Cang was a son of the earth and I knew we would be friends.

"Hey, that's the boy I told you about!" he said, waving toward a couple of other boys, obviously from the same kind of background as us. The first was a timid child of seven, maybe, named Du Yuan. The second looked a good couple of years older than me and answered to the name of Pei Yuanshao. He was tall, with long arms dangling helplessly by his sides and blank eyes reflecting nothing but emptiness, though it would prove to be misleading.

"Nice to meet you," Du Yuan said, his voice nothing but a whisper compared to Zhou Cang's.

"Hey!" barked a boy who must have been ten at least. "We're not in your fields. Move."

I was about to show him what I thought of his tone, but Zhou Cang took me by the elbow before I could do anything and pulled me inside, laughing as if it was the best day of his life. This was another way to answer a conflict I had never considered before—laughing it off. It might sound easy, but I never managed to do it.

The building was nothing but a roof, some pillars, and three walls, the exterior ones of the courtyard, and the inner one, which was full of holes. The back wall, from where we entered, was nothing but two decrepit pillars. I wondered why Cao Cao, who lived a life of opulence and comfort, had chosen such a wretched place to host his project. But since the building was already packed with students, I locked the thought in my head and proceeded toward the few empty spots.

I say spots, but they were nothing more than thin straw mats on the dusty floor, with long, low tables laid at regular intervals. I guess it is the kind of thing that happens naturally, but the room, already divided in two by a path between the tables, was also split according to the students' upbringing. The left side, near the hollowed wall, was occupied by the rich kids, who, while much quieter, were talking behind their long sleeves at the expense of the right half, where the orphans of war sat in a cacophony worthy of a market day.

At the end of the room, to the west, stood a higher, more solid table with a cushioned dais for a seat. In a greater building, the dais would have been set north, but this house stretched from east to west, so there was really no choice. No one sat on it, meaning I was not late yet. There were, however, no longer any wide spots of empty mats for us, so we had to split, with Du Yuan and Zhou Cang staying together and Pei Yuanshao by himself. I moved to the second row from the dais, where something of a space could still be found. Excusing myself as I tiptoed behind the rank of my new comrades, I finally reached my spot, right next to another boy who was already napping over the table. He looked big, and when I sat down, our knees touched, which awakened him. He then sat back up a little, his eyes still half-closed through his slumber, and I realized that *big* did not cover it; he was a giant. For a second, I wondered if he was an adult who had gotten himself lost.

"Sorry, it's a bit crowded," I said.

"It's fine," he answered. His voice had not broken yet, which gave an incongruent impression for such a big boy. He wasn't just tall; he was meaty, for lack of a better word. I wondered if the comrades behind him would see anything.

"I'm Liao Chun," I said, trying my luck with a respectful salute.

"Xu Chu," he answered. Yes, this is how I met the man they would call the *Mad Tiger*, though at this moment, he reminded me more of a certain ox back at Fa Jia Po. While for most of the children around me, I was left to wonder what could possibly have attracted Lord Cao's eye, with Xu Chu, it was fairly obvious. He did not breathe of intelligence, but just like Zhou Cang, sitting almost at the back now, you knew you had a good, honest fellow here.

I only had time to learn that he came from Qiao county in Pei, where the Xiahou and Cao originally came from, which made me wonder if he was indeed a former rebel, when our teacher arrived. We knew of it because the left side of the room quieted and stood at once. Our side took a longer time to react, but we still stood before the man took his place behind the high table, though not before Xu Chu knocked our table with his knees.

To my great surprise and pleasure, Lord Cao Cao entered the building, accompanied by four servants carrying trunks. My lord went straight to the dais, a scroll of wooden slips in his hand like some statue of Kong Zi, while the servants dropped the heavy chests on the floor in front of him, raising clouds of dust as they did. Cao Cao took a good look at the room once the dust settled and sighed.

"I had hoped the room would be more evenly shared," he said as he shook his head. He then sat down, cross-legged. We imitated him, but I was barely halfway through crouching down before his voice boomed through the room.

"I did not tell you to sit." We all stood back up, straight as spear poles. I heard a few chuckles from my left, and of course, the rich kids had known of this. "While I am sorry for the divide between the students assembled here, it is neither surprising nor unfixable. It will do for now, but let me tell you this, from the moment you step through that door"—he pointed at the small gates at the outer wall—"to the moment you leave this courtyard, you are all the same to me. It does not matter who your father, your uncle, or your ancestor is, and it does not matter that you have been invited by me or a member of my staff. Disrespect one of your teachers in any way, whether by missing a class or interrupting their teaching, for example, and you *will* be punished. As you can see, there are three wooden poles in the yard." I had not seen them, but now that he mentioned it, they were hard to miss, standing at the southern side, not too far from the wall. They had chains at their base. "I let you, or more accurately, your teachers, imagine how to use them best to discipline the bad apples among you."

We might be all the same to Cao Cao, I thought, but it was unfair, nonetheless. Those kids on the left knew how to behave properly in this kind of situation. They were used to sitting for long periods of time, listening to someone else. But for us who grew under the sun and had been lolled with the songs of birds and the streams of rivers, this was against our nature.

"This school should have started a few months ago, but as you know, the empire waits for no man. And I will not wait for any of you either. You will show me what you are capable of, the kind of man you will become, and if I find this man lacking, you will be taken out of this project. Find yourself among the best, and your future is set."

This was no news to me, but some baffled faces here and there on both sides said otherwise.

"You will have two lessons a day, as long as your teachers have the time for you. The morning one will be dedicated to your general education, the afternoon to all things military. And though I don't expect any of you to shine in both, the same level of effort will be expected. Is this understood?" he finally asked. The answer was not perfectly coordinated, but we all agreed.

"Each and every one of you will receive a brush, an inkstick, the material to grind it, and ten sheets of paper per week. Do not waste them; you will have no replacement." The second he said that I twisted my head and saw Cao Ang looking at me. His intentions were clear, and I knew I would have to protect this brush with my life.

Lord Cao proceeded to tell us about the meals being brought to us during the interval between the morning and afternoon classes. I remember wondering why we would be fed for basically sitting on our asses all morning, until the first class ended. Then I understood how exhausting a lesson could be. I was famished. There were more rules, most of them making no sense, such as washing our hands before entering the courtyard. All the while, the servants had opened the trunks and distributed the materials mentioned earlier, as well as a bowl and a pair of chopsticks. I was amazed, most of all, by the paper. The genial inventor Cai Lun had created a whole new way of fabricating paper with tree bark, fishing nets, or other things a few generations ago, thus rendering it cheaper and more accessible, but I had only rarely seen some and never blank. Though I was not and never became a scholar, I remember looking at those ten sheets of paper as if I had reached a new step in my life just for owning them. Once the novelty wore off, I still preferred wooden slips, if only for their durability, but I must admit the feeling of paper between your fingers is a pleasant one.

"Now that everything has been said, this is the first and last time I ask you this in my class. Are there any questions?"

No one raised their hand for a few seconds, during which I studied the faces of my new comrades. I did not count very well then, but my experience within the Yellow Turbans had taught me how to split men into groups and roughly estimate numbers. I think we were about seventy children, the youngest looking somewhere around six, while the oldest might have been thirteen years old.

The giant next to me lifted his hand. "What about if we need to… you know?" he asked. The entire class erupted in laughter, and I shuffled a little away from him out of embarrassment. But Cao Cao did not look bothered, except by our reaction.

"What are you laughing at?" he asked, which silenced us immediately. "Basic problems should be dealt with first. There is a latrine behind the building. You may go once a day, at mealtime. Two of you will be chosen at random to empty the latrine every evening."

When I first arrived in Chenliu, this had been one of my primary concerns as well. Not the capacity to empty yourself, but the way to get rid of the waste. In the countryside, we just let it slide to the closest pigsty if there is one connected, or we carried it to the river. However, there was no pigsty around, and the river looked far too clean to be used as such. It so happened that some people were making a living of gathering the contents of the latrines and selling them to the neighboring farms. All we had to do here was carry it to those people. We didn't have to, they would have done so by themselves, but it was part of Cao Cao's plan to humble us, I guess.

A few more questions followed until Lord Cao shut us off and finally opened his scroll of wooden slips.

"There is a *shi* left until your meal, and you will spend it learning the greatest of arts," he said before clearing his throat and focusing on the characters spread on the slips.

My heart raced with impatience. What would my lord teach us? Some of the war classics? The basics of transportation or the military law? Whatever it was going to be, my biggest regret at this point was not being able to write it down. Frankly, I did not know what he expected us to do with those papers, but while the left half was already working the inkstone, we were left to gaze blankly at our teacher.

Then he spoke and shattered my hopes.

*"To my wine I sing
of the times of peace,
when officers shall not make calls at the door.
The ruler is bright and virtuous,
His ministers loyal and trustworthy.
Abiding by propriety and courtesy,
The people have no cause for lawsuits."*

Poetry. Cao Cao would teach us poetry.

To say that I was not enthused would be the mildest way to put it. I looked at my neighbors, who all bore the same confused look, while our comrades on the left behaved as if in a trance, eyes half closed and weaving their heads left and right. I had seen the same attitude from the most devout of the Yellow Turbans.

This was my first class ever, and I couldn't say the future looked good.

Things improved a lot with the afternoon class, which was taught by my lord's cousin, Cao Ren.

Barely out of his teens, Cao Ren had an unmistakable air of competency. He was not particularly warm to us and treated the whole affair as a chore, but I enjoyed his time with us. To put it simply, he taught us about weapons, and just the fact of seeing him standing next to a rack of blades in the yard rekindled my hopes for this school. We did not touch any, but Cao Ren demonstrated the use of some, instructing on the strengths and weaknesses of each. The last one he took from the rack was a crossbow, which he cocked with incredible speed.

"This," he said, looking at the weapon with something like love, "is what kills the most in battle. Half of you, or any soldier really, will only ever use this in war, and most of those who die, die because of it. You will learn how to maintain it properly, load it, and finally shoot until you are able to do so in your sleep. Then, and only then, will we move to blades, spears, and the rest."

I was disappointed, but it made sense, and I had already decided I would respect all the teaching from the afternoon classes as if it came from the mouth of the Founding Emperor himself.

Despite his youth, Cao Ren was a patient man and did not hesitate to repeat himself if any of us asked. He did not look much like Cao Cao, which made sense considering that they shared no blood. His nose had been broken at some point, and a scar ran down his lower jaw, cutting through a young beard. Cao Ren was what you'd expect of a veteran, and that was before he was one. As the years took him through countless battlefields, he became something of a legend.

It surprised me to see how many of the rich kids, who we would soon call the left-wing, cared about such military matters. Sure, a good third or more of them looked as if they might faint just by looking at a sharp blade, but the others showed interest, Cao Ang among them. All I regretted from that afternoon was not being able to show what I knew already. This would have shut the arrogant ass up, I thought.

There was another glorious moment for the right-wing, mealtime. A cart was pulled inside the yard a few seconds after Cao Cao finally relented with the poetry. My head felt empty, as did my stomach. I already knew then that I would never love poetry, and I certainly never did. My lord invited us to form a line toward the cart, on top of which rested an enormous pot of clay. The servant who had pulled the cart now removed the lid, and after the cloud of steam gave way, the first in the ranks could see the nature of the day's meal. The face Cao Ang made was worth the morning of mental torture I had just gone through.

"What is that?" he asked the servant who was shoving a ladle down the pot.

"Porridge," the servant replied before emptying the ladle inside Ang's bowl with a wet splash.

"That's considered a treat while on the march,"

Cao Cao said as he came to stand next to the servant. "Isn't that right?"

"Right you are, sir," the servant replied. "And that's if we still have water."

I can't say I was happy at the prospect of porridge, but at least we had food halfway through the day, which was more than what I had been used to. But I'm certain some boys of the left-wing chose to remain hungry, while many of the right-wing took a second serving, or three in the case of Xu Chu.

By the time the second class finished, I was both exhausted and full of energy. I walked back with Zhou Cang, Du Yuan, Pei Yuanshao, and some more new friends who all lived in Cao Cao's estate. Xu Chu had been assigned the first latrine duty, along with a left-wing boy I didn't know. Zhou Cang spoke for us, not letting enough time between his sentences for us to comment. He was so full of life, and his grin spanned so wide that it proved impossible to resist. Halfway through the road back to Xiahou Dun's, I surprised myself with the sound of my own laughter. When was the last time I had laughed so?

I waved at them for a long time after we split, and I waited until they vanished before I ran toward the stable. I still had my duties to attend to. This was yet another injustice. The rich kids would return to their life of silk and rice while rakes, shovels, and brooms waited for us. At least I had Xin Ping and horses. Zhou Cang and the others had nothing of the sort.

By the time I had shoveled all Xin Ping needed me to and mended the horses, probably with less care than usual, I was completely beat. I don't think even Lady Cao could have forced me to wash before stepping inside the house, so I just lay in the straw next to Brown Wings and spent the last few seconds before slumber took me thinking about the next day's lessons.

Over the next couple of weeks, we got to meet most of our teachers, each of them specializing in one part of our education. Many of those eminent men would become the pillars of Cao Cao's rise, and their names will be known for many generations. But back then, I cursed them more often than I praised them, for I did not know of my luck, and some of them could be downright vicious.

Without surprise, Xiahou Dun spent a good part of his time attaching boys to the three pillars, though he did not do much in terms of beating. I believe he was particularly displeased at being a morning mentor. He taught us our numbers and some basics of campaign preparation. I must admit, he could speak without pause on the best ways to get an army ready, and everything he said sounded logical as well as practical.

His cousin, the forever joyful Xiahou Yuan, taught us how to fight another man, not in pitched combat, but in duel or smaller conflicts. At first, he kept the teaching to hand-to-hand combat, and it was quite amazing to see a man with such a stature capable of moving the way he did. We had our first experience of fighting amongst ourselves under his supervision. And I think he had underestimated how bad it could get. I wasn't the only one with an open conflict against our left-wing, and the first martial arts class turned into a brawl that only stopped when Xiahou Yuan cracked a few heads with the flat of his sword. Lucky for me, I had been paired with a young man I did not know yet, a distant cousin of Ang named Cao Xiu. While the hatred due to our respective sides ran clear, it was not personal enough to deserve to pummel each other, and we avoided Xiahou Yuan's ire.

His second class, despite his warning, turned out the same, and I believe this was when Lord Cao understood something had to be done. He gave us an impromptu class the next morning, but first forced us to change seats. Nothing was random with Lord Cao, and I can only imagine how long it took him to rearrange the classroom by himself before he stepped into the school that day. He did not just make us move around but paired us with a member of the opposite faction.

This is how I met a timid young boy, the youngest among us and probably the most discreet as well. He reminded me of our own Du Yuan, though the latter was turning slightly more aggressive already.

Somehow, even though I hated all those kids who looked down on us, I could not bring myself to be mad at him. He had those puppy eyes, forever watery, incapable of meeting anyone's gaze, and couldn't control a stutter that only worsened when people talked directly to him.

His name was Sima Yi. His family had produced exceptional talents since the founding of the Han dynasty, the western one, and some said their great ancestor had been a king. His father was currently serving as a prefect in Luoyang, and his elder brother, while only being thirteen, was already a cadet at the court. He did not know why his father had sent him to Chenliu, but one thing was certain, he was scared beyond his wits of Cao Cao. I learned all of this on the evening of our pairing, as we were put in charge of latrine duty. I actually liked Sima Yi, and while being two years younger than me, he could already recite the Confucian classics by heart and knew more Han characters than I knew existed. And since we sat next to each other, he helped me a great deal with those, at first.

Zhou Cang had picked the short straw from the pairing as he was forced to cooperate with Cao Ang. If anyone could manage that piece of shit, I thought, it was Zhou Cang. Of course, the numbers did not match, so several boys of the left remained together.

Among our most notable teachers was the tallest man I would ever meet and one of the most educated scholars in the empire, Cheng Yu. Any man walking by his side looked ridiculous in comparison, and that explained why he naturally slouched, despite being only in his mid-forties. He taught us the Confucian classics, the *Shiji* of the great historian Sima Qian, and other topics like the proper etiquette for a gentleman of the court. I did not pay as much attention as I should have to his classes, and neither did he. Cheng Yu was a traditionalist and believed the only proper form of education came from emulating a teacher. Whether you listened to him or not was none of his concern, and I guess this was just a big waste of his time to him.

Chen Gong, Lord Cao's young secretary, focused on teaching us the military classics and battle tactics, and this was by far my favorite morning class. He could not spend much time with us, for our lord kept him very busy. He was a nice enough man with a sense of humor, which was rare in his line of work. But his mind tended to scatter here and there as he spoke, and we sometimes had to call him back to the now. He once gathered enough boards of *weiqi,* and enough black and white stones for the whole class. I might have liked this game from the beginning, had I not been playing against my partner. Sima Yi shamed me, and it took a few days for our young friendship to resume.

Chen Gong's lessons also gave me one of my most gleeful moments as a student. I believe we were studying the second chapter of Sun Zi's *Art of War*, and master Chen made us discuss one of the strategist's ideas on how to motivate men. Sun Zi claimed that when chariots were involved in a conflict, a leader should reward the first man to capture an enemy chariot. Chen Gong then asked what could be said against this idea. He was the first and only teacher who ever invited us to criticize the masters of the past, so the practice was far from being a habit. Nevertheless, I was baffled that no one else seemed able to find the answer. It was obvious. So obvious, in fact, that I hesitated to raise my hand.

"No?" Chen Gong asked. "No one?"

"The chariots," I said, my voice barely more than a whisper.

"What about the chariots?" Master Chen asked.

"We don't use them anymore," I said.

No one in the class had seen as many battles as I had, of that I was certain, and not once I had seen chariots. The only times I actually spotted one of them, it was to carry Dong Zhuo in and out of the camp.

"Ridiculous," I heard Cao Ang whisper after he snorted.

Thankfully, Chen gong heard it too and reacted before I could insult my rival.

"Apparently, Liao Chun is the only one here with some critical mindset," he said, which made the Cao boy cringe. "He is right; chariots went out of fashion a while ago. If you wait for your men to capture one before you reward them, they'll revolt and call you an old-fashioned bastard."

We loved when the morning teachers swore, which made Chen Gong quite popular among us. And since I was gloating at his praise, I laughed louder than anyone else that day.

There was another class I actually did appreciate from the morning sessions, and it surprised everyone, including myself and the teacher, that I showed some skill in this particular topic, calligraphy. The man in charge of forcing the characters into our brains was Zhong Yao, and he was as cold as he was talented with the brush. Even Cao Cao openly recognized the genius of the man with Han characters, though they practiced two rival schools of calligraphy. Zhong Yao was a master of the *kai shu*, which is considered the standard style, while Cao Cao preferred the *cao shu*, a more flamboyant scripture, as if one is writing using a strand of grass. I liked Lord Cao's handwriting, but I never managed to grasp it as well as the other. Zhong Yao typically congratulated me by not smacking my fingers with his thin cane of bamboo. I was not the best of all the students, but I stood far ahead among the right-wing. It got me a few jealous glares at first, but it only took a poetry class for my comrades to remember I was one of them.

In any case, if there is one art that came almost as naturally as horse riding, it was calligraphy, and since I must have disappointed my lord with my terrible aptitudes in poetry, I was eager to show him my worth with a brush. So, one evening, with the excuse of giving him some news about his mare, I went to find Cao Cao.

He was in his hall, a single turtle-shaped lamp illuminating the desk over his legs, and for a moment I was tempted to just observe him for a while. We were not in his house but in the building behind it, where he dealt with his private matters, so there was little risk of being interrupted by his wife or sons. I was only allowed in because I brought *urgent* news of his favorite mount.

I saw him put down his brush once done with a long series of characters, and just after he finished inspecting his work, he said, "Yes?"

I stepped in, gave him a perfect military salute, as taught to us by Cao Ren, and let him know Xin Ping found his mare to behave well through her pregnancy but could use some fresh pasture to keep her energy up. This was all true and was as much of a rebuke as Xin Ping could give our lord without sounding disrespectful.

Cao Cao smiled when I relayed the message and was about to resume his writing task, but I did not move. I had meant to ask him for some advice for a perfect vertical *shu* stroke, the calligraphy technique I struggled the most with. An immature attempt at getting his attention, but once again, he beat me to it.

"Ah, I meant to congratulate you," he said as he sat back straighter.

"My lord?" I asked.

"Master Zhong Yao told me a certain brat with fiery eyes displayed a surprising talent for the characters. I do not believe I ever heard him speaking well of any student before." I blushed, thankful for the darkness of the room.

"Master Zhong Yao is too generous," I said, bowing as Cheng Yu had taught us.

"Hardly," Cao Cao commented with a scoff. "But he has his eye on you."

"I'm honored," I replied.

"If only such beautiful characters could be used to write fine poetry..." he commented, and I had to chuckle. Of course, I wanted to please him in his favored art, but I had no talent for it, and there are some things that cannot be forced. I'd rather laugh about it.

"May I ask something?" I said and regretted it right away, for Lord Cao brought his fingers to the side of his head as if hurt, an eye closed against the pain. I had nothing to do with it, as he said to reassure me before inviting me to ask my question. "Why do we learn poetry, the classics, or even calligraphy?"

He crossed his arms over his chest, and as the wind made the small flame of the lamp wave, I was once again amazed at the handsomeness of my lord. I am not a man's man, but some people carry too much physical charisma to be ignored. Cao Cao was one.

"All my officers need to be able to write and read," he replied.

"I understand," I said, "but why should we write so well or recite poems?" I already included myself in the count of his officers. It was very arrogant, but this was to be my life. Nothing else would do.

"Why do you think I ask them to read and write?"

"To read messages and write reports," I guessed.

"Among other things, yes," he said. "And how do I know I can trust a message supposedly coming from one of my officers?" I had learned nothing about these tactics and could see no suitable answer to this problem. "By knowing them," he said. "Every man has a particular handwriting and a unique sense with words. If one day I receive a message signed Liao Chun, with dry, dull words written in a perfect *kai shu,* I will know it's really from you."

"Maybe the enemy caught me and forced me to write those words," I said.

"Nonsense," he replied right away. "Once you are done with your training, no enemy will ever be able to catch you. And if they did, you'll just have to use *cao shu* or even to worsen your characters, and I'll know they are not your words."

I thanked him for his confidence and felt like I could fly, but a good soldier does not display those emotions, so I tried to keep my regular attitude.

"But don't you think we need more time on more practical matters?" I asked. "I mean, especially the right-wing. It's not like we'll ever catch up with the others on those educated topics."

"You're right," he said after a few seconds of pondering. "You won't mend the gap at this rate. Thank you, Liao Chun. I'll make sure to double the morning class time for the right-wing students."

I immediately stuttered that this was absolutely not what I had meant. If he did what he just said, and the word spread it was my fault; I would have both sides of the school willing to skin me alive instead of just one. But Lord Cao suddenly laughed and could not stop himself until a tear fell from his left eye.

"I am just making fun of you," he said. "I would not do that to your teachers. Believe me, they are going through enough as it is."

I breathed with relief and thanked him for his time. He was still chuckling when I stepped out of his working space.

My lord had joked about it, but the situation was truly getting worse by the day among the two wings. Pairing us had been a good idea, but it backfired quickly. I cannot count the number of pieces of paper that got accidentally stained by a clumsy neighbor, the gobs of snot magically landing inside a bowl of porridge, or any of those ideas germinating from the mind of young boys. So far, the worst that had happened was an ambush set against Zhou Cang as he and Cao Ang took their turn at the latrine. The barrel wasn't completely out of the hole before three boys grabbed him from behind and forced him head down in the shit. He was laughing when he mentioned it the next day, but I knew him well enough by then to recognize his hidden frustration, and the spirit of vengeance made itself known in my stomach.

It wasn't just that we worked against each other any chance we got; we also created factions and planned our next attacks. It became something of a war, with all the planning, the spying, and, inevitably, the treason. Xu Chu was the first to join the ranks of our foes. He had been easy to turn, the promise of food being enough to twist his allegiance. I don't think he saw it that way, but he was betraying his folks, and they had gained a lot of muscle with this coup.

But what we lost in strength, we gained in brain and will. Two boys, neither nobly born nor peasants, switched to our side when they had enough of being treated like the lesser of the left-wing.

The first of our two new allies was Yue Jin, a nine-year-old boy who stood shorter than me and pretty much everyone else. He compensated for his lack of stature with an overly aggressive nature that left no doubt about his intentions should anyone mock him on his size. I found the hard way that he was not just barking but could back up his threats with real combat skills. His hair sprouted at random angles, no matter how much he tried to smooth them down, and one of his front teeth had never grown back, which made him look even more like a younger child.

Yue Jin was the son of a village chief from Dong. Not someone considered noble or powerful, but with enough influence for his firstborn to be enrolled in this school.

I grew to like and respect Yue Jin a lot, especially after I caught him pummeling Xu Chu's skull from the giant's back. Thankfully for him, Xu Chu was not a naturally violent boy, for he would have made little work of this short-ass child, but I was nonetheless impressed by his daring attitude.

The second of our new members was a clever kid answering to the name of Man Chong. He had a familiar look, but I could not put a finger on who he reminded me of. No one knew why he was among us, and he refused to comment on the point, but he was already educated and very intelligent. But while some kids like Sima Yi are clever the way teachers want us to be, Man Chong impressed with his cunning. Most of the time he just looked like an average, well-mannered boy, but once in a while, I caught him looking at someone else like a crow observing a worm, as if studying it before turning it into its meal. He chilled my blood when he acted so, but it was my great luck that, for some reason, we became friends, and he seemed to respect me. Man Chong also seemed to grow a personal hatred for Cao Ang and Cao Shuo, and that too served us well.

I had yet to calm down a week after the ambush on Zhou Cang, and despite my noisy friend's request, I fumed with the will to avenge him. The opportunity offered itself one afternoon.

We had our first horse-riding class, and with it, our first excursion, though in my case, it was a bit of a letdown because we just went to the corral where I spent my evenings. Our teacher was yet another cousin of our lord, Cao Hong. He had much in common with Cao Ren, starting with his rather short stature and strong, angular face lines. But while Ren looked like a born leader of men, Hong was more drawn back and gave me the feeling of someone who would follow more than anything else. Whatever the case, he was highly skilled with horses and not only knew how to mount but also how to get them ready to be ridden.

On that day, he chose two beasts from the stable, none of them known to me except by sight. Cao Cao had taken Brown Wings to Luoyang, and of course, Moon Shadow would not be used by anyone but him. I assumed those two were his and were old enough to remain calm while he demonstrated how to saddle a horse, force the bit into the mouth, and all those other tasks I already knew about. I guess I must have looked pretty smug.

After a *shi* under the early winter sun, he finally called for two volunteers. I don't think I left much of a choice to anyone and was picked to ride the tallest of the two. The second was given to Cao Ang, who, to my great pleasure, had to use the stirrups in order to climb on his mare's back. Call me old-fashioned, but real men don't use stirrups, neither for mounting nor for riding. I'm not saying they are useless, and when charging in line, they help to keep it tight, but otherwise, I find them cumbersome, and understand why they were still rare within the cavalry.

Cao Hong made a game of the lesson, which means Ang and I turned it into a contest. The teacher wanted to test our balance, and to do so gave us a rope, which each of us had to grab from one end. Then on his signal, we were to pull and destabilize the other until one of us either let go or fell.

I waited for Cao Hong's hand to drop, my heart beating hot in my chest. I looked at Cao Ang with months of hatred gathered behind my eyes, while he did the same, probably thinking about the slap. He looked far less comfortable than I was, but he rode better than I expected. When the hand fell, we both pulled with all our might. Immediately, our comrades went on cheering for one or the other, and I am proud to say my name rang louder.

Our horses naturally started to walk in a circle because we both used our knees to gain as much strength as possible. Even then, Cao Ang was strong, but he had not spent years behind a plow or pulling on a stubborn ox. His palms were not rough from the extended use of shovels and ropes. And he had not traveled throughout the land on the back of a horse as I had. After a few seconds of adjustment, I took his measure and knew I could win in a number of ways. But the one I wanted required a bit of work.

Forcing my horse against his, I pushed us both deeper inside the corral, and for a second, I was worried Cao Hong would stop us, but he kept his amused observation going. Then I let my mount resume her circle. All the while, Cao Ang forced himself to let go of the mane in order to pull with both hands.

When his mare arrived exactly at the right spot, I pulled a little harder, increasing the tension on the rope. Cao Ang's jaws were tightly shut. He even started sweating. Oh, Ang wanted to win. And somehow he did, because I let go of the rope.

It all went exactly as planned. Ang waved his arms helplessly, the sudden release of the tension taking him backward better than if I had pushed him. And when he understood he could no longer stay in the saddle, he cursed.

Cao Ang landed right on top of a fresh pile of manure. It splashed all along his left side, and some even splattered on his face. The crowd of students broke into a burst of laughter, and even some of the left-wing joined in. Cao Hong shook his head, but I could see the same smile on his face that was probably on mine. I jumped down gracefully and crouched to Cao Ang's level. And that's when I made a mistake.

"That's for Zhou Cang," I said.

He was shaking with rage. I thought he might punch me right there and then, but the humiliation was too great for him to react. I stood up and offered my hand, which, of course, he refused. Not looking at anyone, Cao Ang stormed out of the corral and did not wait for us to be dismissed before he left the compound.

"You'll regret this," Cao Hong said as he came to gather the horses' reins. He had not meant it as a threat, just an observation, and I knew he was right.

Up to that point, the conflict between the left and right wings was merely what you would expect between two gangs of young boys, but it all changed that day. So far, while the left-wing clearly followed the lead of Cao Ang, no one on our side could claim that spot. After my little stunt in the corral, I became the de facto leader of our faction. I did not ask for it, but I did not shy away either.

Soon enough, walking alone became a risk, with many of the students on both sides receiving a beating. Within a week, we had our first broken bone, to which we replied with a few broken fingers. They ganged up on Pei Yuanshao while he gathered the leaves in Cao Cao's garden and peed on him. We grabbed Cao Xiu and forced him to eat straw until he puked, which took a long time. Our ingenuity grew by the day, though most of the time Man Chong found the most twisted ideas ever. When one of ours was hurt, he or his friend came to me for help, and I dispatched commandos of boys to claim vengeance.

Sima Yi remained off-limits, and we avoided Xu Chu as much as possible, but everyone else was game.

On our side, Man Chong wasn't the only one to shine; Pei Yuanshao did his part too.

He had been "invited" by Lord Cao to join the school after the fall of Runan, when the victors penetrated the city and the boy managed to steal a string of coins from Xiahou Dun without getting noticed. He was caught by a soldier, who found it odd that such a poor-looking kid could buy wine with a string of one hundred *wushu*. Why he had bought wine, Pei Yuanshao did not say, but the point was there, he was a natural-born thief, and we put his talent to good use.

We once ambushed Cao Shuo and Cao Anmin, who had thought themselves protected by walking together. We roughened them up a little, not enough to leave obvious marks, but that wasn't our goal, anyway. They ran back home naked, and the sight of their little asses hugging the walls until they reached their homes made for many evenings of laughter among us.

Pei Yuanshao managed to sneak out of the district and sold the clothes from the two Cao boys. I'm sure he stashed some of the money but brought enough back that we could now replace the stolen inkstone and buy some other items. At the top of our list was an idea coming from the devious mind of Man Chong. I forgot the exact composition, but he gave a list of herbs and roots to acquire, which Pei Yuanshao took a week to gather. Then, on the next meal, our thief was to drop the mixture inside the porridge.

To be honest, I think the left-wing students should have known something was off when they formed the line to serve themselves, with none of us trying to overstep. We still filled our bowls and pretended to eat, and I saw many curious gazes from our enemies. But they only understood the truth when it was too late. I believe it was Xu Chu who first rushed to the latrines. Within a couple of minutes, they were fighting for the hole in the ground, clutching their bellies with pain, and, of course, not all of them made it in time. I don't think I ever laughed so hard in my life. Many of us were rolling on the floor, tears pearling out of our eyes as we fought to regain control of our delirium.

We went hungry for the rest of the day, and Cao Ren was so furious that he canceled the class, but it was worth it. At least this is what we thought then.

Then the *brush incident* happened.

It all started rather quietly. My brush vanished as I went for a service of dry millet, something we had switched to after the porridge incident. This was not such a big deal, and I was already on my third brush at this point. We had a stash of five spare brushes at all times. Either those we stole ourselves or some we bought through Pei Yuanshao. Man Chong kept them on himself, and nowhere was safer than there, for everyone feared him. So I did not pay much attention to the missing item.

I had a sick feeling in my stomach as I went back to the stable that evening. Its origin, I understood, was the lack of attention we of the right-wing had suffered that day. The most worrisome moment of a battle is the silence preceding the chaos, and this is where I stood. My lack of experience prevented me from realizing all of this, but I went to sleep with a gnawing sense of anxiety.

The first sign that something terrible had happened came as I stepped into the classroom the next morning. I could sense eyes on me and even heard a few snickers accompanying me to my usual spot. It took me a couple of seconds to recognize the brush on my desk, but it was without a doubt the stolen one from the day before. Something was different about it though. Its bottom had a different color than before, as if it had been used to stir some soup. As I picked it up, I also realized that it smelled terrible and had a sticky feeling to it.

The snickers rose higher, and following the Cao boys' stare, I noticed Zhou Cang entering the building. That's when I understood what had happened. He was walking strangely, as if each step hurt, his eyes closing with pain. Du Yuan and Pei Yuanshao surrounded him, and the latter was supporting our friend by the elbow. If that wasn't enough, the care with which he sat down on his mat made it plain.

The grip of a burning anger tightened around my bowels. I felt its heat all the way to the tip of my fingers. They had not just hurt him; they had completely shamed my friend and had used my brush to do so. The message was clear: *we won't hurt you, but we will hurt your friends because of you.* If eyes could kill, Cao Ang would have dropped dead. I became oblivious to everything else around me. All that existed was the boy grinning at my friend's pain, and for the first time since Uncle Cheng's death, I wished to kill someone. I slammed my hand down, startling poor Sima Yi next to me. Whatever was to happen next, I did not plan, but Zhou Cang did not let me finish.

"Chun!" he called. His smile cooled me down with a great sense of shame. He shook his head as if to tell me that everything was all right, but I knew him well enough by then. He was full of sorrow. And if *he* could swallow it, why shouldn't I? I sat down, but I promised him in my heart that this would not go unpunished.

When we left that evening, Du Yuan gave him his coat to tie around his waist, for the bottom part of Zhou Cang's robes had turned red. I meant to support him as we walked back to Cao Cao's mansion, but he gently rejected my help. I insisted, saying that there was no shame in accepting some help from a friend. That is when Zhou Cang finally broke. It came all of a sudden. One second he was faking his genial smile, the next, his tears ran free. I did not know how to react, so I grabbed him by the shoulders and meant to pull him against me, but he pushed me back violently.

"That's all your fault, you know," he said. "Before you came, they were mean, but it didn't go any further. But you couldn't just learn your place; you had to fight the bullies."

"What am I supposed to do?" I asked, feeling vexed by his just rebuke. "Let them treat us like dirt?"

"We are not Yellow Turbans anymore!" he replied. "There is injustice in the world, and we can't fight it. So why don't you accept who you are and leave us alone?"

"But we fight to protect each other," I replied weakly.

"We do?" he asked, his face a mask of agony at this point. "Where were you then when they shoved your brush up my ass again and again while laughing? Did you protect me then? No, because you don't live with those monsters, I do. And I've been here longer than you." With each sentence, he poked his finger against my chest, making me take as many steps back. It hurt more than a blade would have because he was absolutely right, and he wasn't done. "And let me tell you one more thing, *Golden Eagle,* you might be in the good graces of your beloved master, but he is not a good man. He gave *you* a choice, but he simply took us. It was either that or death. You know what? My parents' blood was still fresh on the ground of Yingchuan when he put me inside a cart for this cursed city. So screw you for making my life even worse than it was already. Screw you, Chun!"

I thought he was going to punch me then, but instead he just sighed and turned his fists to open hands. Zhou Cang had been keeping so much inside, preserving us with a warm smile all those months, but I had failed to notice how much he suffered. I remembered then the sad-looking boy I had seen when I first visited Cao Cao's mansion. He probably did not know anyone observed him then, and that had been the real Zhou Cang.

One of my greatest regrets in life was not apologizing then. Zhou Cang had been the first to greet me with friendliness in Chenliu and had been nothing short of a brother since. While I had focused on my vendetta with the left-wing, he had suffered in silence, especially when I could not defend him. But I was also hurt by his words, for no better reason than he was right, and that my ego had grown wide. So I acted like a brat and walked away to my evening's chores.

The next day, Zhou Cang was gone.

I did not doubt Pei Yuanshao and Du Yuan had assisted him in his escape, though they never confirmed it. And once outside the city's walls, Zhou Cang would never be found. The story went that he had been taken by Cao Cao in the first place because he had managed to outrun Xiahou Dun's horse over a long distance. Zhou Cang could run faster and longer than any of us, and he claimed to be a superb swimmer as well. So by the time his absence was noticed, I'm sure he was already beyond the hills and the rivers.

I was among the first to enter the school's courtyard that day, determined to apologize to my friend, and with a sense of anxiety I waited for Zhou Cang to enter the building, but he did not, of course. When Du Yuan and Pei Yuanshao came in without the third member of their trio, I knew in my heart he was gone. I turned just in time to see the eyes of the Cao boys avoiding mine while they chuckled and snickered like the snakes they were. And this time, my friend was not there to stop me. I don't think he could have.

Before I knew it, I was jumping over the desks, the soiled brush in my fist. I passed Xu Chu before he noticed me, kicked Cao Anmin with my knee, and landed flat on top of Cao Ang, bringing the full weight of my wrath down with my fist. The room erupted at once. There was no planning, no low blows or vicious tactics. We had finally boiled over.

Cao Ang's head banged against his desk after I pummeled my knuckles into his face. Blood splattered from his nose, but I did not let it stop me. My fist came down once more. Xu Chu caught me from under the arms, but I head-butted him with the back of my head and heard him fall on his ass. Yue Jin was on him next, a flurry of small fists raining on the giant. It was chaos. Even Man Chong, who usually favored more sophisticated methods, took part in the brawl, using his bowl to hammer a helpless Cao Shuo.

Ang shook his head, but I did not let him regain much of his senses. Pinning him down with my legs, I raised my hand, ready to strike him with the brush this time. I shook with rage. I braced myself, looking at the artery pumping blood with haste along his throat. This is where I aimed. I brought the brush down with a great roar, which ended in my mouth as a fist landed against the side of my head.

I did not lose consciousness, but it was just as if I had. Nothing made sense for a while. Blurry images came and went as someone dragged me through the building, then left me on the ground of the courtyard. I heard the clunk of the metal hoop locked around my ankle and knew I was now tied to one of the three poles. A voice rang, echoing in my head like a dozen more. I thought I recognized my lord but told myself it could not be so, for today was not his class.

It was indeed Cao Cao, and I was about to witness the scope of his anger. To say that he was furious would not even begin to cover it. His face was distorted with rage as he shouted for my comrades to step outside. While they did and formed a line facing the three poles, I realized Cao

Ang was next to me, equally tied, drying blood all over his face screaming for murder. The father and the son looked very much alike at that moment.

"Remove your shoes!" Cao Cao shouted, the first words that sounded clear to me. The students obeyed. Then they knelt, exposing the bottom of their feet behind them. I knew what was going to happen next. Xiahou Dun, and of course it had to be him, walked through the ranks of kneeling boys with his infamous cane in hand and flogged a pair of feet randomly. The sounds came in pitiful squeals followed by whimpers, and all the while, Cao Cao reminded us of the shame we had brought on ourselves and him as well. The side of my head was killing me, but not as much as his words. I dared not look anyone in the eyes, but when I saw Xiahou Dun stepping behind young Sima Yi, I could not stop myself.

"Not him!" I yelled. "He's done nothing." I don't know why I said so. Sima Yi had indeed done nothing, but he was not my concern at this instant.

"But you did!" Cao Cao barked, stepping in front of me and pulling me by the back hair so that I had to watch. He nodded to his cousin, and Xiahou Dun whipped the poor boy, who already looked terrified. I'm sure that bastard struck harder than usual. Cao Cao did not let me go until the whole sixty-something students received their punishment. "You made me do this," he whispered in my ear before he let go of my hair.

"Today," he said to all of us, "because of your stupidity, I lost a precious student. I put great faith in Zhou Cang's future, but he is now gone." I don't think Cao Cao cared much about my friend. Zhou Cang failed to impress most teachers, and besides his strong legs and some aptitude in combat, he had little to offer our lord, but Cao Cao had a point to make. "And just as I was coming to inform you of his decision to leave, this is what I found, animals! Beasts fighting like barbarians in the very place where their future is made. I gave you everything!" He slammed his hand against my pole as he said the last, and it was like his words vibrated all the way to my sorry mind. "This is the greatest chance of your life, and you spit on it. For what? Because you are born from different backgrounds? No! You fought because you were badly led. Chun, look at me!"

I lifted my gaze to meet his, and he appeared undulating through the water accumulating in my eyes.

"You wanted to become a soldier, correct?"

"Yes, my lord," I replied.

"You still intend to be one?"

"Yes, my lord."

"And a leader of men?" he asked, forcing me to pause for the briefest of moments.

"Yes, my lord."

"And in the army, what is the punishment for an officer inciting a riot?" he asked. I actually had no clue on the question, for we had yet to study the law, either civil or marshal. But I took a guess.

"Death, my lord," I replied, looking down again. I was answered by the sound of his sword leaving its scabbard, then felt the cold steel gently falling over my neck.

"Liao Chun here led some of you against the others. The punishment is death. Should I apply it?" I did not look up and focused all my energy on keeping my tears from dropping. Zhou Cang's warning came back to my mind. Was Cao Cao truly a villain? Was he going to execute a child for acting like one? I did not believe so, but I was mad with fear and wondered if my life was approaching its end.

My friends, and many of the others, all said no, though they sounded more pleading than anything else. His sword slid over my neck, and Cao Cao moved toward his son.

"What of Cao Ang? He acted the same way. Should I execute him?"

"Father!" Ang said.

"Do not let your feelings for me affect you," he told the students, ignoring his son. "I told you you were all the same to me here. I have other sons and will have more." As far as I knew, he had only one other son, but the rumor claimed that his new favorite was pregnant, though that was beyond the point then. "Do I execute him?" he asked again.

The same answer came from the children. Now that I had cooled down, even I did not want Ang's death.

"So, what do I do?" Cao Cao asked, removing his blade from his son's neck. "Ang? Chun?"

"Spare us, Father," Ang said through his sobs. "We will behave, I promise!"

I was sorely tempted to say the same, but I found his attitude so pitiful that it actually helped me regain my wits. Pleading would get us nowhere, neither would empty promises. But acting like true leaders of men might, I thought. So I gambled.

I dropped on my hands as if kowtowing and stretched my neck ahead, even going as far as working on the collar of my shirt to expose more of the skin.

"Liao Chun?" Cao Cao asked.

"I have failed you, but my comrades only followed my lead," I said. "Punish me any way you want. The military law is clear. Officers bear the responsibility in this situation." Again, I knew of no such things, but I got a sense of the army's logic, and I was right.

I could feel Cao Cao's unease. I had put him on the spot. And he could not just punish me and not his son, not if he wanted to keep our respect. But someone else was already a step ahead.

"My lord," Man Chong said, raising his hand, "if I may." Cao Cao allowed him, pointing his unsheathed sword at him. "Officers of the past have been allowed to escape punishment against future services. Maybe Cao Ang and Liao Chun can receive the same treatment. I suggest you postpone their execution until they redeem themselves in your service."

The blade found the scabbard right away.

"*That* is an idea worthy of my students," Cao Cao said, to which Man Chong bowed with his arms extended. "Cao Ang, Liao Chun, you are sentenced to death. Your sentence will be postponed to a future time until you prove yourselves in my eyes or until you commit another crime. Should you incur my wrath again, no amount of support will save you; you have my words."

"Thank you, my lord!" we both said as our foreheads touched the ground.

I don't know who was the most relieved, Ang, me, or Cao Cao, but the three of us breathed better from that point. The tension also dissipated a little from the crowd of students, and several of them sighed.

"But I cannot just let you go free after the events of the day. So, you will both remain chained here for three days, with no food and one cup of water a day. No one is to help you unless they want to face the same punishment. Am I understood?"

We understood. And thus started three days of torment.

The classes for the next three days all happened inside the building, and it could not have been easy for my friends. But no matter what they thought about listening to our most educated teachers, it was nothing compared to what Ang and I went through.

He got sick on the first night, and since we were then in the coldest part of winter, it was a miracle that I lasted until the second before bouts of coughing took me.

I was determined not to speak to Cao Ang, at first. But hours turned interminable, especially after we were left to ourselves in the late afternoon. So, sometime during the second evening, I started wondering how I could break the ice without sounding as if I had lost. I probably thought about it for the best part of a *shi*, until the sun was already down behind the wall on our backs, though at this time of the year, it happens quite early. And I still got nothing.

Thankfully, Cao Ang did.

"All of that for a cake," he said. His gaze remained straight. It was so like him to put the blame on something or someone else.

"Which you stole," I replied, cursing myself for not accepting this truce offer.

A heavy silence fell back on us, the price of my stubbornness. Ang did not let it settle for too long.

"I guess we did some terrible things," he went on. At least we were going somewhere. He now included himself in the misdeeds.

"We did," I replied, which was as much as I was willing to say in order to meet him halfway.

"Should we apologize?" he asked.

"You first," I answered. He had been the first to strike by stealing the tea cake and blaming me, so he was to apologize first, as I explained. He did not, but I could see he had more to say.

"You think your life was hard because you are poor," he said. Not a question. I don't think there are many things that could have angered me more than what he had just said, but he went on before I could curse him. "I know it can't have been easy, but if you think my life is simple because I was born the son of Cao Cao, you're dead wrong. At least the wife of your father did not poison your mother. Is yours alive?"

I told him she wasn't and that I did not remember her, which gave us something in common. I refrained from saying that most fathers did not have a concubine.

It might have been because he opened up about his mother or that we shared something, but suddenly Cao Ang could not stop talking. And while at first, I could not believe he actually threw me his privileges in the face, the more it went, the more I wanted to understand him.

He might have been born in comfort, but from a very young age, his family had put him under an amazing amount of pressure. Being the firstborn could not have been easy. He was taught to sit and listen before he could even run and speak. By the age of six, he was supposed to recite the *Chunqiu*, simply because Cao Cao had been able to, and since he could not, he was given more tutoring. Even noble-born kids want to play, but Cao Ang grew up without the feeling of the sun on his skin, while his cousins and neighbors were playing *cuju* in the courtyard. And all this pressure and hundreds of hours being schooled could amount to nothing as soon as his father pupped a son from his wife. If by some miracle it never happened, Cao Ang could still be replaced if deemed unworthy, something which happened quite often among the powerful clans. Once a first son was removed from the list of potential heirs, his life was measured in days. The prospect of a family feud overshadows the affection of a father for his son. And seeing where we sat at this moment, I could see why he felt a little anxious.

"And I *hate* poetry," he went on, another point we shared.

I gave it to him; while he finished his days sleeping on a mat, warmed up by a cozy blanket and a full belly, I never had to worry about my own father ordering my death or about poison removing a threat within the family.

Since he had told me more about himself, I shared a bit of my life, focusing on the toughest moments. Then, because I was far from forgiving him for Zhou Cang, I told him about the boy he had hurt the most.

"I am sorry about your friend," he said once I was done, looking sorry.

"I'm sorry for the horse manure," I replied, which was a lie but made for a nice gesture.

"I must admit, you ride well," Ang said.

"And your poetry is good, I think," I said. "Especially for someone who hates it so much."

We got out of things to apologize or congratulate for pretty quickly, but we had moved in the right direction. I started shivering and felt the uncomfortable feeling of a coming cold in my throat. Cao Ang was already past that and blew his nose in his sleeves every few minutes.

"I must admit," he said again after a chuckle, disturbing the silence once more. "The porridge idea was brilliant."

"All right. I'm sorry for that as well," I said.

"Don't be. The face Xu Chu made when he realized the way his bowels moved was priceless. Sure, I soiled myself, but I don't think I ever saw something as funny as those big eyes turning white with confusion."

"And did you see how Hare-lip held his ass with both hands while he waited his turn at the latrine?" I asked. Ang burst with laughter at the memory. Hare-lip's name was Meng, but we only called him by his nickname, so I did not remember his given name.

I had never heard Ang genuinely laughing before, and I must admit he had an infectious laugh. Before we knew it, we were revisiting every detail of the porridge incident, then some of the other tales from the past months. The moon was high in the cloudless sky when our laughter died, and we finally got some light, interrupted sleep.

Cao Ang and I would never become best friends, but our enmity died that evening, and with it, the conflict between the two wings. We kept calling each other according to the side of the classroom we had picked, but only because we had become used to it and were proud of our distinction.

Sure, there would be many occasions to rekindle the conflict, but it remained within the bounds of a sane competitive spirit.

While our little drama shook Chenliu's Cao's district, the rest of the empire did not simply rest. There was a never-ending number of rebellions to put out all over the Great Han land. Or at least this is what the general-in-chief claimed. The emperor's brother-in-law should have relinquished his title from the moment the rebellion of the Yellow Turbans met its end, but every bit of riot was an excuse for him to keep a tight grip over the army. Of course, it also meant the situation in the capital was close to a full-scale riot. Soon enough, the government split into two sides. The followers of the *butcher* on one side, many of them being young men with ambition, while the others followed the faction of the Ten Eunuchs, who not only had the ear of the emperor but were also protected by He Jin's sister, the empress. I think she was the only reason the capital did not go up in flames right away. And in all of this, no one seemed to care about Emperor Ling, who by all accounts was content enough to indulge himself in debauchery while the people went poorer and hungry.

I say that the capital did not go up in flames, but it actually did, or part of it at least. The imperial palace suffered a great arson, and as usual, when this kind of thing happens, an extra tax was levied on the common folks, and I guess a few thousand were sent to the capital for forced labor. The stupidity of the government of the time still amazes me. We just got out of the greatest rebellion of our history, and the first thing the people in power did was to take more money from the common folks just to repair their fancy palace.

The year that just passed also saw one of the worst plagues in memory. We were miraculously spared in Chenliu, and Cao Cao claimed it was all because he made us wash our hands regularly. Of course, we thought he was joking, but now I am not so sure.

All those signs were hard to miss, and I constantly remembered what Lord Cao had told me back in his tent of command in Julu. The world as we knew it was ending. We just had no idea how chaotic the passage to the next one would be.

CHAPTER ELEVEN

Chenliu, Chenliu commandery,
3rd year of Zhongping era (187), Han Dynasty

Not everything changed as radically as my behavior toward Cao Ang. In fact, for nearly six months, Cao Cao remained closed off to me. He did not treat me any different from the other students, but neither did he show me the attention I used to benefit from before. I would lie if I said it did not hurt, for I respected him above any other man, but I also knew he had other things on his mind than the worshiping of a nine-year-old boy.

Among the many worries that kept his life difficult was his lack of an official title. Cao Cao had distinguished himself during the Yellow Turban uprising, and later as well in Ji'nan, but nothing came of it. The great flaw of my lord was his obvious ambition. You knew, from the second you met the man, that he would rise as high as the world let him and then even further. But the government did not give him the opportunity. And while he remained in Chenliu, fuming over the stupidity of those above, another man soared. Sun Jian, the Tiger, became the hero of the Han government. He was absolutely everywhere. At one time, he helped put down a rebellion in Liang, all the way in the northwest; then you heard how he quelled another in southern Changsha commandery a month after taking office there.

While the man claimed to be Sun Zi's descendant, in reality, he was a nobody. His father was probably a rich merchant from the southeast, and everything Jian got, he owed to himself. He was brilliant in war, and since his birth did not offer him much, he was also not a threat to anyone in the capital. Cao Cao could not say the same.

As such, the Tiger soared while my lord bided his time.

Cao Cao proved difficult to approach, but then came a moment when I had no choice, as his mare gave birth to her foal. He had insisted on being there when it happened, and when the time came, it came faster than Xin Ping had anticipated. I was sent running to my lord's mansion, where Cao Cao had just extinguished his lamp for the night. Since there was no time to play it quiet and apologetic, I woke a servant and sent her to her master.

Ten minutes later, we were rushing toward the stable, or what Cao Cao would call rushing.

Moon Shadow gave birth to a foal as black as the night, with only two white socks on her rear legs. Xin Ping claimed the foal would become a fast runner, and Cao Cao could not be happier, especially since his mare behaved well after the birth.

It was an exciting moment, which left me panting as if I had helped Moon Shadow myself. In all the elation, I only noticed my lord's hand on my shoulder when he removed it.

"What do you think, Chun? Will she be a great warhorse?" Cao Cao asked; the first time in six months he addressed me.

"I'm certain she will, but I know little about young horses," I replied.

"You will have to," he went on. "Because you will train her. Under Xin Ping's supervision, of course."

I thanked him, going as far as bowing. He said there was no need for that, but in my mind, there was every reason to. Not so much for giving me an extra task, but simply for including me back into his world.

He called the horse Shadow Runner, and she would become the most amazing mare.

Not much happened for the rest of the year. We fell into a comfortable routine, with our ten-day weeks following each other astonishingly fast. Just like government officials, we had two days off every week. The students of the left-wing used those days however they wanted, but for us, if we wanted to keep up with our educated comrades, we had to spend them studying. Man Chong, Sima Yi, and sometimes Cao Ang organized extra sessions for those of us with the greatest difficulties. And, of course, I was kept busy with my chores at the stable, plus the training of young Shadow Runner, though at first, it was more mothering work than actual training.

We also practiced with weapons more often from that summer onward. Cao Ren had trained us with the crossbow for several classes over the last year, and I was confident enough in its use by then, but I ached to swing a blade. I later regretted my eagerness. Not so much because of the weapons, but because of our instructor. Xiahou En was actually a member of Cao Cao's father's staff, but my lord had called him specifically for our training, and it must be said that he was highly skilled with both the *jian* and the *dao* sword. He was also the only man I knew who approached Xiahou Dun in terms of viciousness. Every strike was not only taught to us, but carved into our skin by his expert hands. By the time he was done with us, we all wished him dead, even his family members, but at least we could all use a sword without hurting ourselves. Of course, we were never truly done learning swordplay, but Cao Cao probably saw the impact En was having on us and asked Cao Ren to resume our training.

We also learned new topics, such as the geography of the Great Han land, some basics of law and administration, and some very complicated, hard-to-digest engineering classes. Our teacher was Cao Cao's chief engineer, a man lacking any sense of pedagogy, to the point that I did not even retain his name. It sounded so simple to him, but for almost all of us, it was as if he spoke a foreign language. Raising an elevated platform for a siege or undermining the integrity of walls with tunnels looks like easy enough tasks, but once you listened to a professional, you realized how much thought had to be put into every little detail. The type of ground, the proper angle, the humidity level at the beginning of a project, the expected rain, all those factors, and so much more were to be considered. The only one who seemed to follow this weird man's speech was my partner, Sima Yi, who looked as if drinking the man's knowledge.

I much preferred geography. Within a few months, I could recite the names of every important city, county, and all the commanderies of the empire, as well as the greatest rivers, mountains, and passes.

Maps came easily, at least reading them. Some of my fellow students showed a capacity for drawing them, but I was not as skilled in that practice.

The next year proved a lot more eventful, not only for me but for all of us in Chenliu.

The first notable event was the departure of Zhong Yao, our calligraphy teacher, who was called to the capital and given the rank of magistrate of some county. I can't say we missed him much, but since no one replaced him, we were to practice by ourselves.

He wasn't the only one to leave Lord Cao's service. In fact, the more it went, the fewer guards seemed to roam the district. By that time, we were allowed to leave the compound, as long as we remained within the limits of the city, which sounded fantastic at first, until we realized the best part of Chenliu was the one we lived in. I first assumed that the decreasing number of armed men came from Cao Cao's increasing trust in us. We were, after all, not making as much of a mess. But I soon theorized that his lack of official position probably took a toll on Lord Cao's revenues, and, as such, he had to let go of some guards. He kept a semblance of training for his militia one month a year, but that was it. Another reason why I believe my lord became more conscious of his expenditures is that we switched from paper to wood in our classes.

On a personal level, two amazing events happened during the third year of the Zhongping era.

To begin with, it was the year when I first fell in love.

It was a few days after the beginning of spring, which means I was slightly over ten years old and found myself inside Lord Cao's mansion for one of those extra classes organized by Cao Ang. If I were to guess, I would say he needed to get back into his father's good graces for some reason and had offered to school us on poetry. We arranged four small desks in a square and quickly got some ink ready. I was pleased that Cao Ang had managed for us to use paper, and from their faces, both Yue Jin and Cao Anmin felt the same.

We were halfway through the afternoon, and I was struggling with an impossible verse when *she* stepped inside our makeshift study room and into my world. Lady Bian, Cao Cao's concubine. The rumor that she had been pregnant was just that, a rumor, which is probably why Lady Ding had not gotten her assassinated. It would have been a shame, for the world would then have lost its most beautiful creation.

Lady Bian was in her late twenties, but looked as ageless as the jade adorning her wrist. She had kept the beauty of the flower while already showing the sweetness of the fruit. Her eyes batted like the wings of a butterfly, with long eyelashes covering an impish yet adorable gaze. No wonder Cao Cao had fallen head over heels for her.

"Would these young poets like some fruit?" she asked, a voice like silk.

"Yes," I replied before I realized it. Cao Ang should have been the one to accept the offer. "Sorry, yes, my lady," I said, forcing my voice to gain a lower, more masculine tone.

She smiled. She knew how I felt. Just like her lover, Lady Bian could read you like an open book.

"I'm sorry," I told Cao Ang the second she left. "I shouldn't have spoken."

"It's all right," Ang replied. "I can see your etiquette got overpowered by something else." I hated his smirk then, but not as much as the way the two others snickered. Despite myself, I felt my cheeks turning red and hot.

"Don't tease him," Anmin said. "Lady Bian could make a eunuch grow back its member." We laughed as prepubescent boys do at this kind of joke. "I am myself fond of thinking about her in my most intimate moments, if you know what I mean," he went on.

"We don't need to know that," Yue Jin said as he started grinding some ink. I actually did not know what he meant but chose not to ask. "Is it true, though?" our short friend asked. "Is she really what they say she is?"

Cao Ang shushed him with a finger on his lips, then slightly bent over to talk more privately. We copied him so that he could whisper.

"Yes," he said. "She was a singer when Father found her."

Now it was Yue Jin's turn to blush, though I did not understand why. Sure, powerful men never married for love, but she wasn't his wife, only his concubine. Surely a man like Cao Cao could name whoever he wanted as one. And a singer would make a fine companion.

"Does she sing well?" I asked, which got a chorus of mocking laughter.

"You should ask her to show you *how well she sings*," Cao Amin replied a few seconds before Lady Bian returned. Upon hearing her footsteps, my heartbeat increased its tempo, and I found it impossible not to look from where she would arrive.

She came to us carrying a platter of fruit, which showed she had not been raised in this environment. Another lady would have made a servant do it. Instead, she dropped the platter on top of Ang's desk and sat between us to cut some of the fruit. I didn't even know it was possible to sit so elegantly. A light breeze blew her scent into my nose, and I thought I was going to drown in it.

"My lady," I asked before I could think on it and stop myself, "do you sing well?" I asked. The three other boys snickered and hid behind their sleeves. Yue Jin especially could barely control himself. I must have turned as red as the apple she currently peeled. Lady Bian threw the three others a glance containing reproach and amusement in equal part.

"Would you like me to sing for you?" she asked. I nodded, and Cao Ang almost fell backward with laughter. She gently slapped him on the wrist, but there was no violence whatsoever in her gesture.

She sang, and it was like time froze, or I wished it did at least.

Lady Bian had a voice as pure as the clearest lake, soft like the smoothest silk, and if I had not been completely under her charm already, her singing would have put me right into it.

The song she chose was one of love. I don't remember the lyrics, for they mattered little. All that did was her presence in my world, the vibration of her voice, and the glances she granted me. The song ended, too fast, just as she finished peeling a piece of apple, which she then handed me. I remembered to breathe and blink then.

"Was my singing to your liking?" she asked.

Speechless, I nodded, or I think I did. Frankly, I don't remember how I reacted, but it made her chuckle.

"Well, enjoy the rest of the day, my young poets," she said as she stood up.

The silence after she left was most curious. I think we all fell a bit in love with her that day.

"She can sing," Yue Jin said, agreeing with himself with a nod.

"Yeah," Cao Anmin went on. "I will think about her again tonight."

Yue Jin punched him as hard as he could in the shoulder. If I had known what he had meant, there is no telling what I would have done.

Needless to say, I made myself a frequent visitor to Cao Cao's domain after that day and accepted every invitation from Cao Ang to study poetry. I don't think I got any better in this art though. And to my great disappointment, I did not see Lady Bian for a long time, for she was soon pregnant, for real this time.

Cao Cao fathered another son, a healthy boy named Cao Pi. And my lord had learned from his experience with Cao Ang's mother, for he moved his concubine to another domain in the town, with her own guards and cooks.

I was summoned to Lady Bian's estate shortly after Cao Pi's birth, and I must admit my mind was reeling with the idea of being in her presence. I knew how birth worked and had become accustomed to the process with horses, just as

I knew women were not supposed to go outside their houses for one month after, during which they are not allowed to bathe. So I did not expect much and kept telling myself that whatever she looked like, this would not be the real Lady Bian.

In the end, I did not see her but met with my lord in what passed for a hall in this smaller mansion. He had moved his desk and sitting mat over there, as well as the perpetual hill of documents he had to go through.

"Come here, Chun," he said without looking over a scroll of bamboo slips.

"My lord," I said as I reached his level, "I didn't know I was to meet you here."

"So you came expecting to meet someone else?" he asked, keeping his stone face for a second before letting the mask peel away.

"Not really," I lied. "I did not question my order and simply came where I was expected."

"Well put," he said.

"How is the lady?" I asked before hurrying to add, "And the baby?"

"They are fine," Cao Cao answered with joy. "Cao Pi already opens his eyes. Can you believe that?"

I told him it was the sign of a great destiny, though I knew nothing of the sort. It was uncommon for noblemen to care about their babies. Too many of them died early on, and it was not before they turned two or three that fathers really paid attention to their progeny. But Cao Cao, as usual, was different. You could even say he was the opposite. He loved observing his sons and daughters in their baby and toddler years. But when they started running around and asking questions, he willingly left them to their tutors.

"I have your first assignment," he then said out of the blue.

This was the second great event in my life that year. I had become a messenger for Lord Cao Cao.

My natural talent in horse riding, coupled with my newfound skills in geography, made me an obvious candidate for the post. It had been a month since Cao Cao had informed me I would carry his missives in the commandery or even further in case of emergency. And for a month, I had impatiently expected to be called on such a mission. I had not been out of Chenliu for over two and a half years, and the call of the wild could not have been stronger.

"Where to?" I asked, standing straight as a flagpole.

"To a good friend of mine," he answered.

I was to meet with Qiao Xuan, a name I had heard before but could not remember why. I was also disappointed because the man lived in the next county, a day by horse, at most.

Cao Cao hadn't been riding Moon Shadow recently, despite his many trips to Luoyang, and could not yet mount Shadow Runner. As such, he offered me to use his mare. This was a great honor, and since she was used to me, I had no issue with the idea.

This is how I left the city of Chenliu for the first time in over two years and headed straight for Qiao Xuan's estate. I left early in the morning, taking only what I needed to eat on the way, a few coins for a night at the postal station if needed, and a scroll of wooden slips.

The weather was fair, the sun bright, and both Moon Shadow and I enjoyed this long-awaited freedom. I did not tarry, but I did not press the mare too hard either. She needed a bit of getting used to the road after so many months of semi-captivity, but once she broke a sweat, she was just as fresh as I had first seen her.

With the help of a few locals, finding Qiao Xuan proved easy enough.

The man was a former minister with a list of past titles long as a day without water, yet he lived in a very simple house of earth. When I jumped from the mare, an old man came out of the door and was soon followed by two adorable girls of two or three years old. It was early evening, and I imagined the old man must have been slightly worried by the sound of a horse approaching. When he saw I was just a child, he seemed to relax and waved the girls away.

"I am here with a message for master Qiao Xuan," I said, giving a respectful bow.

"You found him, young man," he replied.

Qiao Xuan was easily in his seventies, with a venerable white beard reaching down to his sternum and a face so riddled with wrinkles it reminded me of the bottom of my *Yeye*'s feet. But his smile was young and fresh.

On the way to his abode, I remembered where I had heard his name. He was famous in Chenliu for having foretold the kind of man Cao Cao would become while still in his teens. This old man was supposedly a great judge of character, and people came from far and wide to ask his impression of young men. Should he praise them, those men could then spread the word and gain some favor from local officials. When Cao Cao first met him, Qiao Xuan said that he would be *"a good servant in times of peace, a ruthless hero in times of chaos."* I don't think he ever knew how right he had been then.

I handed him the scroll and watched him work the string keeping it rolled. The two little girls came back to the door, looking with a curious expression at this older child who had been riding a big horse. They were full of life, those two, with similar pairs of bubbly eyes and just enough teeth to give a beaming smile. I could imagine their grandfather enjoyed their company as a source of youth. Qiao Xuan must have followed my gaze and understood what I was thinking.

"They are my daughters, you know," he said, a hint of reproach in his voice.

"They look lovely," I replied.

"They are," said Qiao Xuan as he read the first slip. "And they keep this old man's days full. Ah! That's Mengde all right." The last part he said as he reached the end of the message. Older people, especially those who had gained a high status, did not need to use another man's *zi*. That Qiao Xuan did was proof of the respect he gave my lord. "Do you know what this is?" he asked. "Your lord is inviting me to meet his son, which is a nice way to ask for me to grant the baby a nice future. Mengde does not believe I will live long enough to evaluate his son when he's old enough. Well, you tell him I'm feeling as full of life as a young stallion, and those are my proof," he said, bringing his two daughters to him.

"You won't come?" I asked, surprised that anyone would refuse my lord.

"Young man," he replied, "Mengde does not just want a few sentences about his son. He wants my input on the situation of the empire. If I know him, he must be pacing like a tiger in a cage, stuck as he is in his district." He was absolutely correct. "There was a time when I lived at the center of the Great Han. Look where it got me. I am poor; I have been abandoned by my friends, those who yet live at least, and would make a poor company to your lord. But we all have to pretend we are in a better situation than we actually are. So tell him my health is declining, and the journey would take too much out of me." As he said so, he faked a cough and we both chuckled. There was no anger or sadness in his voice. He simply stated the facts, but I felt sorry for him.

"The thing is," I said, veiling myself with a look of embarrassment, "this is my first mission for Lord Cao. If I fail, I think he'll just be done with me."

Qiao Xuan sighed. I had guessed right; he was a good man.

"You can tell Mengde that he is always welcome here. He can wait for his boy to be of age to travel if he wants. I'll still be here. If not, he can just ride by himself. I will always have some *baijiu* ready for him. As for you, young man, I can see from your horse that you rode all the way from Chenliu without taking a break. So let me give you a little something. Come here."

I thought he would hand me something to eat, or a few coins maybe, but as soon as I stepped close enough, he took my face between his hands. He peered through me; there is no other way to say it. My head moved with his wrists as he inspected my ears, my hair, and even the shape of my nostrils. The little girls laughed when he forced me to make a grimace by stretching the skin of my face. And he finished with a longer, slightly uncomfortable observation of my eyes. He did all of this with the light of a single lamp, and I wondered how accurate his reading could be. But when he clicked his tongue, I was more worried about what could have bothered him.

"What is it?" I asked.

"You have too much fire," he seriously said.

"Fire?" I asked.

"You know of the five elements, right?"

I did, of course. The five elements, the scholars claim, are the fundamentals of everything in the world. All, from the smallest ant to the sky above our head, are the subjects of the interaction between fire, water, earth, metal, and wood. This is the same for people and dynasties. To guarantee one's success, a certain balance between the five is necessary, but most human beings favor one element above the others by nature. This was as much as I knew and told him so.

"But you, my young friend, have no balance. I only see fire," Qiao Xuan.

"Is it bad?" I asked.

"Bad? No, none of the elements are bad, or good even. Fire is the greatest tool ever mastered by mankind. But in the wrong hands, it can kill. It depends on you to use your fire to keep your allies warm or to incinerate everything around you. From what I can see in you, you are capable of both. This is what I say of you, *a man with enough fire to lighten the path, or to burn it down.*"

With that, he stood straighter again, and somehow he looked more tired, as if checking me had taken the remaining of his energy for the day.

"Now go. Tell Mengde to come here if he wants. And keep my words for you. Do not tell your lord what I said about you, understood?" I told him I did, which was a bit of a bummer. And I was smart enough to listen to this advice. Years later, when I truly understood the meaning of his judgment, I also realized how bad it could have been for me if I had told Cao Cao about it.

I left this old man and his two little girls and made my way back home, only stopping for a couple of *shi* at the local postal station. Qiao Xuan had given me much to think about, especially with this fire story. In the end, I decided it was all utter dog fart, and he had only said so to make an impression on me. Even then, I found him to be an interesting character and hoped I would meet him again.

Sadly, he died less than a year later from an old disease.

Once in a while, I thought about those two little girls and if they were doing all right. If he ever inspected them as well, I wonder if he saw that his daughters would one day almost cause the death of Cao Cao.

CHAPTER TWELVE

Chenliu, Chenliu commandery,
4th year of Zhongping era (188), Han Dynasty

From the very beginning of the fourth year of the current era, we could feel a difference. I've already spoken about the silent tension building up before a battle; well, this was exactly how I would describe that year. The flow of news from the capital suddenly dried up to a trickle. We knew battles were taking place in faraway places such as Liang or near the Taihang mountain at the border of Julu, but the government's reaction was so swift that the issues seemed to get fixed in a matter of days.

The only topic that shook the conversations among Cao Cao's staff concerned the government's idea of appointing provincial governors. Up to now, the highest a local official could get was administrator of a commandery. The province units were left to the supervision of the inspectors, who held in reality very little authority, and whose job was simply to report to the court. But in that year, the government gave three men the title of governors, including a certain Liu Yan, who took command over the southwestern province of Yi.

About half of the officers in Chenliu supported the measure, claiming that it only made sense to put powerful men in charge of provinces, while others believed it would just stir the embers of chaos in a dry land.

Cao Cao seemed undisturbed by those talks, but he kept working without rest on some plan of his. I went on more and more missions as weeks went by, meaning that I missed more classes than anyone else. It wouldn't have been such a bad thing, if Cao Cao hadn't announced our first test for the end of the year.

I traveled to the four corners of Chenliu commandery, then to all major cities of Yan province. I even went once to Runan, a trip I managed to accomplish in seven days. Which not only got me the praise of Cao Cao, but an unexpected reward as well.

The day after I returned from Runan, Cao Cao was waiting for me by the stable. Shadow Runner was turning into a strong filly, though, to my regret, I had little to do with her training. I still gave her some time whenever I could during my days off, but those available times became scarce.

"Chun," Cao Cao greeted me, excusing himself from a conversation with the horse master. "I thought you would never come," he said.

"Sorry, sir, you gave me the day. I didn't know I was expected," I replied, baffled.

"I was joking," Cao Cao said, giving me one of his signature smirks. "I would sleep for three nights if I rode to Runan and back in seven days, but I had the feeling you might show up here."

"Anything I can do for you, my lord?" I asked.

"This time, I am the one with something for you," he said, holding a rolled-up piece of paper between two fingers. My curiosity piqued right away. Cao Cao usually handed me messages, not waving them like a bone before a dog.

"What is it?" I asked.

"An old promise being fulfilled," he said. "Or partially, at least."

As soon as he said so, I remembered the bearded warrior, and it was like I was back in the ravine, witnessing the death of Uncle Cheng. My anger resurfaced as if it had never left.

Cao Cao had found the trace of my uncle's killer, or rather he had obtained a name, Liu Bei. There had been four officers in that ravine. The only official one had been Zou Jing, but it was no secret, even then, that another actually led the militia. The only time I saw him was when he interfered to prevent his subordinate from beating Dong Zhuo, the second and most vicious general during my time in the cage.

The three officers, including the bearded warrior, had left the camp soon after, and I had never heard of them since. But now I had a name.

Liu Bei, according to Cao Cao's letter, had been appointed magistrate in a county of Pingyuan commandery, just north and east of here. But a few months back, he had been driven off by bandits and had since vanished. No one knew of his whereabouts, and there was no mention of any champion in the message, but I knew in my heart that my enemy lived and waited for me to change that.

"Sorry, Chun, that is all I have," Cao Cao said.

"I have a name, my lord. You have my thanks," I replied. It wasn't much, but it was a start.

"I will keep my eyes open for this Liu Bei," Cao Cao went on, shaking the letter with conviction. "You just keep serving me well, and one day you will have your revenge."

"Understood!" I replied in my most soldier-like tone.

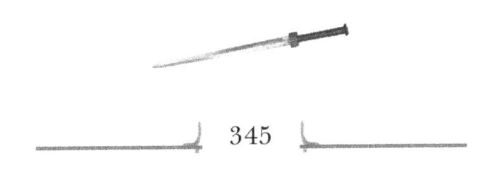

My motivation rose to new heights. I now had the faint trace of a path leading to my revenge, our first examination would be held in a few months, and Lady Bian had not only recovered from her pregnancy, but to my eyes she had gained in beauty, if that was even possible. I had just turned eleven, so my feelings for her changed a little to accommodate different needs, but I was just as deeply in love as before. My friends were teasing me to no end on the topic, and I am certain as one can be that Lord Cao knew how I felt about his favorite concubine.

He was not threatened by it, of course, and even though I grew faster from that year, I was far from being capable of seducing a woman, let alone a beauty such as Lady Bian.

Some of the other boys, especially those with a few more years, were changing in more obvious ways. Xu Chu not only kept growing, but also seemed to get stronger by the day. His roundish face became more angular, and his big, fleshy arms reshaped with young, supple muscles. One year later, he would leave the school program to be trained as a bodyguard, but for now he was something of a legend among us, capable of defeating even the likes of Xiahou Yuan in wrestling.

Yue Jin did not seem capable of growing taller, but his stringy arms and legs filled with meat as well, and since he was a natural fighter with no fear, he became our greatest combatant. Even more surprising, he managed to get his temper under control and sometimes looked like a quiet lake when he sat by himself. Cao Cao's interest in him grew strong from that point.

To my great sadness, one of our students left Chenliu in the early days of summer. Sensing the rising tension in the capital and surrounding commanderies, Sima Yi's father called him back to their hometown. He was still a child and had not overcome his fear of our lord, but he was my friend, and we had been paired up for almost three years. So when we said our farewells, I was touched to see him shed a few tears. I would not hear about him for a very, very long time.

With the natural departures that had taken place over the years, I believe around fifty-five students remained.

The dynamic of the district also changed rather drastically at the time of Sima Yi's departure. Cao Cao, along with his secretary Chen Gong and several officers and teachers, left for Luoyang and did not return for the next three months. Over the last year, I'd say my lord had spent half of his time in the capital, though he still managed to come back regularly enough. This time, however, was different. Something was going to happen, and I could feel it was the result of months and years of planning. It was as if all the messages I had carried in Yan province and further had been delivered for a single purpose, and this purpose was about to be revealed.

Because of the absence of Lord Cao, along with so many of our teachers, the summer of that year became something of a semi-vacation for us. We were supposed to be tested in the autumn, exactly three years after school started, but since I had no message to carry, very few horses to take care of, and at best two or three classes a week, I enjoyed some freedom. Best of all, Xiahou Dun had accompanied his cousin to the capital, and Cao Ren remained behind this time.

Every day we expected news from Luoyang, or the return of our lord, but since it did not happen, we kept ourselves busy. The older boys seemed to make some regular visits to the other parts of Chenliu, but I preferred to remain in the district. When I managed some time away, I used it to train Shadow Runner, and with all this available time on my hand, I could finally give her the attention she deserved. Cao Cao had taken her mother with him for once, meaning that she was excited whenever I came to her stall.

She was still a bit young to be mounted, but since I was not a grown man yet, Xin Ping declared

I could get her used to a rider already. This was the first time I tried to break a horse to ride, and it proved both frustrating and exhilarating. Shadow Runner was stubborn, but so was I.

To keep her safe, physically and mentally, I could only get on her back for two days in a row before letting her be riderless for three. I think it took about a month of this routine before she seemed to accept me, and that was without a saddle or bridle, so I was covered in bruises by the time the month ended.

The next month, I moved on to saddle her, which she took well enough. However, she absolutely hated the bit and kept fussing over the bridle. Some horse trainers prefer to introduce the gears before mounting, and it certainly works as well, but I just enjoyed this process better.

When, after two months, she proved ready to be mounted for longer periods of time, Xin Ping told me we would have to wait for the next step of her training.

"Why?" I asked, vexed.

"Because if we go any further, she'll only accept you, you idiot," he answered, which made sense, but did not stop me from calling him an *old donkey*.

I had an idea on how to solve the problem of Cao Cao's absence, and I would lie if I said it wasn't born of some personal motivation.

The guards manning the entrance of Lady Bian's mansion eyed me suspiciously when I claimed to have some business with the lady. But they knew me well enough by then and let me pass. I wonder if they would have agreed three or four years later when I looked more like a man.

Lady Bian was holding her baby and singing to him in the garden when I stepped in. I let her finish her song before I approached her field of vision and judged the time right when the baby cooed happily.

"My lady," I called, far enough not to startle her.

"Isn't that the young poet?" she said. That she recognized me pleased me more than I can say. I didn't want her to see me as a poet, though.

"I can assure you I am everything but a poet," I said, trying hard to copy her lover's genial smirk.

"So my lord says," she replied, which made us both laugh. Not only had she remembered me, but she and Cao Cao had even talked about me. The knowledge filled me with joy. "How can I help you?" she asked.

"If it's not too much to ask, I would like to borrow some of Lord Cao's clothes," I said. She shot me a confused look, and I blushed when I realized how odd my request could sound. I blabbered an explanation about the filly I was training and how I meant to get her used to Lord Cao's scent.

"That is very thoughtful of you," she said as she stood up. Her belly was rounder than I remembered, and sure enough, she was halfway through her second pregnancy. "Wait here," she then asked, handing me her baby before she went back inside her mansion.

Cao Pi was about to turn one, I believe, and he was a very energetic child already. He could not yet walk, but he had a cleverness in his eyes that never left him. As I said, I am not great with children, but I played with the young son of my lord while the woman I loved went to fetch some clothes. Had I known I was holding a future emperor, I would probably have shown more deference and stopped making faces.

He was laughing when Lady Bian returned, a folded jacket in her arms.

"Would that do?" she asked as she unfolded it and held it for my inspection. I had seen my lord wear it above his robes several times in the early spring, and it was indeed perfect. The sleeves were not too long, and it did not reach too low, meaning that I could wear it despite being shorter than Cao Cao. I had not considered I would wear his clothes at first, simply that I would let the horse smell them, and I realized once again how strange my request must have sounded.

"It will work perfectly," I said as she folded it back and put it on the granite bench I had been sitting on before she returned. "Thank you, my lady."

"Pi-*er* likes you," she said as she took her son from my arm. Her nails grazed my wrist, and I shivered with pleasure. "You must come back to play with him."

I promised I would and held onto that promise a couple of times, though never for Cao Pi's sake.

I felt rather silly when I stepped into Shadow Runner's stall, wearing an unwashed jacket belonging to my lord, and I prayed very hard that no one saw me. The young horse seemed confused, but since she could still smell me, she accepted my presence.

By the time Cao Cao came back, right after *Qiufen*, the autumn equinox, I was already on his second jacket, the first one having lost any trace of his scent, and Shadow Runner was as ready as I could get her.

I was thrilled at the idea of showing him how much she had improved and was determined to stop him from the moment he dismounted, but Cao Cao proved even more excited than I was and had dismounted before the stable in order to rush to his concubine with some great news.

My lord had finally received a nomination.

Lady Ding must have been furious that her husband neglected her when he returned to Chenliu, but I think nothing negative could touch him.

This was the closest I had seen Cao Cao from euphoria, and that was the following day. He had summoned all the students for an impromptu class in the morning to share the good news, and it was nothing short of a miracle that we all showed up on time.

I can still see him clapping his hands with delight as we sat expectantly. Our good fortune depended on his, so as you can guess, we hung on each word coming from his mouth. And Cao Cao had every right to be gleeful.

For over four years now, He Jin had retained the rank of general-in-chief, refusing to relinquish his authority even when there was little for him to do in his post. This made the emperor nervous, and that was understandable. For the past hundred years, almost every emperor had to contend for power with their brothers-in-law, who had risen because of them. It had created unnecessary conflicts in the capital and diverted the government from more urgent matters, and some blamed those conflicts as the source of the misfortune presently striking the Great Han land.

YELLOW SKY REVOLT

To restore some balance and regain the upper hand, the emperor, or more likely the head of the Ten Eunuchs, ordered the creation of a new army in charge of the defense of the capital. For some reason I could not understand, he named this corps *The Army of the Western Garden*. Far from imposing fear, we found it unnecessarily flowery. One could imagine how a battle between the Army of the Western Garden and that of the Rapid Tigers or the Feathered Forest would turn.

Nevertheless, this new army was a big deal. There was now a new professional force, which responded first to the emperor and not to the general-in-chief. Eight men received the rank of colonel, each in charge of a regiment in this corps. Their leader was the head of the Ten Eunuchs, Jian Shuo, and if all of us claimed that one of these creatures had nothing to do with leading an army, we all agreed it actually paired well with the name of this division.

Cao Cao ranked fourth among those eight men. His childhood friend, Yuan Shao, ranked second, and this in itself showed the difference in power between them. While Cao Cao had based his life on his grandfather's fortune, the Yuan family of Runan had produced so many excellencies and ministers over the two Han dynasties that you could fill a mansion with their amassed fortune.

Whatever the case, Cao Cao could not be prouder, and I can only assume how much of this army came from his great mind.

There was only one drawback from this nomination; at least as far as I was concerned, he would have to move to Luoyang. The Army of the Western Garden had one role—to defend the capital—so all its colonels had to be present. It also meant that the men filling its ranks would be chosen from there, and Cao Cao could only join Luoyang with a limited followership.

Since he was to return to Luoyang as soon as possible, he advanced the date of our examination to two days from his announcement. Just enough time for us to despair and for him to prepare its contents.

I won't go into the details of the whole affair, but it turned out to be a huge bummer. Since there were not enough examiners, and not enough time to get ready on both sides of the test, it felt like a rushed event. Two-thirds of the examination were spent on the morning classes, with little time given to the more martial and practical matters.

It is with no shame that I ended up at the bottom of the first tier in the written and spoken tests, while I ranked second in the others. Yue Jin had dominated the martial tests, and Xu Chu came right behind me. If not for a hastened cavalry test, I would probably have been lower than that.

Man Chong came first for the morning class examinations, and I often wondered what would have happened if Sima Yi had stayed in Chenliu.

But more than those, I had to recognize with mixed feelings the results of Cao Ang, who ended up fourth on both examinations. It might not sound so amazing, but it put him right on top of the general grading system. Cao Cao obviously prided himself on his son's success, for he put him at the first table by his side during the following feast.

Our examination was overshadowed by our lord's nomination during this event, but Cao Cao favored us with several toasts. All the officers, teachers, and important personalities of the city came to the feast, as well as all the students. Cao Cao had organized the feast inside the unoccupied palace of Chenliu, though how he got an authorization, or even if he did get one, I do not know.

Five by five, we came to congratulate our lord on his new title and emptied a cup of wine in his honor. When my turn came, he returned the favor and looked me in the eye as he did, probably remembering what had happened the last time we shared a drink. I did not drink yet but had tried the beverage often enough that I did not puke this time.

I got drunk for the first time in my life, though not the last, far from it. I did not just drink but also ate until I thought I would burst. There was so much meat, so many dishes I had never tried, and even a few I did not know existed. This is how I pictured the feasts in the emperor's court.

I do not know how it came to happen, but I spent the night in Brown Wing's stall and woke up with my first hangover. I could not have been the only one in Chenliu, and it took the better part of two days to get a semblance of activity in the Cao district.

Then, four days after the feast, Cao Cao left again. And not just him, but seemingly everyone who mattered in Chenliu. I didn't even have time to show him his young horse. To be honest, I felt a little abandoned.

This turned out to be the dullest of winters, with so few classes that even I missed Cao Cao's poetry teaching.

To my great surprise, my friends, with the help of Lady Bian, prepared a birthday dinner in the lady's mansion, and that's as much fun as I had in those long, boring months. The lady sang for me, which was the best present I could ever ask for.

Then, halfway through spring, just as I thought the boredom would never stop, came news none of us expected.

Emperor Ling died in his thirty-third year, which effectively put an end to Lord Cao's dreams of grandeur.

CHAPTER THIRTEEN

Chenliu, Chenliu commandery,
5th year of Zhongping era (189)—
1st year of Chuping era (190), Han Dynasty

Emperor Ling died during the fourth month of the year, and all I can say is that as emperor, he made a mess of everything, including his succession. Two sons survived the emperor. The first was Liu Bian, the son of the empress, Lady He, sister of the general-in-chief, He Jin. He was also one year older than me. While Liu Bian should have been the obvious heir, his father had not favored him and found him lacking. So, many people believed his second son, Liu Xie, son of a consort who died shortly after his birth, poisoned by a jealous empress, would be named heir. This eerily reminded me of Cao Ang's story, with the exception that the young boy was raised by his grandmother, Empress Dowager Dong. Liu Xie had a fine reputation all the way to Chenliu, and many people who had never even been to Luoyang rooted for him. The latter also happened to be supported by the Ten Eunuchs and the rest of their factions, if for no better reason than he was eight and could be controlled for a longer period.

Neither of them was the official heir when Emperor Ling died, and the men of the court did as they always do; they bathed the capital in blood.

It started with a trap set by Jian Shuo, the leader of the eunuchs and of the Western Garden Army, intending to lure He Jin to his death. With He Jin gone, the eunuchs would have had free rein over the succession, and Liu Xie would have become the next emperor. This was without counting on Yuan Shao being a two-faced son of a bitch.

Yuan Shao was playing both sides of the conflict, and seeing how things unfolded years later between him and Lord Cao, I wonder how much my lord actually knew of his old friend's duplicity.

While being the second in command of the Western Garden Army, Yuan Shao also plotted more secretly with He Jin and leaked the plan of his murder. The Butcher got Jian Shuo arrested and executed, then made Yuan Shao his Director of Retainers. And since no one seemed to care about the Army of the Western Garden anymore, he was also the de facto leader of this division.

He Jin placed his nephew on the throne, and he himself became the regent in a duo with Yuan Wei, the imperial Grand Tutor, who so happened to be Yuan Shao's uncle. It should have stopped there, and for a couple of months, we thought the thunder had passed, with no more raindrops than Jian Shuo's death. As far as the Han dynasty was concerned, it was the closest thing to a peaceful transition we could expect.

But there too, one has to be amazed by the sheer absurdity of those in power. Jian Shuo was not enough, and He Jin felt threatened in his every move. The eunuchs had to go if he wanted his power over the young emperor to become permanent. Some claimed he was once again pressed on by his close advisor, Yuan Sho, but I never found out the truth about this, and in the end, it did not matter. In a great act of profound stupidity, the general-in-chief summoned all the great warlords from the empire he could think of to join him in a fearful attack on the eunuchs. I can't imagine what pushed him to act as such. Without a doubt, the eunuchs had amassed a great number of supporters, along with their soldiers, but this should have been nothing compared to the might of the general-in-chief—there was no need for extra armies.

And in a last blunder, He Jin accepted a parley with his sister, the empress, who had acted as a buffer between the general and the eunuchs for years now. Except that his sister had never invited him and the whole thing proved to be a trap from the eunuchs, who seized He Jin, killed him, and sent his head to Yuan Shao as a warning not to bring the army inside the walls of Luoyang.

What they did not know was how close the first warlords were to the capital. Yuan Shao did know, and he would be damned if he let any of those ambitious lords steal his opportunity. All Yuan Shao had to do was to punish the eunuchs and support the young emperor, and in this swift move, he would become the most powerful man in the empire. By all accounts, Luoyang turned into a scene of a nightmare that night. The armies under the command of Yuan Shao stormed the city, looted the palace, executed anyone remotely looking like a eunuch, and burned down a few buildings.

And despite all the zeal with which they exacted their revenge for the dead general, they still managed to miss a few members of the eunuchs' faction, who escaped the city with the young emperor and his brother.

It was their great misfortune that led those last eunuchs on the path of a warlord answering the call of He Jin, and it was an even greater sign of their sordid fate that this warlord happened to be Dong

Zhuo, who had come all the way from the frontier with his army of former convicts and barbarians.

Dong Zhuo, may he rot in the afterlife, immediately understood the great chance that had fallen on his lap, for he came back triumphantly to the capital, restored peace, and placed the emperor back on the throne, for a grand total of three days. Dong Zhuo not only forced the empress to dismiss her own son, but soon had Liu Bian and the new empress dowager poisoned. He then put the little brother, Liu Xie, on the throne and bestowed on himself the title of chancellor.

One of the men I hated the most was now holding power over the Great Han land, and not only abused his power at every turn, but just did not seem to care about his image of a tyrant. This was his great strength. While most men are slowed down by their honor and the desire to leave a polished legacy behind them, Dong Zhuo just took as much as he could, and that made him ruthless, dangerous, and unpredictable.

This all happened within six months of Emperor Ling's death, and not one day passed in Chenliu without a new rumor from the capital. At one time we heard Cao Cao had been killed in the palace's massacre, then that he had not only survived but was standing right by Yuan Shao's side as they exterminated the Ten Eunuchs. Every few weeks came a delegation informing us of the name of a new era, to the point that we soon started betting on the name of the next.

We joked about it, but all of us were feeling the tension rising by the day. We were holding our breath, expecting the next rumor involving blood and death, praying that it wouldn't be our lord's.

But when the new *Chuping* era was declared with the following spring, matters seemed to calm down a little. Cao Cao sent letters to his wife once in a while, and his staff came back to Chenliu one by one until it was just him and Chen Gong, his secretary and our teacher of battle tactics, facing the farce Dong Zhuo was turning the court into.

A month after the latest change of era, we received an imperial missive in Chenliu claiming that Cao Cao had been given the title of Colonel of Resolute Cavalry from the hand of the chancellor. The empire was still in turmoil, but we thought Chenliu would resume its peaceful life now that its leader once again had an official rank.

We could not have been more wrong, for the next day, Cao Cao rushed into the district, accompanied by Chen Gong, both of them covered in blood.

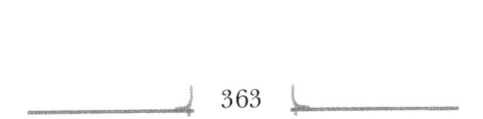

YELLOW SKY REVOLT

I heard many stories about the escape of Cao Cao from Luoyang and his journey back to Chenliu.

Some ludicrous tales claimed that Cao Cao had attempted to assassinate Dong Zhuo himself, using a legendary blade given to him by the Excellency Wang Yun. The attempt failed, and Cao Cao pretended to give the knife to Dong Zhuo, which gave him just enough time to flee the capital before the chancellor found out the truth and sent his troops after my lord.

Another story, clearly aimed at hurting Lord Cao's image, told how he sought refuge in the domain of a certain Lü Boshe, an old friend of his father. Boshe would have been like an uncle to Cao Cao, and welcomed my lord, despite knowing of the danger such an act represented. Leaving Cao Cao and Chen Gong to rest, Boshe went to buy some wine while his people prepared a feast for their honored guests. Cao Cao would have woken up to the sound of blades being sharpened, and thinking that he had been betrayed, killed all the servants and family members in the domain with the help of Chen Gong. When they realized their mistake, the ground was more red than brown. This tale went as far as claiming that Cao Cao met Boshe as they fled and killed the old man to avoid any mortal feud in the future. When interrogated by Chen Gong on the reason for this murder, my lord is said to have replied, "I would rather betray the world than let the world betray me."

If you ask me, all of those stories are utter horse shit.

For a start, no matter how highly I think of the man, I do not believe Cao Cao was capable of assassinating someone by himself. The risks were just higher than any potential reward.

As for Lü Boshe, I had never even heard the name before, and Chen Gong might have been a master strategist, but he was as capable with a sword as I am with a loom.

I do, however, suspect that Cao Cao spread the latter part about him betraying the world. This was poetical enough to sound like him, and it also sent a message about anyone who might consider doing him wrong.

What I can say with confidence, though, is that they both arrived in Chenliu looking as if they hadn't slept in days, their clothes drenched in dry blood and their horses beyond the point of exhaustion. Sadly, this was the last time Moon Shadow would ever be ridden. She came home lame, and Xin Ping immediately declared her days roaming the land to be over.

"I hope she is ready," Cao Cao told me, nodding toward Shadow Runner.

"She's ready," I replied. And ready she was. Even Xin Ping had declared her to be one of the finest steeds he'd ever seen. "What's happening?" I asked, a feeling of panic setting inside of me at the sight of the gory image they presented. They moved well, so I assumed none of the blood was theirs.

"You'll know soon enough," Cao Cao said without looking at me. His gaze wavered left and right as if he was trying to find something, maybe his wits. "Get everyone you can think of from the district and tell them to come to my hall in half a *shi*."

"Yes, my lord," I replied, bowing.

"I'll see you there," Chen Gong told our lord as he stretched his back and was about to leave.

"Don't wash," Cao Cao said, to which Chen Gong replied he was too tired for that, anyway.

I ran through the district, yelling at anyone I could spot to gather in Lord Cao's estate and to spread the word as well. Then, when I ran out of houses to visit, I rushed to the red district of the town and to the only "singers" house I could spot. Sure enough, a few of my comrades and some staff members of Lord Cao were inside, despite it being only late morning.

I kicked myself in the butt for not having first come here because I now had to run back to Cao Cao's mansion if I wanted to be on time. It also meant that the establishment lost half its current patrons, who scurried away from the buildings like mice from a granary, many of them readjusting their garments while running.

Breathless, I reached Lord Cao's gates on time to spot Xiahou Yuan and Xiahou Dun a few steps ahead.

"Do you know what's happening, sirs?" I asked as I caught up with the two cousins.

"You tell us," Xiahou Yuan said. "You're the one who's been running around yelling at us to come here."

"It better be important," Xiahou Dun said, sounding threatening, but only because his cousin was present. I had stopped fearing the man a year ago. Sometime during my twelfth year, I understood that my master was no match for me if it came to a fight. Of course, if I raised my hand against him, I would lose my head, but the simple knowledge of my superiority was enough to extinguish the last traces of fear he used to inspire in me.

"I think it is," I replied, which did not satisfy any of them, but the sight of our lord, standing at the end of his hall in the same state as when I had left him, convinced them.

They pushed through the crowd amassing itself at the entrance and inside the hall, then spoke to Lord Cao before he gestured for them to be quiet. I could not hear what they said because I remained at the entrance, where most of the students stood.

I had never seen so many people in this place before, and it overflowed with anxious-looking fellows. So much so that the latest arrivals had to watch our lord from the windows.

"Silence!" Xiahou Yuan bellowed from the bottom of his barrel-shaped chest. It got very quiet, very fast. I was just telling Pei Yuanshao all I knew, which was very little, but like everyone else, my attention went to the end of the hall, where Lord Cao stood, arms raised for our attention, Chen Gong standing by his side.

"*Xiongdimen*," Cao Cao said, and I immediately knew this would be a peculiar speech. Lord Cao rarely used words like *brothers* or *friends* to address us. That he now called us *brothers*, even though half of his staff was older than him, showed the importance of his coming words. "I thank you for joining me so fast. This is a terrible day, and I need you now more than ever. As you can see from the looks Master Chen and I share, we almost did not make it back to Chenliu. Do not worry about us; we fought for our lives dearly and came out unscathed, if only terrified by the state our beloved empire has fallen into."

There was a tremor in the audience following those last words. As the officers and staff members returned to Chenliu over the previous months, we heard amazing stories about the capital. You could not call what Dong Zhuo practiced corruption, for corruption requires a certain discretion, while the Chancellor couldn't care less what it looked like. What happened there was extortion. And this was just the top of the pile of horrendous actions taken by Dong Zhuo. Murders, rape, and public thievery were conducted daily by his officers and soldiers. No one was protected, and if anyone tried to leave, they would be arrested, dragged back to Luoyang, and executed. As far as we knew, only Cao Cao and Yuan Shao before him had managed to regain their provinces.

"I will tell you all you need to know about Luoyang and what this… pig is doing there," Cao Cao said. I have to give it to him; he was acting perfectly. I had spent enough time with my lord to know when he was faking it, but even I wondered for a second how much of his ire was real. That he used a word like "pig" tipped me off. Even at the height of his anger, he would have found something more poetical to call Dong Zhuo.

"But first, I need to apologize to you all," he went on. The global murmur rippled loud enough that Xiahou Yuan had to silence us again. "I have to apologize for two reasons. First, less than a week ago, I was offered a title by the murderer of our young emperor. A cheap, meaningless title of colonel with no substance and even fewer responsibilities, but a title nonetheless. Had I accepted, all of you would be protected from his wrath, and your lives would be simple in Chenliu. But while I wish to protect you, I could not accept placing myself under the thumb of a traitor like Dong Zhuo." Lord Cao spat at the mention of the chancellor's name, and it was a nice touch. Cao Cao simply never spat.

"As you probably know by now, the empire has been raped by this greedy bastard from the north. Everything sacred, every temple, every palace, minister, and imperial tomb has been soiled by his vicious presence. And I am not even talking about the imperial harem, which became his private chamber. The law has been forfeited, and not a day goes by that good men pay the price of his perfidy. Even dogs refuse to walk in the streets of Luoyang, afraid to meet one of Dong Zhuo's men."

This was a grim picture my lord put in our head, and I wished he had been exaggerating, but from what we heard from people living in Luoyang at the time, it was the whole truth.

"So I beg your forgiveness for not being strong enough to endure this madness. When the choice was given to me to join the ranks of those dynasty killers, I refused and left the capital, along with my brave secretary, Chen Gong. My brothers! Do you forgive me?"

The response was nothing short of an uproar. What could you possibly reply to that speech? We did not only forgive Lord Cao but thanked him for his noble actions. He played us like a flute.

"My life is worthless if not bound by honor, and yours do not matter against the preservation of the empire. I am now a rebel to the court. But do not misunderstand my actions; I only rebelled against the traitor and will fight to bring the Great Han under the rule of its true leader. But none of you asked for this. So, if any of you wishes to go, I allow it and there will be no rebuke. There is no dishonor in avoiding a conflict with the most powerful man in the world." But there was, and because he had mentioned it, no one would be coward enough to accept his offer. He gave us a minute of silence, just enough time to let the doubts of a few men be killed by the stares of his neighbors.

"Then I need to give you a second apology," Cao Cao went on. "We all knew the day would come for the Han dynasty to face a challenge of this sort. It was just a matter of time before an opportunist came to grab the dragon by its tail. And I meant to prepare you for such a time so that once again we would rise to the cries of help of the emperor. However, it came sooner than I had anticipated, and we are not ready yet." I know he was talking about us students, and I thought he was being unfair, for I believed us to be ready for war. This was just the teenager in me thinking, for of course, we were not ready.

"And while I had wished to share in the glory of our victory over evil with all of you, many will stay in Chenliu."

"Silence!" Xiahou Yuan called again, which was not enough to calm the uproar. All of us wanted to be part of Lord Cao's plans. To think that we would be left behind after years of training was unbearable.

"I understand your frustration, and this is why I ask for your forgiveness again." I think this time his apology was sincere. Not that Cao Cao cared much about our frustration, but just like he expected the best from us at all times, he did the same for himself. And he had failed to plan for the current events accurately. Though how one could be expected to foresee the death of a young emperor, I do not know.

"Know that more conflicts will require your brave swords and sharp minds. This, if I am not mistaken, is only the beginning. Many ambitious men will rise to steal a piece of the Great Han for themselves, and they will need to be put down before the four-hundred-year-old Han dynasty meets its end. And do not mistake me!" he shouted, just as he produced a square of silk from behind his back and held it high for us to see. It was a golden square, stained with characters of red ink, as far as I could see. "We will cover ourselves in glory, in the emperor's name, for we have been chosen by Emperor Xian himself to gather the lords and kill the traitor. Not a day before we left Luoyang, the young emperor wrote this edict with his own blood and, with great peril, passed it down to me. I will not let him down. Will you?"

The ground shook with our answer. Cao Cao put the fire of war in our bellies, and each of us pictured himself as a savior of the Han dynasty. We dreamed of stabbing Dong Zhuo for the pain he had inflicted on our young emperor, his dead brother, and all the concubines of the harem.

Not all of us would join our lord, but he nevertheless used our assistance. Those who could write copied the edict, and those who could ride were sent to dispatch the copies, meaning that I did both. Some of the students and staff members were sent to gather men from their counties and villages while I rode through Chenliu commandery to pass the word that war was at our doorsteps and the empire needed our help. Though I offered to bring the messages to the great lords of the other provinces, Cao Cao dispatched other men, claiming that he needed me in Chenliu when he left for war. I misunderstood his meaning, thinking that I would sit the war out. But Cao Cao had other plans. I would be one of the three students to accompany him.

Cao Cao made me his personal aide, a great honor. In this role, I was to follow him like his shadow and answer all his requests, which sounded awfully vague. But he gave me one more specific order.

"Protect Cao Ang at all costs," he ordered when he summoned me for my nomination. Cao Ang was coming with us as well. He was almost fourteen and would need the experience if he ever was to become a man worthy of respect. Cao Cao could not spare men to guard him, and when the battles happened, we were to remain at the rear. But if that failed, Cao Cao ordered me to pull Cao Ang out and ride to safety. I was a bit vexed, and said I would prefer to fight, but Cao Cao told me I wasn't to use my blade.

"If I see blood on your sword," he said, "I will kick you out of my army. Is that clear?" he asked, and since Cao Cao looked tired beyond words then, I just accepted and only pointed out that I did not have a sword. He fixed this issue by giving me a full set of light armor, a leather cap helmet, and a *dao* sword. While back in those days, the *jian* sword was more popular, I had always preferred its one-edged, more solid counterpart. Being a horse rider first, the *dao* is just more practical. I wasn't supposed to fight, so I did not receive a shield, not even the light *gourang* hook shield I was just learning to appreciate.

It is a mark of Cao Cao's legendary swiftness that only two weeks after he came back, almost three thousand men answered his call. They were far from a professional army and reminded me of the Golden Eagle division, but they were eager to join our lord. Soldier Guo Wen was among them, and he was the one who came to find me while I assisted Cao Cao with one of the hundreds of tasks required of a war leader before going on a campaign. Soldier Guo made a show of not recognizing me, saying that he was looking for a runt reaching about his nipple's height. He had gained a few gray hairs in his beard, but otherwise looked just as healthy and energetic as when I last saw him, more than five years ago.

A week later, we received a missive informing us that seventeen lords were marching in answer to the imperial edict and were to gather at Suanzao, in Chenliu commandery.

CHAPTER FOURTEEN

Zitong county, Yi province
12th month, 4th year of the Jingyuan era
of the Cao Wei empire (263)

"What about the blood?" Chen Shou asks as he finally puts down his brush. As usual, he takes his right wrist in his left hand and proceeds to massage it. To be honest, I am glad he seems to have forgiven me. Not that I care about his impression of me, but writing is a painful task at my age, and I much prefer the young one to take care of recording my story.

"The blood?" I ask.

"On Cao Cao and Chen Gong's clothes. You didn't say where it came from."

"Ah, that! It's actually a question I asked Cao Cao while on the way to Suanzao." We'd been on the road for a couple of days at this point, and with an untrained, rusty army as was ours, it required Lord Cao to ride back and forth between the vanguard and the rear to make sure everything advanced properly. When I asked him, we were looking down at a small group of soldiers busy pushing a cart out of a pothole.

"What did he answer?" Chen Shou asks.

"He said it came from the goat they had killed on the road to Chenliu, he and Chen Gong."

"A goat?" he asks, understandably baffled.

"I guess they stole it from some farm, and since neither of them had ever butchered an animal before, they made a mess of it and the blood splattered all over them. They probably nicked an artery or something."

"I'm sure they could have bought some ready meat," Chen Shou says, and it takes me a couple of seconds to realize what he meant.

"They didn't mean to eat it," I say. "Though I hope they did. Damn of a waste otherwise." Chen Shou still does not understand. It's fine; he's never met Cao Cao and cannot grasp the way my former lord thought. Many people died for the same reason.

"They used the blood for the edict," I tell him.

"The edict was a fake?" he asks, making a face worthy of Xu Chu when he ate that porridge.

"Of course it was a fake! Everyone knew it was a fake! Do you truly imagine an eight-year-old boy cutting himself so that he could write an edict and have it passed on to some obscure court member?" I don't mean to speak ill of Liu Xie; he was a great young man, but not *that* great.

Chen Shou slumps on his mat just as our wagon hits a bump. It's like I killed a bit of his childhood with this revelation. I will never understand those scholars.

"But you did meet up with the Loyal Rebel Lords, didn't you?" he asks, hanging on to another bit of his fantasy.

"Oh yes, we did, though we didn't call them that then."

"What did you call them?" he asks, picking up his brush again in order to note my answer. He is going to be disappointed.

"The Seventeen Pompous Fart-Breathers," I tell him before roaring with laughter. They were eighteen lords, but we did not count Cao Cao in this particular tally. I can see Chen Shou does not find it amusing. But, again, he wasn't there. "All right, we did call them the *Loyal Rebels,* but only because they came up with the name and forced us to use it. The name was actually the first item on their agenda, and even that took the better part of a day. That should tell you how well we thought of this association of *lords.*"

"But that's when you met with Lord Liu Bei again?" he goes on.

"Yes, and that's when I saw Guan Yu, my nemesis, for the first time in six years, and all my hatred resurfaced once again."

YELLOW SKY REVOLT

Suanzao, Chenliu commandery,
2nd month, 1st year of Chuping era (190),
Han Dynasty

I do not wish to belittle those seventeen eminent men too harshly. They were probably brilliant in their own domains, just not war. Each and every one of the eighteen lords came with a retinue of lesser commanders on top of their troops, and among the eighteen, with a little under five thousand men, Cao Cao was the least powerful one. Since he had been among the highest ranked colonels of the Western Garden Army, and since he had started this whole affair, Cao Cao was tolerated among the inner circle, but it was a close call.

Once the question of the name of this alliance was settled, they spent another couple of *shi* giving each other some fancy titles. Cao Cao became General Who Displays Firmness, a title he couldn't give a pig's ear about. Yuan Shao was chosen as the leader of the alliance, and since his troop had the greatest numbers of men, and he also had been the most vocal opponent of Dong Zhuo from the beginning, no one argued the point except for his brother. Yuan Shao was the same age as Lord Cao, thirty-five years old, and could contend with him in terms of handsomeness. But while Cao Cao's appearance was accompanied by a raw, natural charisma, Yuan Shao's was vain and forced. He was nonetheless fairly impressive in his polished armor, and even though I, for one, remembered most of the current situation was of his making, I could also see why he was respected. His brother, or cousin, some said, was the opposite. Yuan Shu was just as vain as Yuan Shao, but with none of the results. He just gave me the feeling of a greedy toad, obviously jealous of his brother's luck. The universe can be cruel, and when their father passed his genes, he gave the better part to Shao. Yuan Shu was named General of the Rear, meaning that he was put in charge of the supplies.

The only warlord of renown among those people in Suanzao on the first day was the famous Sun Jian who had so infuriated my lord when he held no official title. And if I thought Yuan Shao impressive, Jian was in another league altogether.

He was not only tall and strong; he was simply genial. His arms and shoulders were muscular, marking him as a true veteran, while his eyes shone with a practical cleverness born of experience. Though he'd been invited by Yuan Shu, the lords gave him a spot within the inner circle, if only because his name would frighten Dong Zhuo the most. I don't think he received a title, but just like Cao Cao, it probably did not matter too much to him.

Not all the lords arrived on the first day, and since the first of many gatherings proved a boring affair, this is as much as I remember of it.

Cao Cao was not impressed, to say the least, and when he retired to his tent that evening, I could see the beginning of a strong headache drawing itself on his traits. He told me to let Xu Chu know he wouldn't be needed as his guard the next day, but I was to stay with him and to bring more wine.

An endless stream of soldiers poured into the plain over the next few days, each led by one of the eighteen.

Few of them left an impression on my young mind. I can name Kong Rong, but only because he was the descendant of Kong Zi, the man to whom we owe most of our culture, as well as some of my worst student memories.

I have to mention Zhang Miao as well. While not a war leader, he was a decent man, discreet and thoughtful. I spent many hours close to him because he and Lord Cao always sat next to each other. Zhang Miao was the administrator of Chenliu commandery, meaning that technically he was my lord's direct superior. In truth, they behaved like friends, and I do believe Cao Cao thought of him as such.

The last great lord to arrive was also the one I expected the most, for his reputation was fearsome, and his cavalry was said to be the most impressive of the empire. His name was Gongsun Zan, a warrior lord from You province in the northeast, whom our Wuhuan neighbors feared so much that few of them dared to cross the frontier under his jurisdiction. People called him Gongsun Zan of the White Horse, for he only accepted white horses into his cavalry. While it was a bit of an exaggeration, most of them were indeed white or light gray. They were also mounted by a mixture of Wuhuan and Xianbei riders rather than Han people. Gongsun Zan owed his reputation to the skills of those auxiliaries, and if I prided myself on being a great horse rider, seeing how *they* mounted their steeds put me back in my place. I would have many occasions to speak with people from those two tribes and learn more about their skills, but even then, I could see how formidable they were. Gongsun Zan, though, not so much. He was a pudgy man with an easily triggered temper, and though he rode well indeed, I think most of his victories came from his allies and from an eagerness for violent measures.

I did not see him much after he arrived because as soon as he joined the inner circle and received whatever dog fart title they had cooked up for his benefit, we learned that Dong Zhuo was meeting our challenge with his own forces.

This was the most significant difference between the two armies. While we had to deliberate about each tiny detail, especially when it came down to sharing responsibilities and rewards, Dong Zhuo was leading alone. Our numbers were at least twice his, but ours were non-professional soldiers for the most part, while he controlled an army of veterans from the frontiers, men with actual experience of war.

There were just too many soldiers for us to move at once, so the army of the Loyal Rebels was split into four groups, with the main one advancing toward Luoyang by the main road, where we knew Dong Zhuo would meet us.

On the first night of the march, my lord invited Sun Jian for dinner and asked me to attend the meal as his aide, and for the first time, I was tempted to refuse a direct order. He was about to ask me why I did not acknowledge the order, as was expected of me, then seemed to remember that Sun Jian was the man who had conquered Wan when my baby sister lived in it, meaning that her death was on his hands. I had received no news from Fat Ling and took it as a sign that he had never found her.

"I'll ask Cao Ang," Cao Cao said. He was not happy, I could see, but he probably understood why I did not feel like pouring wine for my sister's murderer.

"No," I said after swallowing a painful bit of saliva. "My general gave me an order. I'll see it done."

I pushed my hatred as deep inside my chest as I could until Sun Jian came inside the tent, and then it just vanished. The man had such a powerful charisma that midway through the meal, I smiled back when he gave me a wink.

Sun Jian and Cao Cao had fought together against the Yellow Turbans in Yingchuan and Runan, but from their behavior, I could see they had not shared much time together then. But with a bit of help from some hot wine, they became good friends and seemed to agree on many things, from the quality of the other lords in the coalition, to the future of the empire. Most of what was said in the second half of the evening could have gotten them in real trouble, but I think they understood each other and knew they had found a kindred spirit in one another.

Deep in the night, while I fought for my eyes to remain open, Sun Jian gave a loud yawn, bringing me back to the moment.

"You remind me of someone," he said, and it took me a second to understand he was talking to me.

"Lord?" I asked, not sure what else I was supposed to say.

"How old are you?" Sun Jian asked. Despite being in his early thirties, his voice sounded like those old men who smoke too much. A good voice for a lord of war.

"Thirteen," I answered.

"My son is fourteen," he said, adding, "I guess that's who you remind me of. He, too, has a lot of fire in his eyes."

"My firstborn is about to be fourteen as well," Cao Cao intervened. "I hope they can meet in the future."

"It's settled then," Sun Jian said, just as he stood up. "When all this sad business with Dong Zhuo is over, let's arrange for our sons to become friends."

"And for their fathers to remain as much," Cao Cao said, copying Jian. Both picked up their half-empty cups of wine and extended their arm toward the other.

"*Qing!*" they said before downing the cups in one go.

As Sun Jian left, my lord's gaze did not leave the Tiger's back. He was looking past the moment, toward the future. Though whether Sun Jian was an ally or not in his vision, I cannot say.

It only took a couple of days for us to reach the army of Dong Zhuo, though *they* had marched at a professional speed and had taken hold of one of the most formidable passes protecting the capital: Hulao pass, the *tiger's trap*.

Even Cao Cao had not expected Dong Zhuo to move so fast. The chancellor himself wasn't at Hulao but had sent one of his three most fearsome officers, Hua Xiong.

On the first night, Sun Jian was ordered to storm the pass, and being the most junior of the lords, he had no choice but to obey. It was a massacre. Hulao was well-defended, well-provisioned, and the soldiers occupying it had fought for years in this kind of defensive environment. Sun Jian lost one of his four officers, a young man named Zu Mao, who by all accounts behaved bravely but was put down by Hua Xiong himself when the attackers fled. This had indeed become the Tiger's trap.

Seeing that our most fearsome general had lost, Yuan Shao called for an assembly to decide on the next step. Half of the eighteen were present at Hulao, with Yuan Shu remaining in Suanzao and the others having gone north and south to try other routes. We could not just forget Hulao pass and join one of the other two groups, for that would put Hua Xiong's men behind us, and wherever we went, we would have to deal with one of the eight passes protecting the capital.

Our path had to go through the pass, and Hua Xiong had to die.

Fortunately for us, Hua Xiong was as eager to prove himself as we were to eliminate him. Just as the assembly of lords began in the morning, we received a challenge from the enemy commander for a duel. We could send any of our champions to face him, and to a warrior, there is no greater sound than an offer for one-on-one combat. We live by our reputation, and while it can take many years for a warrior to be noticed through countless pitched battles, a duel can change one's station in a matter of seconds.

Naturally, the assembly drowned under the uproar of officers willing to accept the challenge. For each lord, there were five to fifteen officers, plus their aides, some guards, and a few record keepers. The assembly included at least two hundred people, and as Cao Cao's aide, I stood behind my lord, not far from Yuan Shao, all the way at the front. From my point of view, they looked like children brawling.

A man named Yu She was chosen. I don't think he was the fiercest looking among them, but since he was Yuan Shu's man, put under the command of Yuan Shao, he was favored by our illustrious General of Chariots and Cavalry. Our leader served him some hot wine, as was customary, then sent him on his way to fight Hua Xiong.

From what I later heard about Yu She, he was a talented warrior who could fight just as well on foot as on horseback. This, however, did not help him much, and he was killed in two strikes.

Yuan Shao had barely resumed the talks of the day and so strongly believed in his champion's victory that he was bringing up the order through which the lords should pass through the gates of Hulao.

When the guards came to report the defeat of Yu She, no one dared to look the general in the eyes.

The challenge was extended once more. This time, fewer officers offered their swords, but still enough for Yuan Shao to choose from. He picked exactly the man I would have chosen. Pan Feng was his name, the main officer of a lesser lord among the eighteen. He looked like the perfect mix of an ox and a tiger, with enormous arms, even wider thighs, and a big, square head with no visible neck. I would have been scared out of my wits if I met a man like Pan Feng in battle. Even more fearsome than the man was his weapon, a great battle-ax. I rarely met fighters using axes in battle, and if it took all his physical strength to be able to do so, it is not surprising.

His lord, I think his name was Han Fu, served him the wine this time.

Pan Feng fought a few seconds longer than Yu She before being cut down as well, though I put it on his horse being obviously slower.

No officer presented himself when yet another challenge was issued.

In less than a day, Hua Xiong had killed three officers of the coalition, Zu Mao, Yu She, and the imposing Pan Feng. The latest defeat harmed our champions' will the most.

And while the crowd of officers vanished in front of my eyes, another stepped forward. He had not presented himself the first times, otherwise, I would have seen him. But now, he was alone at the center of the assembly, the bearded warrior.

He went down on one knee respectfully, giving a perfect salute to our leader.

"Though of no renown, I, Guan Yu, cavalry commander in the army of Liu Bei, accept Hua Xiong's challenge," he said, his voice as deep as a well. I could hear my heart beat against my chest, but not my thoughts, which seemed to collide in a turmoil of angry shouts.

"Who are you?" Yuan Shao asked with utter contempt as if the man had not just answered this very question.

"My lord," I whispered, which startled Cao Cao. He frowned as he turned to look at me, and he had every right to be mad at me for speaking at this moment. "That's him. That's the bearded warrior."

Cao Cao's frown vanished and his eyes scanned the warrior with more care.

This man was magnificent. His beard now reached down to his sternum, and the years since our last encounter had filled his shoulders and chest even more. There was no doubt it was him. His reddish face, his perfect eyebrows; it was just the same man as the one who had killed Uncle Cheng and so nearly ended my life as well. My hand went to the grip of my sword by itself.

"He's with me," said a voice from down the ranks of lords. Gongsun Zan stood up, which took a few efforts for a man with his paunch. Before he walked to join his champion, he waved at the two men behind to accompany him. The first was Liu Bei, the trio's leader, and the second was the young warrior who had defeated Deng Mao, though he did not look nearly as young. He now boasted a bushy, messy beard, making him look like a tiger or a bear, and his muscles had grown twice more than his comrades'.

"This man is the first oath brother of my comrade Liu Bei," Gongsun Zan went on, "who studied with me under the tutelage of Lu Zhi, and this is Zhang Fei, their third brother. For those who fought the Yellow Turbans, their names might be known to you. *They* kept the north safe from the rebels while you hid in your palaces. I might add that Liu Bei here is the descendant of Liu Sheng, son of Emperor Jing and first King of Zhongshan, so if any of you think his farts don't stink because of their ancestry, Liu Bei's smell like roses."

Frankly, Liu Bei did not impress. He was neither handsome nor ugly, neither strong nor weak-looking, and his clothes looked exactly what you'd expect from a neighbor in Fa Jia Po. And this claim of ancestry could not be less relevant. Emperor Jing had reigned over three hundred years ago. Even if this lineage was true, Liu Bei was as much a nobody as I was. We all thought so, him too. But even then, he was just so silent and dignified that you would think to be in the presence of a Buddhist monk.

"We can't send a nobody to fight an officer," said one of the lords, which was agreed by several others.

"Chun," Cao Cao whispered, looking over his shoulder. "Do you want him to fight Hua Xiong?"

In reality, what my lord had just asked me was if I wanted Hua Xiong to kill my nemesis. I was tempted, even though it meant I would not kill him myself. While the lords argued, I thought that such an occasion might never represent itself. It took me six years to meet this man again. Who knew if our futures would ever cross again? And since we were at war, he might very well die in the following days.

"It would still be because of you," my lord said, perfectly reading my line of thoughts. And he was right. This Guan Yu would never be allowed to fight as it was; this much was certain from the direction the argument was taking. But with my lord's help, he would become our champion. So, even though it was hardly the way I would have chosen, I would still kill him. Instead of a blade, I would just use Hua Xiong. I barely nodded when Cao Cao stood up.

"Lords!" he called, raising both his arms. Cao Cao, so far, had been more discreet than usual, so when he spoke, they listened. "Who among you would believe such a man is not yet an officer of our glorious army? Look at him; he stands as fierce looking as Li Guang himself."

Guan Yu rose on cue and saluted my lord, who made his way to him. They were about the same height, but somehow Cao Cao looked smaller.

"I will let none of my officers fight against Hua Xiong," Cao Cao then said. "Instead, I am willing to support this mighty Guan Yu to represent us. Are we in agreement?" When he asked this question, Cao Cao looked at me briefly, just long enough for me to nod in gratitude.

No one opposed Cao Cao, and my lord went as far as asking me to bring the wine for our new champion.

I filled a cup and walked toward Lord Cao, though my eyes were focused on Guan Yu, the bearded warrior who would die by my choice. When I gave the cup to my lord, Guan Yu gave me a curious glance, and I wondered if he could possibly remember me. It passed just as fast as it came, for my lord was now offering the wine to this warrior.

"Thank you," Guan Yu said, extending his hand. "But I will enjoy your generous gift when I return victorious."

He did not wait for my lord or anyone else to reply and made his way out of the assembly. Cao Cao handed me back the cup, along with a wink.

This time, Yuan Shao did not resume the conversation. We just waited. The most surprising, as far as I remember, was the calm with which Liu Bei patiently awaited his brother's return.

Our leader was getting out of nails to bite when an uproar shook our ranks, and for a second, I smiled, thinking that it marked the end of Guan Yu's life. But the roar sounded different than with Yu She and Pan Feng. It lasted longer, and I understood it was actually a cheer.

Guan Yu came back on his horse, from which he dropped skillfully. In his left hand, he carried his bloody crescent halberd, while in his right hung the head of Hua Xiong, an air of terror forever marking his traits.

Not a word was uttered in the assembly as Guan Yu dropped the head of the enemy's commander at the feet of Yuan Shao. Cao Cao took the cup from my hand and gave it back to our champion. My palms felt empty but still hot from the wine. This is how fast he had dealt with his opponent.

Guan Yu downed the cup, then handed it back to me.

"Thank you," he told me. He was not even shaking or sweating. You could not imagine, looking at him, that he had just fought to the death with such a fearsome warrior or that he had emerged victorious from it.

I had meant to have him killed, but somehow I had transformed Guan Yu, my greatest enemy, into the hero of the coalition.

EPILOGUE

Zitong county, Yi province
12th month, 4th year of the Jingyuan era
of the Cao Wei empire (263)

CHEN SHOU LEFT MY WAGON with a smile on his lips for once. Finally, he has heard about our esteemed Lord Liu Bei and my beloved General Guan Yu, though I was still a long way from thinking of them as such.

Remembering Hulao fills me with nostalgia.

I was so young then, so very young, and naïve. The line between right and wrong had yet to be shattered in my child's mind, and though I cursed my luck for having unknowingly helped my enemy, a part of me also cherished the idea that he yet lived. This would have been too easy.

But even Guan Yu was to face an impossible challenge, for Dong Zhuo had now taken the measure of our capabilities and had decided to send his adoptive son to face us. Soon, we were to fight against the greatest warrior of our time, the mighty Lü Bu. I still shiver when I think about that man and his foul steed.

Though as far as we, the soldiers of Cao Cao, were concerned, there was more to fear than Lü Bu, for my lord was about to commit his first great mistake and so nearly got us all killed.

As for me, despite my promise to Lord Cao, I was about to wet my sword and claim my first life.

To be continued in

HEROES OF CHAOS

BOOK TWO
of
THE THREE KINGDOMS
CHRONICLES

AUTHOR NOTES

You just finished the first book of a series I have kept in my mind for nearly ten years, and for this, I cannot thank you enough.

I vividly remember the day in 2005 when I first heard of the Three Kingdoms. It was, as for many other enthusiasts of this period, through a video game. But what struck me as I smashed the buttons of my controller was how epic and thrilling the story felt. I turned my TV off, went to my local bookstore, ordered a copy of the *Romance of the Three Kingdoms*, and dived headfirst into what would turn out to be my greatest passion. What followed were fifteen years of research, avid reading, and finally, writing.

I obviously love so many parts of this period of China's history, or at least from the way it's been told and retold. We have some amazing contemporary sources of the events that shook China in the second and third centuries, among them the *San Guo Zhi* (the Record of the Three Kingdoms), written by

Chen Shou. Other historians and storytellers worked on the topic over the following centuries, and the characters and events related to the Three Kingdoms took a legendary tone. The final and greatest step to turn history into story came with Luo Guanzhong (fourteenth century), and his *San Guo Yan Yi* (Romance of the Three Kingdoms). This novel is now known as one of the four classics of Chinese literature, a spot it entirely deserves. Some of the most famous moments associated with the Three Kingdoms are taken straight from Luo Guanzhong's work, and many are purely fictional. Some of the characters came from his great mind but have since been accepted in the Chinese culture as if real. In this first volume, among the characters who did not exist, I can name Deng Mao, Cheng Yuanzhi, and Zhou Cang. But another character has benefited from a fair amount of modification: Liao Hua.

While the hero of this tale did exist and became an important member of the Shu Han state, a great part of his life as described in the Romance of the Three Kingdoms is fictional. For instance, Luo Guanzhong claims that he was a former Yellow Turban (so already alive in 184), but also that he lived to see the end of Shu Han (263) while being in his seventies, the latter part being historically true. As you can easily see, there is a gap. This discrepancy served me well in plotting the book you hold in your hands, but I had to advance his probable year of birth by ten to fifteen years.

A lot of my beta readers in China asked me why I had chosen such an obscure character. Liao Hua is not among the most famous heroes of his time, especially in the *Romance of the Three Kingdoms*. So why base a whole series on him? Well, for three reasons.

First, I love his name. I cannot tell you why, but from the first time I read it, his name resonated with me.

Second, he did see more than any other character of this era. Even considering his real date of birth, he saw the rise and fall of Shu Han, and as such, of the three kingdoms, and was part of most if not all of his kingdom's military campaigns. This makes him the perfect witness and reteller. And since his early years are mostly unknown, it gave me the opportunity to play with him and make him meet the greatest man of that age, Cao Cao. In reality, the two probably never met.

Third, I believe history has been unfair to him. While many men from that time gained a fairly undeserved fame, Liao Hua is worthy of being called a hero. I won't go into the details of why I believe so here—that would spoil a lot of fun for you with the future novels—but from a historical point of view, he deserves a more central spot in the great tales of the Three Kingdoms, and I hope to help him there.

This blend of history and legend, not unlike the Arthurian tales, for example, offered a lot of challenges for this novice writer. As you can imagine, one of my most time-consuming tasks has been historical research. While I have lived in China for over two years and have studied its culture for ten, there is a thick line between leisurely research and what is required to write a novel. I have read dozens upon dozens of books, academic papers, and history manuals on topics such as the Han dynasty, Chinese military matters, philosophy, food, religions, etc. But even that wasn't enough. First, we don't know everything. Chinese history is particularly poor on documentation of the life of regular people at that time. I had to fill a lot of blanks with what we know from previous or future dynasties, as well as cultures of the same period but from different places. Of course, I do not pretend my novel is perfectly historically accurate, and if I left blatant inaccuracies, I give you my most sincere apologies. I have two goals in writing this series as far as my readers are concerned: To give a great moment of fiction for those of you who already like and know the Three Kingdoms and to bring those who didn't into the first category.

For those reasons, I have also intentionally changed some historical details. History is an amazing field, but it is not always entertainment friendly, and I have sometimes chosen the legend over the history. For example, Guan Yu's weapon. There is almost no chance that Guan Yu used his famous crescent halberd, and in fact, probably used swords. But he is so often associated with this blade that I found it almost sad to take it away from him. Same with the famous duel between Guan Yu and Hua Xiong. While in reality, Sun Jian's men killed Hua Xiong, the story of the wine being still warm was just too good to pass. For those historical inaccuracies, I am still sorry, but not as much.

And finally, as far as history and legend are concerned, it is my great pleasure to twist those characters into a more realistic mold. In 2010, yet another TV series based on the *Romance of the Three Kingdoms* was released, and for once, the story veered a little away from the original source. Most of all, I was amazed by the portrayal of Cao Cao by actor Chen Jianbin, who made the *Hero of Chaos* a more believable, flawed, and human character. But a lot of people in China criticized the story and the actor for going too far from the novel, while I truly believe it was the way to go. Cao Cao might not be famous in the west, but he is to China what Julius Caesar is to European cultures. In China, the equivalent of the saying "speak of the devil" is "Speak of Cao Cao, Cao Cao arrives." Yet, from the time of his life, he has been given the role of an ambitious, manipulative villain. Whether he deserves this portrayal or not, I find it too simple. I won't hide that I adore Cao Cao for his complexity, his obvious genius, and for the paradox between his image and the results of his life's work. I cannot wait to dive deeper into his story.

As for Liao Hua, who for now is still called Chun, it is time for him to stop being a simple witness and move to a more active role in the drama of the Three Kingdoms.

I hope you are as excited as I am about the next volumes. There is a long road ahead, and if things go according to plan, this series will stretch over ten books. But I cannot do this without you. So, please, if you enjoyed *Yellow Sky Revolt*, take a minute to review the novel on Amazon, Goodreads, or wherever else you acquired it. You cannot imagine how much it helps indie writers (or writers in general) when you give us good reviews. So, thank you for helping me do what I love.

And if you want to get in touch, you can find me on Twitter, contact me through my website, or even check the videos on my YouTube channel, Back in Time Fiction.

Thank you again; good day to you,
zai jian and *à plus*.

Baptiste

ACKNOWLEDGMENTS

No book writes itself, and one person is usually not enough. This one isn't different, and I owe a bunch of accolades, beers, and coffees to those who made Yellow Sky Revolt a reality.

I want to first show my deep gratitude to the awesome beta readers/research helpers from Yunique France, who supported my many, many questions on Chinese culture and patiently fed my curiosity. Thank you, guys.

All my thanks as well to two special friends and role models among the self-published community, Brook Allen and R. W. Peake, who not only guided me on my indie path but also provided an example to follow. If you like great historical fiction set in ancient Rome, you should absolutely check out their work.

I need to thank my two sons, Louis, 6, and Isaiah, 6 months, for all their valuable help. Just kidding, you guys made it impossible to focus more than five minutes at a time. Still, you are my motivation. I write to make you proud and to give you some large boots to fill.

A big thank you as well (for real this time) to my parents-in-law for their support and allowing me to use their name next to mine.

And, of course, my undying love and gratitude to Yun, my beautiful wife. I often joke that I owe her 33% of anything I write, but it is probably closer to 50%. Any word I type, I do so because you are by my side. And any hour I spent over the keyboard, from plotting to publication, was only possible because you took care of the rest. You hold this family together while I play with my characters.

Finally, I wish to thank my followers, readers, and anyone who has shown an interest in my work. Ego is my fuel, and you guys make sure the tank stays full. Cheers to you all.

Ok, a last one. Liao Hua, this book is obviously for you. I can't believe they made a gazillion Dynasty Warriors games, but they haven't yet made you a playable character. Tecmo Koei, what are you waiting for?